THE WATER FROLIC

Chris Crowther

THE WATER FROLIC first published in 2010
as ISBN 978-0-903094-26-9 by
Hamilton Publications – Ventulus – Cross Lane
– Brancaster – Norfolk – PE31 8AE

This edition in 2019 as ISBN 978-1-9998111-2-9 by
Taleweaver – PO Box 1239 – Norwich – NR12 8XF

www.chriscrowther.co.uk

Printed in Great Britain by Barnwell Print Ltd
– Dunkirk – Aylsham – Norfolk – NR11 6SU

Sketches by Sarah Rogers

Other books by Chris Crowther

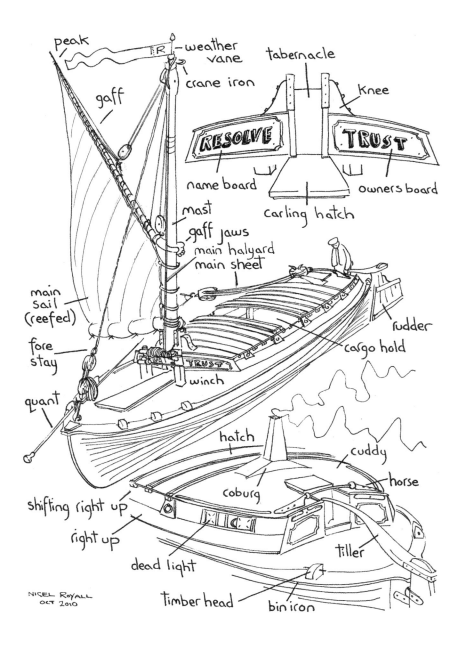

peak

weather vane

tabernacle

Knee

crane iron

gaff

RESOLVE

TRUST

name board

owners board

carling hatch

mast

gaff jaws

main halyard

main sheet

rudder

main sail (reefed)

cargo hold

fore stay

winch

quant

hatch

cuddy

horse

coburg

shifting right up

right up

tiller

dead light

timber head

bin iron

NIGEL ROYALL
OCT 2010

Prologue

Whoooosh!

The first rocket had been fired and the excited crowd let out a spontaneous cheer as its glittering tail climbed high above the broad and into the late summer night. Reaching the top of trajectory, there was a momentary hush of anticipation followed by shrieks of delight as the pyrotechnic exploded into a shower of golden stars, which seemed to climb still higher before beginning their graceful, silent descent back to Earth. Some seemed to die away quite quickly while others continued to sparkle until they reached the water below, throwing into stark relief the hundreds of upturned faces and the tall mast of the wherry moored beside the staithe.

Ranger Jack Fellows watched the stars fall and fade. In many ways, he reflected to himself, they were typical of life's journey. We all start with that glorious first rush of energy and then some burn out ahead of their time while others hang in there, glowing brightly until that last dread extinction. He looked up to the heavens above and had an overwhelming feeling that a spirit was watching over them this night.

Jack shook away profound thoughts, squeezed the hand of wife Audrey beside him, and received a reassuring smile in return. Everyone had looked forward to this night of delayed celebration – a time to forget all that had gone before, a closure of all they'd endured in the preceding weeks.

Ah, those weeks. Was it only six since they'd stood on this very spot surveying the results of all their planning, enjoying the sight of *Resolve* lying at the self-same mooring, bunting flying and giving little hint of the tragedy to follow? Two weeks before that, they'd been dredging where the firework raft now lay in mid-broad, and only a week before that, Jack had been collecting PC Meadows and the whole grievous saga had begun.

*   *   *

Chapter One

'Good to see you again, Jack.'

'Hi, Stan, hope you haven't been waiting long. Jump on board.'

The Norfolk and Suffolk Broads are divided into northern and southern rivers and, despite meeting at Great Yarmouth and their upper reaches being only a few miles apart, the characters of these waterways are very different. A change, however, is always good and Jack was still glad of it as he edged his patrol launch in towards Brundall Staithe on the River Yare.

This was only a temporary change of operational area. Personnel leaves and course assignments had left a shortfall of rangers on the southern rivers and Jack had happily accepted a month's secondment and the change in scene that it would bring. One obvious difference in this old commercial waterway was its faster tidal flow. He was stemming it now as his patrol launch ferry-glided in towards the wooden quay heading. Standing close by its edge, the uniformed figure of the policeman had given a cheery wave and greeting before springing across and squeezing into the wheelhouse and the seat beside Jack.

PC Stan Meadows was a part of BroadsBeat, the Norfolk Constabulary team assigned to policing the 150 miles of navigable waters of Britain's largest protected wetland. BroadsBeat operated their own boats, but often joined the Navigation Rangers to add a police presence to the patrolling launches. For Jack, it was a welcome chance to talk the language of a life, seemingly aeons ago, when he himself had served in the Met. On this early summer morning however, PC Meadows was almost apologetic when he turned towards the ranger and said, 'Another theft, I'm afraid.'

'Yeah, I know Stan. Control told me when they called to request this pickup.' Jack went astern on the engine and pulled slowly away from the quay. 'What's been nicked this time?'

PC Meadows ran a big hand through his close-cropped grey hair. A sudden spate of local thefts in this generally crime-free area of Broadland was causing even this phlegmatic copper to show concern. 'Another outboard, a ten horsepower job this time.'

Jack put the wheel hard over, went ahead on the engine and swung the launch downriver. 'Same place?'

'Afraid so.'

'That makes it three outboards in the last month.' Jack turned towards the policeman. 'Our thief certainly seems to know what he's looking for.'

'Only because boat-owners are such soft targets.' PC Meadows raised his eyes to the heavens. 'We fight a constant battle trying to discourage them from leaving high cost kit lying around just waiting to be stolen.'

'Probably because the boating fraternity's the last to honour an unwritten code of honesty,' responded Jack, easing the power up as they cleared the village boundary. Soon the launch was purring along with a healthy wash creaming away from its lean bow. The River Yare, because of its greater depth and width, allowed higher speed limits than its more sedentary northern neighbours. 'Days were when you could leave anything on a boat and know it would be there when you came back weeks later.'

'But not any more.' PC Meadows obviously felt a change of subject was needed on this bright summer morning. After waving to a passing hire-cruiser, he nodded towards the marshes, still blanketed in their thin veneer of radiation fog, stretching away on either side. 'So, how do you like your new patch, Jack?'

'Different, but it's a good change.' The southern rivers' reputation for being somewhat wild and bleak was an attraction for Jack, who had always enjoyed a bit of desolation. There was no doubt that this wide waterway that had once seen coastal shipping navigating to Norwich, enjoyed few tree-lined reaches and broads, but its vistas of marshes, agricultural land and remote hamlets stretching well back from its banks, produced a charm all of its own.

The policeman smiled back. 'And fewer boats too.'

'You can say that again.' Jack was always glad to have this officer on board his launch, a copper of the old school and as cheerful as he was burly. It was a characteristic of policemen that Jack had come to know well in his own long service with the force where, in spite of being constantly exposed to the grimmer sides of life, they were invariably blessed with good humour. Nurses were the same. It was doubtless a shield that prevented others' tribulations getting too deeply embedded in the soul.

A dyke was coming up to starboard. This led to a small broad with a neat village nestling on its banks. Jack turned into it. 'So who's had his outboard nicked this time?'

PC Meadows grimaced. 'That's the really bad news – it's Harvey Laydock.'

'What, the celebrity chef?' Like the rest of the nation, Jack knew the name of this TV star whose gourmet dishes and brusque persona had made him compulsive viewing and a very wealthy man. 'I knew he lived hereabouts.'

'Just on the edge of the village.' PC Meadows rolled his eyes. 'Biggest house, biggest boat, biggest ego.'

Jack laughed. 'And quite a stunning family to go with it, I believe.'

'Too true. From what I've read in the glossies, his wife's an ex-model and their two teenage kids have inherited her looks.' The policeman shook his head. 'Some blokes have it all don't they – luck, money and a bloody perfect family.'

*   *   *

'God, you must be the stingiest man in the world.' Amanda Laydock scowled at her father across the breakfast table. 'And all for a lousy outboard motor.'

'That's not the point. There's too much thieving around here lately and those responsible have to be dealt with.' Harvey glanced towards his wife, hoping for some support, but Lucy Laydock merely looked down at her plate, pretending not to hear, as she played with her untouched scrambled egg. Next to another family argument, food was the last thing she needed this morning, with a stomach still feeling the effects of half a bottle of vodka from the night before.

The Laydocks lived on the outskirts of the village in Fayre View, a prestigious house well-befitting a "Grade A Celeb". Seated around the large circular table beside the sunlit indoor pool, Harvey pursued his side of the argument. 'Boat theft in this village is getting out of hand and if we don't inform the police, things will only get worse.'

'"Inform the police",' mimicked Amanda in her most sarcastic voice. She wasn't yet nineteen, but already well able to stand up to her father. 'Alright, if you must, but do you really have to call the Chief Constable personally about a pretty worthless outboard motor that you could replace out of the cash in your pocket without even thinking of it?' She pushed away her plate and swung long, glossy hair back behind her towelling robe. 'You've really got it in for the young people around here haven't you, Dad, and you're hell-bent on making trouble for them. How petty.'

'I always believe in going straight to the top.' Harvey poured himself another coffee. 'I met the Chief Constable at a reception last month, so why not make the most of your contacts, I say.' He leaned towards his daughter. 'And, let's face it, it's not really your social conscience that's bothering you is it? What's narking you is that I won't increase your already generous allowance so you can flash money around the county with your new, so-called friends.'

'Well, at least I have some friends,' Amanda stood up and threw her napkin across the table, 'which is more than you do.' Pushing back her chair, she stormed towards the door before pausing and adding, with just a catch in her voice, 'And you'll lose your family too, if you carry on like this.' Then she was gone.

'That young lady needs sorting out.' Harvey directed his verdict towards his wife, who merely shook her head.

It was son Damien who responded. 'She's just a bit het up, that's all, Dad. She didn't mean it.'

'Yes she did.' As always, a bit of contrition was having the opposite effect on Harvey who took an impatient sip of his coffee. 'How can she talk to me like that after all I've spent on her? She's got her own car, an allowance that's more than most girls her age earn and had an education that cost a fortune – like you.'

'Education isn't everything, Dad.' Damien Laydock hated these increasingly frequent family squabbles, during which he invariably ended up as the ineffectual peacemaker. 'Doing what you want to do in life is more important.'

'Oh, here we go again.' Harvey let out a frustrated snort. 'I know where this is leading.'

'Well, have you thought any more of what I asked you, Dad?' Damien met his father's eyes. 'You know how much I want it.'

'You're too young to know what you want.' Harvey slapped his napkin down on the table. 'Thousands, that public school education of yours cost me. And what do you want to do with it? Throw it all away so you can work like a common tradesman.'

'I want to learn a skill doing something I love, Dad, that's what I want to do.' Damien was a couple of years younger than his sister and not a forceful lad by nature. It took much of his nerve to stand up to his father and say, 'How about yourself? You only started as a cook in a café and look where it took you.'

Harvey didn't like being reminded of his humble beginnings and the irritation in his voice betrayed it. 'All the more reason for giving you and Amanda the very best I could, so you could have successful professional careers. I had it all planned for both of you – medical school for Amanda and law school for you.'

'What, so Mandy can look after Mum while she's drying out and I can issue writs against every newspaper that dishes out the dirt on you?' Damien couldn't believe he'd just said those words to his father, and he quickly added, 'It's not what I want, Dad.'

'No, well we don't always get what we want in life.' Harvey pointed a shaking finger at his son. 'Don't expect me to finance your daft daydreams. If you're determined to go against my wishes, then pay for it yourself.'

'I'll do just that.' Damien strode towards the door in the wake of his sister.

'Where are you going?' This was the climax to yet another acrimonious breakfast and Harvey had finished pulling punches. 'Off to join that bunch of hippies again, I suppose?'

Damien paused, biting his lip. 'They're not like that, Dad, but, as it happens, no, I'm going down to the staithe. The police are coming, remember, to see about the theft. Someone needs to be there to meet them.'

'I'll be down shortly.' But Harvey's words were spoken only to the closed door. With incipient self-pity, he turned instead to his wife. 'I don't know where we went wrong with our kids.'

But Lucy Laydock was already at the poolside bar pouring herself another shot of vodka.

*   *   *

As Damien cycled the mile down to the staithe, the ranger and policeman were approaching from the broad via the marked channel. Jack glanced at his depth sounder as they glided slowly across.

'Bit shallow here, Stan. Even in the channel it's only showing a metre.'

'Yep, and it can get lower than that in dry spells.'

Jack raised concerned eyebrows. 'I'll check with the dredging department and see if they've got it scheduled.' They were close to the staithe now, a couple of hire cruisers alongside, but still space enough to slide in the thirty-foot patrol launch. Further on was another dyke and the parish moorings. Most of the boats moored to its banks were of moderate size, though one large and flashy motor cruiser stood decks and flying bridge above the rest. The village itself lay close by the moorings, a mist-shrouded collection of random dwellings showing little sign of life except for a lone cyclist just emerging down its narrow street. Its rider freewheeled onto the staithe and waved, a young teenage lad of fresh looks and slim frame. As the launch brought up alongside, he caught the mooring lines and quickly secured them to posts with a familiar competence. Minutes later the engine was shut down and Jack followed PC Meadows onto the shore.

'Hello, I'm Damien Laydock.' The lad held out his hand, but there was an apologetic edge to his voice as he quickly added, 'Harvey Laydock is my father.'

The PC returned the handshake and introduced Jack before scanning the empty road. 'Considering the urgency with which your father wanted this outboard theft investigated, I'm surprised he's not down here himself.'

'Yes,' Damien glanced down briefly at his trainers, 'I'm sorry, but he'll be here very shortly.'

'That's alright, I know how busy these celebs are.' Long years had given PC Meadows that policeman's knack for cutting sarcasm.

'Is that your father's boat there?' asked Jack, pointing towards the large cruiser. He could understand Stan's irritation, but sensed the discomfort of a young lad trying to make amends. There was a likeable decency about this teenager with a quiet refined voice, but whose paint splattered tee-shirt and tattered jeans spoke of a total lack of pretence.

Damien nodded. 'Yes, and that's where the outboard was stolen from.'

'Right, let's go and have a look then.'

Damien led them down the staithe to where the large cruiser, with Great Taste emblazoned on her canvas dodgers, lay moored.

'Sorry about the name,' said Damien with a pained expression.

'Could be worse,' sympathised Jack, 'and she's a lovely boat.' Indeed, Great Taste was forty-five feet of sheer luxury and obviously capable of speeds far in excess of any ever permitted on the Broads. More impressive still was the boat's well-kept and ordered appearance. Mops and boathooks lay secured in their holders, springs led fore and aft and other ropes and warps, not in use, were either hanging coiled or curled into neat cheeses on the spotless decks. 'Your dad certainly keeps a smart ship.'

'Oh, it's me who looks after her.' Damien obviously felt some further explanation was necessary. 'Dad's not a boat person really. He just likes to ... to ... well, own one.'

'I know what you mean,' said Jack with a smile, 'but you obviously love boats.'

The lad smiled. 'Yes, but not this sort. My choice would be something more traditional, a wooden boat with sails, not engines.' He shook his head, sadly. 'Dad wouldn't even hear of it. If it doesn't have a king-size bed and a cocktail cabinet to match, he isn't interested.'

'Wooden boats do need a lot of maintenance,' said Jack, spreading a little oil on what were obviously troubled waters.

'I wouldn't mind. I love working on traditional boats.' Damien nodded towards the end of the moorings where several small craft were drawn up onto the grass, including a small wooden sailing dinghy. 'That's Once Bittern. Mandy and I sail her a lot, but I enjoy working on her just as much.'

'Mandy?'

'My sister.'

'Oh, right.' Jack turned back to the business in hand. 'But we need to sort out your dad's missing engine, Damien. Was this where you kept it?'

'Yes, on the tender.' Damien pointed to the inflatable dinghy hanging from davits on the cruiser's stern. 'We left the outboard permanently rigged on its transom. It was there on Saturday, but when I came down to check the boat midday yesterday, Sunday, it was gone.'

'Which is when your father interrupted the Chief Constable's cocktail party to report it as stolen,' said PC Meadows, with undisguised disdain. 'The engine was locked on, presumably?'

'Well ... no,' Damien looked again at his feet, 'we never did.'

'And, presumably, it didn't have one of our security covers either?' The PC was referring to the Norfolk Constabulary's initiative of providing marked PVC covers that replaced the engine's usual cowling when not in use. The scheme had proved a great success, thieves consistently avoiding any motor that was going to cost money before it could be sold on. 'Well worth a modest fifteen quid outlay I'd have thought.'

'I did suggest it to Dad,' explained Damien, hesitantly, 'but all he would say was that, being so high-profile, he expected the police to give him one.'

'Did he now,' said PC Meadows, shaking his head and taking a notebook from his pocket. 'Right, give me the details. Make, model and serial number?'

Damien hesitated on the latter. 'Ah ... I'm not sure on that one.' He turned and looked towards the sleek open-topped Jaguar sports car that had just drawn to a halt by the moorings, 'Perhaps Dad will know.'

'I doubt it,' said PC Meadows, noticing the celebrity chef seemed in no immediate hurry to join them. Instead, Harvey was pausing to glance in the sun visor mirror to adjust his highlighted hair and smooth his designer shirt. When he did emerge, it was to reveal a figure far shorter than apparent on TV, and a waistline hinting at the effects of middle-age and good living. After swaggering unhurriedly to join the group, it was Damien who made the introductions.

'Well, what do you think?' asked Harvey, deliberately avoiding handshakes, but glancing towards his engineless tender.

PC Meadows didn't try to hide his disdain 'I think it probably wouldn't have got nicked in the first place if you'd bought one of our covers or taken the trouble to lock it. Simple prevention would save a lot of police time.'

'Yes, well,' responded Harvey, visibly bristling, 'your Chief Constable obviously felt some time should be spent on this case, so tell me what you're going to do about it.'

'List your outboard on the stolen boats website and keep an eye out for it on the river, boat jumbles and car-boot sales.'

'Is that all?' Harvey gave an audible scoff. 'How about conducting searches and interviewing suspects?'

'What suspects?' Jack's rare encounters with TV personalities had invariably revealed a reality far short of that produced by makeup artists and flattering camera angles. Harvey Laydock was no exception, his high-octane lifestyle already producing rings of stress around care-worn eyes. Jack fixed them through narrowed ones of his own. 'Do you have any suspicions who might have stolen your motor, Mr Laydock?'

'Of course. It's obvious isn't it? It was one of those morons on that hippie barge.'

'It's a wherry, Dad, not a barge and don't call my friends morons.' Damien was biting his lip in suppressed anger. 'Why do you have to be so bigoted?'

Harvey shook his head with exaggerated frustration. 'Because they're a bunch of no-goods, that's why.'

Before Damien could respond, he was distracted by a stoutish tweed-clad figure pacing onto the staithe. 'Oh no, that's all we need,' he groaned and whispered to Jack, 'Henry Wanstead, chairman of our parish council and a real pain.'

The man in question came striding up to the group. Fiftyish, balding and with a ruddy complexion, there appeared to be mutual recognition with PC Meadows, but his main attention was strictly for the TV personality. 'So sorry I'm late, Harvey,' he puffed, uttering the first name with the relish of a man delighting in being on such terms. 'As soon as I got your call, I dropped everything and came straight here.'

'It's alright, Henry, I'm sure you came as fast as you could,' Harvey turned towards his boat, 'but we have to do something about security at these parish moorings.'

'Of course, of course.' Shaking his head vigorously, Henry Wanstead affected a look of concern. 'This theft of your motor is very distressing, Harvey.' He turned and nodded towards the river. 'Doubtless the work of members of that damned commune.'

'Too right, Henry.' Harvey shrugged. 'I was just trying to explain to these officers here, how that collection of down-and-outs have blighted the whole area.'

'Absolutely. Nothing is safe since they came on the scene.'

PC Meadows had heard enough. 'If you mean the crew of the wherry Resolve, Mr Wanstead, then ...'

'Councillor Wanstead.' The chairman turned to face the policeman for the first time. 'It's Councillor Wanstead, if you don't mind.'

The policeman scanned Henry Wanstead's five foot five inch frame. 'Well, Councillor, I was about to explain that in spite of all the complaints we receive about that wherry and its crew, we have found no incriminating evidence whatsoever, to link them to these thefts.'

'Pah!' The chairman seemed glad of this opportunity to flex his official muscles. 'The trouble with you and the rest of the police, Meadows, is that ...'

'Constable Meadows, sir.'

'What?'

'It's Constable Meadows, councillor.'

'Oh … yes … Constable … well, as I was going to say, the trouble with the authorities these days is that they bend over backwards to pussyfoot around the more, shall we say, undesirable elements of society, when what we need is some tough, good old-fashioned policing.'

'We'll investigate fully, sir,' said PC Meadows, 'but I suggest you secure your own moorings with a little more care, starting by ensuring that anything movable is locked up, stowed away or fitted with one of our covers.'

'Especially with all the dross of the county roaming at will,' complained Councillor Wanstead. 'Sort out that commune and …'

'Actually, a greater concern to you should be the state of the channel,' interrupted Jack, keen to get off what was obviously a contentious issue. 'It's way too shallow.'

'Rubbish, there's plenty of depth there.' Wanstead glanced around the boats filling the moorings. 'No boats here have a problem.'

'But we do,' interjected Damien. 'Our boat is touching bottom at low water springs and it's got even worse in the last few months.'

Jack could see Henry Wanstead's dilemma. Clearly the councillor wanted to say that having such a big boat was the main problem, but that would be impossible without offending the man he held in almost heroic regard.

'It certainly needs deepening, and will only get worse.' Jack turned again to Wanstead. 'I'm going to see if the authority can fit in an emergency dredge.'

If this news was meant to appease the chairman of the council, it had just the opposite effect. In fact, he seemed quite alarmed at the prospect. 'Dredge the channel. Whatever for? We don't want it dredged.'

'Why ever not?'

'All that noise and disruption,' protested the councillor. 'Clanking dredgers, barges ploughing backwards and forwards, diesel engines running all day. The effect on the village would be appalling.'

'This channel is part of the navigation and as such comes under the jurisdiction of the Broads Authority,' explained Jack. 'I'm afraid you won't have a say in the matter, Councillor.'

'But you can't – we won't let you.' Almost in desperation, Henry Wanstead turned to his celebrity hero for support and found none.

'Of course the channel needs dredging, Henry.' The TV chef seemed far from happy at having the investigation into his outboard theft distracted by issues of navigation. 'But the reason we're here is to sort out this crime wave, and a good place to start will be that wherry.' He turned back to PC Meadows. 'Go there with a search warrant and you'll find my motor.'

The policeman sighed. 'If you feel so strongly about it, we'll at least go and have a chat with them, Mr Laydock,' he glanced at Jack, 'but I doubt it will produce any result.'

'What a surprise,' said Harvey sarcastically as he turned on his heels to leave, 'but I'll check with the Chief Constable in a week to see what progress has been made.' He suddenly remembered the chairman of the council, still obviously agitated and now left abandoned. 'I'll give you a lift home, Henry.'

'Oh, wonderful! Thank you.' The councillor scuttled off.

'Look at him, scampering after Dad like a lapdog,' said Damien, as the small rotund figure of the councillor climbed eagerly into the Jaguar, to be immediately sped off in a cloud of wheel-spun dust. The youngster sighed. 'And sorry about Dad. He wasn't always like this, but he's been bolshie on TV for so long, he's like it all the time now. Lately, he's got even worse, and hasn't a lot of sympathy with the wherry project.'

'So we gathered,' said Jack. 'From what was said, I take it you have a personal interest with Resolve?'

The teenager nodded. 'Like I told you, I love boats and Greg Kennard lets me work on the restoration with him sometimes.'

'Greg Kennard?'

'He's a local boatbuilder who does most of the skilled work on Resolve.' There was an eagerness in his voice as he added, 'I've learned a heck of lot from Greg.'

Jack nodded. 'And you've seen nothing on that wherry to make you suspect any of the crew being involved in these thefts?'

Damien hesitated only slightly before reaffirming, 'Absolutely not. I know them all. They wouldn't do that.'

'Let's hope you're right,' said Jack, with feeling, as they made their way back to the patrol launch. Engine started, they prepared to get away as Damien cast off their lines, coiled them neatly and handed them across. 'Thanks for your help, Damien,' shouted Jack as the light breeze drifted them away from the staithe. 'We'll let you know of any progress.'

As they motored away across the broad, he looked back to where the teenager still stood on the staithe watching them, seemingly deep in thought. Long experience of human nature told Jack this was one youngster reluctant to return to his family home.

*   *   *

At Fayre View, Lucy sat at her dressing table, gazing into the mirror and trying to comprehend how "Page-Three looks" could degenerate so quickly into the haggard wreck staring back at her. After leaving the breakfast table, she'd indulged a twenty-minute shower, three cups of black coffee and still felt like death.

'I'm off out, Mum.' It was Amanda standing in the bedroom doorway, casually dressed in jeans and tee-shirt, her long hair tied back in a ponytail and looking as stunning as her mother remembered she herself had looked at eighteen.

'Where are you going?' Lucy felt she should ask the question even if she no longer really cared.

'Just "out", that's all.' Amanda glanced around distractedly. 'Anywhere but staying here pretending to play happy families.'

'You shouldn't talk that way about your home, Mandy, or answer your father back the way you did this morning.'

'Well, someone's got to stand up to him.' Amanda took some steps further into the room. 'You never do.'

'I don't need to,' protested Lucy, unconvincingly. 'Your father and I have such a close relationship that ...'

'Poppycock!' interrupted her daughter. 'If you want to live that fantasy, that's up to you, Mum, but don't expect Damien and me to play the game. Dad's a bullying trumped-up cook whose womanising has driven you to hit the bottle and become a total wreck.' Amanda crouched by the dressing-table stool, meeting her mother's eyes in the mirror. 'How can you stand it?'

'Your father's provided a good home and life for us all.' Lucy wiped away a tear that was already smudging the eye-shadow applied minutes before. 'He's a little naughty at times, I know, but that's men for you.'

'Well, not my sort of man.' Amanda stood up sharply. 'Divorce him, Mum. You'd get half of everything and have a happier life.' At the door she paused. 'You know, it's me that should be going into law, not Damien. I'd enjoy representing women like you against their pig husbands.' Then she was gone, the sound of her running feet and the slamming front door effectively blanketing out the sobs of her mother in the bedroom above.

*   *   *

Chapter Two

'It's not far,' explained PC Meadows as they turned back onto the Yare and increased speed. 'Resolve is in a farm dyke about a quarter mile downriver.'

'Yeah, I know.' Little passed Jack's eager eyes and he had spotted the old wherry on his very first patrol, or at least her bows, for she was moored in a narrow dyke, in need of paint and, as yet, still mastless. As a lover of all things maritime, he applauded any scheme to restore old vessels, but there had been a plethora of debate surrounding Resolve's unique use, and what he needed now was to cut through all the emotion to hard facts and data. 'So, what's her full story, Stan?'

'A long one. As you probably know, she was one of the trading wherries sunk in Surlingham Broad eighty years ago.'

'The so-called "wherry graveyard". How many of them ended up there?'

'No-one knows for sure but, a decade ago, a syndicate actually raised one.'

'Resolve?'

PC Meadows nodded and repositioned his bulky frame in the wheelhouse seat beside Jack. 'Those salvagers were just the first of a whole series of well-meaning, but financially strapped, groups who found that old wooden vessels needing restoration act like a big sponge on your money. She'd been languishing ashore untouched for a couple of years when Gloria Vale bought her.'

'The present owner?'

The policeman nodded. 'Yes, and quite a lady she is too. She must be pushing fifty, but's still a looker.'

'And, presumably, rich with it.' Jack had heard a lot about Gloria Vale, but never met her. 'Any idea how she came by her wealth, Stan?'

'The hard way, by all accounts. She was born in a working-class district of Manchester, but her father died when she was just two. Her mum struggled to bring her up single-handedly and Gloria admits that she was a difficult teenager, always in trouble. She couldn't find a job and in the end, set up a stall selling cups of tea outside the local factory. Eventually, she earned enough to buy a café and then a restaurant until, ultimately, she owned a whole chain. Her business thrived until a few years ago, when it suddenly went belly-up, and she lost everything. She's one hell of a tenacious lady though and, somehow, she eventually clawed back a lot of money and promptly announced she was going to lead the simple life helping those less fortunate.'

'Which is when she bought Resolve?'

'Yep, and formed the Resolve Trust which, in theory, seemed a great idea.'

'A floating commune for homeless youngsters.'

The policeman nodded. 'Inspired by her own tough childhood. Her aim was, and still is, to take vulnerable youngsters off the streets, give them a home and, at the same time, teach them new skills in a healthy environment.'

'Sounds a worthwhile scheme to me.' Jack scanned the marshes where the mists were beginning to lift, revealing a vista of open fields and scattered sunlit buildings on the rising ground beyond. From the green-covered banks, a grey heron lifted off in lazy flight, its protesting squawk only vaguely resembling the cry of "Frank" which Norfolk folk insisted was the reason behind its colloquial name. 'You certainly couldn't find a healthier life than this,'

'Too right, and Gloria received a lot of applause for her venture – at first.'

'Until ...?'

'Until she tried to find a permanent mooring. That's when she found out that homeless youngsters, some with a bit of a past, aren't exactly welcomed with open arms into the community. In effect, they became scapegoats for any local trouble ranging from anti-social behaviour to break-ins and thefts.'

'Like this spate of crime in Councillor Wanstead's little domain,' replied Jack, frowning. 'As I understand it, the kids do some volunteer work locally.'

'That's right, including a lot of conservation work for your Broads Authority, clearing riverbanks, marshland and the like. But Gloria had a hard job finding somewhere to moor until a local farmer offered them a slot in his dyke in exchange for a bit of free labour on the farm. Now, when the youngsters aren't doing that and other volunteer work, they're busy on the wherry restoring it to its former glory.'

'Under this Greg Kennard.' Jack recalled the name mentioned by Damien. 'What's his story? Who is he exactly?'

'Local boatbuilder, but in a very small way,' explained Stan. 'He has a small workshop in the village where he builds a variety of sailing and rowing dinghies and canoes, but his first love has always been wherries. He offered his services to the trust and, seeing how well he interacted with her charges, Gloria Vale invited him to lead the whole restoration project. The kids do the work under his supervision. The result is a trading wherry being restored and young people learning new skills.'

'Which has to be a good thing,' agreed Jack. Just how well that restoration was coming along, he would soon see for himself. Just ahead, between open fields where cattle grazed, lay the narrow farm dyke in which the wherry was moored.

The dyke was short as well as narrow, and Resolve filled most of it. Low and squat, she lay bow-on to the river, her sixty-foot length seemingly dwarfing Jack's patrol launch as he turned in and glided alongside.

There had been significant improvements since his first passing glimpse. Now, fresh grey paint on the sides of the hold stood out in pleasing contrast to the black clinkered planks of her main hull while, standing on the side-deck, a young girl with close-cropped blonde hair carefully applied lettering to some boards lying on the main hatch. More painting was going on at the bow where a young man in the tender applied a last few strokes to a traditional white "snout". He waved his brush in greeting as Jack edged the launch into a space by the stern. Sitting atop the cargo hatch, another youngster in shorts and check shirt put down the guitar she had been strumming and came to catch the thrown line.

'Hello there. Are you coming aboard?' She was an attractive-looking girl in her early twenties, her slender neck supporting strings of beads that hung and jangled with melodious abandon as she bent and secured the launch's lines to one of the wherry's timberheads.

'If we may.' Jack shut down the engine and clambered aboard as an older woman with striking red hair emerged from the cabin. She could have been late forties, but with looks and vibrancy that cut straight across the boundaries of age. Faded jeans and a tight-fitting hooded sweatshirt showed off a youthful-looking figure but, when she spoke, her faint northern accent carried just a slight note of anxiety.

'Oh dear, the Broads Authority. What have we done now?'

'Nothing I hope,' assured Jack, holding out his hand. 'Jack Fellows, Navigation Ranger and you must be …'

'Gloria Vale. Welcome to Resolve.' She smiled, and held out a hand devoid of rings. Her hair was shoulder length with undisguised streaks of grey only slightly marring the glorious red. ' She glanced over Jack's shoulder to the stocky figure of PC Meadows just joining them on deck. 'And the police as well. This must be serious.'

'No need to worry, Miss Vale, just routine enquiries as before.' PC Meadows glanced about the wherry's decks. The young girl who'd taken their lines had moved to do the same for the young man in the tender, who was ready to return on board. With him back on deck, the two headed for an open hatch amidships, closely followed by the blonde girl who seemed to have finished her sign-writing and who paused to give them a cheerful wave before disappearing below. It was more than they received from the teenage lad lethargically sanding the long tiller. His face was clouded by acne and an expression soured by latent hostility. It wasn't lost on PC Meadows. 'Is there anywhere we can talk privately, Miss Vale?'

The wherry's owner nodded towards the tabernacle. 'Let's go for'ard.'

The two men followed her along the side-deck, pausing as they went to admire the name-boards. There were two of a size and shape to fit the for'ard bulkhead either side of the tabernacle, painted light blue with yellow surrounds. It was the standard of the lettering though that was truly impressive. On one, the young sign-writer had crafted the name RESOLVE and on the other, TRUST, both in red lettering with skilful curving flourishes at beginning and end. 'Rita Wakefield's our artist,' explained Gloria, noticing their admiration. 'I found her spraying graffiti artwork on the walls of a disused building where she was squatting.'

'But, obviously a girl of considerable natural talent,' said Jack, as they moved on. Like all wherries, Resolve's foredeck was twelve feet in length, the after part split by open carling hatches through which the mast counterweight would normally drop when the mast was raised. At the end of this and immediately ahead of the hold was the tabernacle, the huge upright bracket on which the mast would hinge. They gathered around it, Jack careful to avoid the tools scattered about. 'Resolve must have a way of bringing out hidden talent.'

'So many down-and-out youngsters have skills to offer the community, if given the chance.' The answer came not from Gloria, but from a young man in his late thirties who had just joined them from below. He had the tanned, healthy look of someone well-used to activity and fresh air. After wiping a hand on greasy dungarees, he held it out. 'Greg Kennard.'

'Jack Fellows.' The ranger indicated the tin in the boatbuilder's other hand. 'Linseed oil?'

The young man shook his head. 'It would have been boiled linseed in the old days, but that takes too long to dry. We collect our new mast tomorrow, so I'm preparing the tabernacle with teak oil mixed with a little varnish.' He shrugged. 'We're trying to be as authentic as we can, but we have to be practical at the same time.'

The boatbuilder's hands were big and firm with a roughness befitting a craftsman, and his eyes carried the gleam of a man who loved his work. The presence of uniforms, however, was something he was less than comfortable with. As he shook PC Meadows' hand he frowned. 'More trouble?'

The policeman's answer was another question. 'What makes you say that, Greg?'

'Just that any wrongdoing around here always gets put at our door.'

'Not everyone is against us, Greg.' Gloria Vale turned to the two officers. 'Greg is my right-hand man in this project, so anything you want to discuss can be said in front of him.'

'Fair enough.' The PC glanced from one to the other. 'We're here investigating the theft of yet another outboard motor on Saturday night.'

'And, as usual, you think we're somehow involved?' There was bitterness in Kennard's voice.

'No, we don't, Greg, but there are those that do.'

'Yeah, and I can imagine who they are.' The boatbuilder nodded in the direction of the village. 'That puffed up celebrity Laydock and the chairman of the parish council. They've had it in for us since we got here.'

'Wanstead's just a lacky,' said Gloria. 'It's that bastard Laydock who stirs him up and tries to get us evicted.'

'That might be,' acknowledged PC Meadows, 'but the fact remains that in the few weeks you've been here, there's been a spate of local thefts from boats. It's certainly a coincidence.'

Gloria drew her slim figure to its full height. Insinuations regarding her charges were obviously something she took to heart. 'The only crime these young people ever committed was to end up sleeping on the streets. Now they're trying to make a new start if people would just let them.'

Jack stepped in as pacifier. 'This is a wonderful project, Gloria, but what you've created here is an alternative lifestyle, and people are always sceptical of those outside the norm. It's human nature that, when trouble strikes, local people will always point their fingers towards strangers, especially those with dubious pasts.'

'Or that well-to-do people automatically assume those less fortunate are the likely criminals. In reality, it's the rich who are often the real villains of society.' Gloria made an obvious effort to calm her voice before saying, 'I hear what you're saying, Jack, but I know these young people and I know they wouldn't let me down by stealing.'

'How well do you know them?' asked the constable. 'For example, that lad there ...' he pointed to the young man now applying a coat of primer to the tiller he'd been so carefully sanding, '... has he ever been in trouble with the law?'

'John Flint? Why him?'

'Policeman's instinct.'

Resolve's owner hesitated before reluctantly acknowledging, 'Well yes, I do believe Flinty has been in trouble at times in the past, but he's promised me that's all behind him now.' She nodded towards the girl who had first taken their ropes and who was now taking a mug of coffee to the tiller painter. 'And his sister, Jenny, is determined to keep him on the straight and narrow.'

'Was she sleeping rough as well?' asked Jack, surprised to find them brother and sister, and that a girl blessed with charm and looks could share such a forlorn lifestyle.

'Good grief no!' exclaimed Gloria. 'Jenny had just graduated from Sheffield University when she discovered her brother was sleeping on the streets in Norwich. Being the girl she is, she put her own bright future on hold to come and help him. That's how they ended up onboard Resolve, and why she's determined to stick close by until she's confident he's turned over a new leaf.'

'What were his previous convictions?' persisted the PC.

A trace of anxiety momentarily clouded Gloria Vale's fresh complexion. 'I believe there was one charge of appropriating money.'

'And where was he the night before last?'

'We were all onboard here. Saturday is our musical evening. Flinty's really good on the harmonica.'

'That's nice. And was he playing his harmonica all night, Miss Vale?'

'No, of course not,' answered Gloria, pretending not to notice the policeman's sarcasm. 'We all turned in at ten-thirty.' Jack could tell that her smile of reassurance was more for their benefit than her own as she added, 'We encourage early nights on board Resolve.'

'But if any of your youngsters decided to go ashore, would there be anything to stop them?' asked Jack.

Gloria frowned. 'They're not prisoners, Mr Fellows.'

'What about transport?' PC Meadows looked around at the open farmland stretching from the dyke. 'It must be a fair way from here to the road. Do you have a vehicle?'

'We don't need one,' answered Greg. 'We live a waterborne life here. The river's our highway and boats, our transport.'

Jack looked down at the small craft, including two canoes, surrounding the wherry. 'Can your charges take these boats at will?'

'Yes.'

'And could Flinty have taken one on Saturday night without anyone knowing?'

Greg shook his head. 'Pretty unlikely. Everyone sleeps below together and wooden boats always creak when you walk about. Someone would be bound to hear him.'

'Would you like to take a look around?' asked Gloria.

It was a natural invitation from a woman justifiably proud of her project, but Jack knew it was also an offer to search without a warrant. Besides, he was keen to have a closer look at this historic old vessel. He smiled and said, 'Lead the way.'

Greg Kennard led them to the midships section where the hatch boards had been removed and steep steps led down into the wherry's innards. Sunlight flooded down from this opening, but it was the only natural light penetrating the great cabin in which they now stood. The two other youngsters were just finishing their coffee, but stood up and left as the ranger and others entered.

'Presumably, this was originally the main hold,' said Jack, stooping beneath the low deckhead as Gloria ushered them to some rough benches flanking a large table. The latter was suspended by chains from the beams above, also of plain wood, and liberally scattered with unwashed crockery and the remnants of breakfast.

'Yes, but an ideal communal living area.' Gloria sat down opposite and picked up a coffee-stained mug with "Flinty" crudely painted on its side. 'Housekeeping's still casual, I'm afraid, but it's how we like it.'

This living space was indeed basic with few additions to the vessel's original layout. Hinged to the frames, three on each side, were bunks which obviously also doubled as couches and could be folded away like the table when more space was needed. At the aft end, a simple counter separated these main quarters from a small galley area. Throughout, the frames, planking and beams had all been painted with white gloss which certainly brightened the interior, as did the polished brass oil lamps bracketed to the ribs.

'No electrics then?' asked PC Meadows.

'No power at all on board,' answered Greg. 'This boat is run just like when she was built in 1901.'

Jack had been counting the plates and mugs on the table. 'So, Gloria, apart from you and Greg, there are four inmates on board?'

'The Resolve Trust prefer to call them "team members", Mr Fellows.' Gloria smiled, tolerantly. 'But, yes, there are the Flints, who I've already told you about, Rita Wakefield and Freddie Catlin, who was the lad painting the snout.'

'And do you live onboard, Greg?' asked PC Meadows, writing the names into his notebook.

'No, not all the time.' The boatbuilder cocked his head upriver. 'My workshop in the village has a studio flat above it. I sleep there some nights and others here with the crew.'

'Communal living indeed,' observed Jack, scanning the open space of the accommodation.

'Yes, but with some segregation between the sexes,' explained Gloria with a smile. 'That curtain,' she nodded to the far end where a canvas sail-like screen hung suspended from a brass rod running longitudinally along the deckhead, 'is drawn across at night, and it's girls on starboard side and boys to port.'

'And never the twain shall meet,' completed the PC, with a knowing chuckle.

'That's the intent, Officer,' replied Gloria. 'I know what the locals think of Resolove – the rumours about dope-sniffing hippies who indulge in nightly free love – but it's just not true. Of course, it's inevitable that relationships might well form between young people living in close proximity, but we aim to provide a fresh start for them, focussing on a clean, healthy lifestyle free of drink, drugs, cigarettes and promiscuity.'

'I really admire your principles, Gloria, and I'll spread that word around,' promised Jack.

'Not that it'll do much good,' said Greg, cynically. 'The likes of Harvey Laydock and the parish council will still do all they can to force us to find alternative moorings or, worse still, have us shut down completely and undo all the good we've achieved so far. These youngsters need understanding, not hostility.'

'Well, we'll see about that,' said Jack as he turned towards the gangway ladder and the upper deck. Back in the sunlight, he glanced towards the boat-builder's tools lying scattered on the hatch covers. 'There's a lot of work to do.'

Greg nodded, seemingly glad to talk about a subject obviously dear to his heart. 'Yep, like I said, we're picking up the new mast and counterweight at Brundall tomorrow and we have to be ready, but we're getting there.'

It reminded Jack of one question he meant to ask. 'Harvey Laydock's son, Damien; he works with you sometimes doesn't he?'

'Yes, a great lad. Nothing like his father. Damien's never happier than when he's working with me, and desperately wants to go on the boatbuilders' course at Lowestoft. He certainly has the enthusiasm and aptitude to do really well, but his father's dead against it.'

'Harvey doesn't approve then?'

'Not a bit. Thinks Damien's letting the whole family down. Father had a legal career mapped out for the lad.' Greg shook his head, sadly. 'Snobs, heh?'

Jack grimaced, but thoughts of the wherry positioning to Brundall for her new mast had raised another question. 'Without auxiliary power, how do you get Resolve along the river?'

Greg indicated the large dinghy that Freddie had been using. 'We stick an outboard on the tender and push her with that. Gets us along at a couple of knots which is all we need if we work the tides.' He looked up to the big sky overhead and the first wisps of cloud moving to the urging of incipient breeze. 'Can't wait to get her rigged and sailing again though.'

'And to be able to cruise the Broads at will,' added Gloria. 'That way, we won't have to outstay our welcome in any one place.'

They'd reached the aft end of the wherry now and Jack turned before climbing down into the launch. 'It's been great talking to you both. I'll look forward to seeing what progress has been made when I'm here again. Let me know if I can be of any help before then.'

PC Meadows followed. 'Sorry to have bothered you again, Miss Vale, but thanks for your co-operation and honesty.'

Gloria gave another of her disarming smiles. 'It's easy when you have nothing to hide.' She nodded back towards the main hold. 'You sure you don't want to do a full rummage for this stolen outboard?'

The PC smiled. 'That won't be necessary, Miss Vale.' He glanced across to Jack who gave a confirming shake of his head. 'I think we know integrity when we see it.'

'Oh, well, that's progress, at least.' Gloria handed across the lines. 'I'm glad someone has faith in us.'

'More than you think,' replied Jack as he slid the engine lever into slow astern and backed away. On Resolve, the two girls and Freddie Catlin smiled and waved. Still painting the tiller, Flinty gave a hostile scowl and turned away.

'I wouldn't trust that one an inch,' said PC Meadows.

'I know what you mean,' agreed Jack, though his own experience in the police had taught him it was all too easy to misjudge one's fellow man or woman.

Going ahead on the engine, he turned back upriver and the policeman's drop-off. The morning had given Jack much to think about and he needed to talk to the works department about water depths in the village channel.

Strange, he thought, that Henry Wanstead, chairman of the parish council, should be so plainly opposed to having it dredged. And why did all the animosity between Harvey Laydock and Gloria Vale seem so very personal?

*   *   *

At this same time, Amanda Laydock was swinging her two-seater sports car off the narrow road and edging carefully into a gap between the trees. This small area of woodland, just a few miles from the family home, was one of her favourite haunts. It was where she came most often to find peace, gather her thoughts and contemplate the future.

Switching off the engine, she sat for a few minutes listening to a favourite CD while allowing her eyes to wander over the dashboard's dials and switches. Amanda loved her car. It had been a present from her father as a reward for excellent A-level results, the typical gesture of a man generous to a fault if it suited him, but unbelievably tight-fisted and obstinate if it didn't.

In fact, her dad was the most two-faced person she had ever come across, unspeakably rude and obnoxious most of the time, but charming to those he was trying to impress, like the star-struck hussies ever-ready to fling themselves at him. How could he be so gullible and how could Mum put up with it? Perhaps it was a simple case of there being no other option.

Amanda shook her head and switched off the music. Longing to be independent of her father's handouts, she loved wandering amongst the trees with the very definite purpose of earning money. Once out of the car, she took her rucksack from the boot.

By now, her little business was earning more than just a few helpful pennies and showing all the promise of a livelihood. That gave her as much satisfaction as the increasing size of her personal bank account. Evermore determined to show her dad she could make it on her own, she shouldered the bag and strode into the wood.

How Amanda loved the sense of isolation this remote habitat gave her. As she made her way deep into the interior, the sunlight no longer cast dappled shade onto the woodland floor. With the canopy thickening overhead, an eerie peace filled the air but, despite the silence, Amanda could sense the intense activity of creatures around her. She stopped and bent down to turn over a log and smiled to herself as she uncovered a living community of mini-beasts and fungi, all deriving sustenance from the rotting wood. A sudden rustling in the leaves made her turn round sharply to see a squirrel scampering back up into the high branches of a beech tree. If an elf or fairy had appeared in these magic dells, she wouldn't have been in the least bit surprised. In the meantime, though, there was work to be done and she continued to pick her way around fallen trunks and branches.

To Amanda, this business initiative was more than just a useful money-spinner – it was a welcome escape from an unhappy home life. Her brother Damien likewise found solace amongst his boats. It made her sad to think of them both becoming estranged from their increasingly dysfunctional family.

Ah well, so be it. Amanda's gloomy thoughts were soon distracted when, a few yards ahead, she spotted just what she was looking for. Soon she was kneeling down, opening her rucksack and removing the plastic bags. It was as she slipped on rubber gloves, that her eyes were drawn to something nearby – something she'd never seen before – something best left right where it was.

*   *   *

23

Chapter Three

The Broads Authority dockyard lay on the north bank of the River Yare where the rural wildness of the lower reaches started to give way to the urban sprawl of Norwich. Rivers and moorings had to be maintained and the tugs, barges, cranes and dredgers working from here were a very necessary part of that commitment. It was also the rangers' base for this section of the southern rivers. Jack brought his launch alongside the quay-heading, secured his ropes and headed straight for the offices of the Head of Construction and Facilities.

Tom Maynard looked up from maps spread across his desk. He was wearing a colourful check shirt and the look of a man who would rather have been outdoors on this fine summer's day than inside amongst his papers and files. Nevertheless, he gave a cheerful smile as the ranger entered his office. 'Hello Jack. How's your new patrol area?'

'Fine thanks, Tom, but there's one thing I'm a bit concerned about.'

'Which is?'

'The marked channel here.' Jack pointed to the small broad marked on the very map Tom Maynard had been studying. 'It's really shallow, only a metre at high water. Is it scheduled to be dredged?'

The manager sighed. 'If only. We've had it down to be done at least three times in the last few years, but every time we've had vigorous resistance from the chairman of their parish council, Henry ...'

'... Wanstead,' completed Jack. 'Yeah, I met him this morning.'

'Then you'll know what I mean.'

'But why does he object? We usually have to ward off complaints for not doing enough dredging.'

'He says it would cause too much noise and disruption.'

'Yes, that's the reason he gave me,' said Jack, 'but I can't help feeling it's a contrived excuse.'

Tom nodded. 'Yep, me too, but he's not the sort of person you feel inclined to spend time arguing with.'

'Do we need to? Can't we just go ahead and do it anyway?'

'Nothing to stop us,' agreed the manager, 'but there's always another part of the system needing dredging and plenty glad to have us.'

'The trouble is,' continued Jack, 'there are boats at that parish mooring that can't get out at low water. They pay their tolls and have the right of navigation.'

'Quite so,' said Tom, walking over to a large plastic-covered chart on the wall that depicted the year's dredging schedule. He tapped the block covering the present week. 'We're dredging on the Chet right now, as you've probably seen. The job's gone faster than we planned and the next one is down the Waveney.' He gave Jack a questioning look. 'If we're going to do that channel it makes sense to slot it in between these two.'

'When?'

'We could probably get started in a couple of days.'

'Great. Let's do that.'

The manager grinned. 'No problem, but I'll leave you to tell Henry Wanstead.'

'Tom,' said Jack, pausing at the door and smiling himself, 'it'll be my pleasure.'

*   *   *

'Where does Amanda go in her car? She's been gone for hours.'

Back at Fayre View, Harvey was attempting casual conversation with his wife. It was an exercise he found increasingly laborious. It hadn't always been like that. There had been times at the start of their marriage when Lucy had been the most exciting person in this whole world.

They had met at a fashion show, she the leading model on the catwalk and he the caterer on his first big gig. Their relationship flourished and the press were quick to publicise their unlikely match in the tabloids. The knock-on result was that Harvey not only got lucrative catering contracts but, ultimately, his own cookery series on TV. By this time, he and Lucy were married with two beautiful children and a very healthy bank account. He had it all.

Or, at least, he thought he had. Unfortunately, those years of increasing fame and fortune had the reverse effect on both his wife's career and pin-up looks. Two pregnancies, over-eating and an ever-increasing reliance on drink had increased both her dress-size and apparent age. Lucy had never been a natural mother and, although she cared for the children's general well-being, she seldom demonstrated the heartfelt love and affection for which they craved, resented the restrictions parenthood brought to her life and was secretly relieved when they started boarding school. Harvey, all too aware of his wife's shortcomings, had tried to compensate Amanda and Damien by giving them everything they wanted. Unfortunately, that rarely included affection because personal contact required him to be home - a situation Harvey found increasingly difficult to stomach.

Luckily, his TV work and its associated promotions had demanded more and more of his time and provided a ready-made excuse for his frequent absences. Another "plus" had been his string of female admirers, who didn't continuously bleat on about all that had gone wrong in the day, but merely wanted to share the night.

In all this maelstrom of high life though, it did secretly bug Harvey that his wife didn't seem to care about his philandering. With the children at boarding school and money to do as she wished, the odd tipple had fast-escalated into chronic excess. It was only when the doctors started talking in terms of mortality that Lucy had agreed to go into rehab. That had been the first of a whole series of admissions, costing Harvey a fortune and the children any chance of a loving stable home-life.

And now, as Lucy sprawled on her lounger, glancing increasingly at the poolside bar and running shaking fingers through the straggly remnants of her once-radiant blonde hair, Harvey pursued his fruitless quest for information. 'Doesn't Amanda tell you where she's going or what she's doing?'

'Why should she?' Lucy brushed the gin she had just spilled, from her blouse. 'She's got her own life.'

'Yes, but it's a life we don't seem to know anything about,' said Harvey, standing up and pouring himself a rum. 'And all those clothes she keeps buying – I know we give her a pretty fair allowance, but she's spending money like water. Where the hell's she getting it from?'

'Good luck to her, however she does it,' mumbled his wife. 'At least she's doing something with her life.'

'And I mean to find out just what.' Harvey slumped down into the other lounger and took a gulp of rum. 'At least we know where Damien is, even if it is with that weird crew on that bloody wherry.'

'Oh, don't start on that again,' groaned Lucy. 'You know what the boy wants. Why don't you just help him achieve it?'

'Because I want my son – both my children – to achieve more in life, and I'm going to make damn sure they do.' Harvey wagged an all-knowing finger at his wife. 'Starting by finding out what that daughter of ours gets up to.'

'Yes, well you might have to stay home for more than five minutes to do that,' said Lucy into her glass before looking up and asking, 'When are you off again?'

'Tomorrow for a couple of days,' answered her husband, somewhat guiltily, before summoning up a sliver of mock-professionalism and adding, 'they want to discuss this new series I've got in mind. I want to include some classic desserts.'

'Well, I hope for your sake they include plenty of tarts,' said Lucy, gulping back the remains of her gin before slinging the empty glass into the pool with all the feeling she could muster.

*   *   *

26

In fact, Amanda was only a mile from her fretting father, onboard his cruiser Great Taste. Having found what she wanted in the woods, she was now all set to continue with the next procedure in her little enterprise, and for this she needed facilities, equipment and, most important of all, total privacy.

There was no way she would have found that at Fayre View, but her father used Great Taste so little that here she was reasonably assured of secrecy. It was an illicit use, for earlier attempts to secure a key of her own had met with adamant refusal. Harvey might not have a lot of interest in his boat, but he was damned sure his daughter wouldn't use it for the wild parties he was convinced she wanted to throw. Amanda allowed herself an inward chuckle. Had he realised her real need for Great Taste, parties would have been the least of his worries. It didn't matter anyway, because Damien had been far more accommodating. Having responsibility for caring for the boat meant her brother had his own set of keys and, against his better judgement, he'd had a spare set cut for his sister.

Perhaps that was because she had been totally honest with him. With only eighteen months between them, they got on well and the usual teenage squabbles that often afflict sibling teenagers were rare. Although their characters were somewhat different, with Amanda being the more assertive of the two, sharing trials and tribulations at home had brought them ever closer. Knowing she could trust his confidence, she had told Damien of her new venture and why she needed the boat for at least a few hours once a week.

The nature of her scheme had worried her brother considerably, not least because exposure could bring the family name into sharp disrepute and, possibly, the courts. On the positive side, he was business-savvy enough to see the lucrative possibilities of her venture. There was also the joint satisfaction of defying their father.

So, Amanda had her own key and the use of the boat, which seldom left its mooring. Now on board, she wasted no time in the saloon with its designer furnishings and fittings, instead making straight for the small cabin she occupied on the few occasions the family had gone cruising. She liked her little cabin and, more than anything now, she liked the fact that it gave access to a section of the bilges. Leaving the cabin door open, she rolled back the thick navy-blue carpet and opened the hatch cover beneath. The slightly sickly odour of bilge water came up to greet her, but she was prepared for that. Below was the bilge pump, the primary reason for this access, and beside it, a metal case. Amanda hauled the case out. It was a type designed for use by photographers, light but sturdy and, best of all, well-sealed against damp. Pausing only to wipe off surface condensation, she carried it through to the galley.

Predictably, for a luxurious boat with such a name and owner, Great Taste's galley was impressive indeed. Into this shrine of high-tech appliances and top-of-the-range décor, she brought her slightly smelly case and laid it gently on the marble worktop. The smell would be dealt with later, along with the even more suspicious odours that this evening's work would produce. She opened the lid and removed her equipment.

Amanda had excelled in the sciences at school and gained four top A-level grades. Her favourite of these by far had been chemistry. She loved the challenge of converting formulae into visible and working compounds and mixtures and delighted in all the apparatus used to achieve it. This boat's galley would never be a match for a fully-equipped laboratory, but laying out the highly accurate weighing scales, measuring jug and glass jars, gave Amanda an indefinable thrill. She was using her knowledge, and making a bit of money as well. She filled a kettle with water, placed it on the gas hob and lit up. Sterilisation of these bilge-stored implements was the first priority. While waiting for the water to boil, she delved into her rucksack and brought out a new supply of collected matter from the small plastic freezer bags. Then she went back to her storage box and removed a large sealed container.

Very soon now and her little production line would be back in full swing. She couldn't help wondering what her father would think.

*   *   *

Wondering was what Councillor Henry Wanstead was also doing a lot of, in his white pebble-dashed detached bungalow at the far end of the village, and he was doing it alone. For the chairman of the parish council's life was a lonely one indeed. He had no wife, and all his children were on the other side of the world, and seemingly happy to stay there. There was not a single person he could say was a true friend.

He'd hoped Harvey Laydock might be one. It had been a great thrill when the TV celeb had built Fayre View and moved into the village. Henry had made a real effort to foster a friendship by making a personal visit of welcome. He'd been a little hurt by Harvey's offhand manner, but this had been compensated for a few months later by being told to call the chef by his first name. It was an honour he never failed to parade whenever he could.

That slight familiarity, however, didn't extend to being invited to one of the many parties and barbecues at Fayre View. Finding his name consistently omitted from the guest list, Henry had deluded himself that this was merely an oversight by the man he held in such high regard. Certainly, Harvey never failed to contact him when he needed some concession from the council. He knew he could always be assured of the chairman's immediate attention to his every wish and his present wish was the eviction of the Resolve Trust.

Henry wasn't totally sure why Harvey was so intent on kicking Gloria Vale, her wherry and her motley crew out of the parish. But if that was what

Harvey wanted, then he would do everything in his power, and perhaps a little more, to ensure that was what Harvey got. Success would surely result in an invitation to Fayre View and cement his personal friendship with the chef.

And Henry sorely needed a friend this miserable evening, for the councillor was a very worried man. That morning, he had gone to the staithe as summoned, and met this new ranger from the Broads Authority. It had not been a happy meeting. In addition to being patently unimpressed by Henry's position on the council, the ranger had dropped that bombshell about having the channel dredged.

It was a prospect that he had dreaded for years, but always managed to avoid. Now, this new chap seemed all set to ride roughshod over his objections and get it dredged anyway. The ironic thing was that it was Harvey Laydock's boat that needed the extra depth more than any other in the parish. Henry, as chairman, might well convince the parish council to send another letter opposing the dredging on grounds of noise and disruption, but if he did that he stood the risk of incurring Harvey's lasting displeasure and being struck from the social list before he ever got on it. On the other hand, if he let the dredging go ahead, it could be personally disastrous.

Henry put his head in his hands and wished he were very far from this village and his whole miserable life.

*   *   *

Someone who did have a willing ear that evening, was Jack Fellows. Wife Audrey had shared all his challenges, successes and stresses for the last thirty odd years and was the perfect partner to come home to.

This secondment to the southern rivers meant the journey from work to home was a longer one for Jack, requiring a car journey through peak-time traffic instead of the pleasant village walk from the boatshed at the end of his road. But it was only for a few weeks and Audrey's welcome was all the warmer for it being a little later.

'Get your shoes off, Jack, while I make you a cup of tea.'

'Thanks love.' Jack washed his hands in the kitchen sink while asking over his shoulder, 'Any word from Jo?'

Joanna was the Fellows' eldest daughter, married and living in London with her first child due in two weeks time.

'Yes, she's fine,' said Audrey, pouring a fresh brew into her husband's favourite cup. 'She went for a check-up this morning and everything seems okay.'

'Good,' said Jack, who shared a special relationship with his elder offspring. 'When do you think you'll need to go down there?'

'As soon as baby's born, I expect,' said Audrey, pouring her own tea before considering again the singular aspect of her husband's question. 'You will be coming with me, won't you?'

'Ah… well…' Jack spooned sugar into his tea, 'could be tricky work-wise.'

'Yes, well giving birth to your first baby can be tricky too, and it would help Jo having both her parents with her.' She pushed across a plate of homemade biscuits with a degree of frustration. 'So you just get things sorted for a quick getaway, Jack Fellows, and no more excuses.'

'I'll try,' promised her husband, lamely, 'but, remember the reason I'm down on the southern rivers in the first place is because they've got other rangers away.'

'Well let's hope at least one is back for two weeks' time,' stated Audrey firmly before softening and asking, 'How are things going down there?'

'Fine, but not without the usual agro you'll find anywhere you go on this planet.' Jack explained the day's events, telling Audrey about his visit to the wherry and the antagonism between Resolve and village.

'I would have thought most people would applaud such an initiative,' said Audrey, helping herself to a biscuit.

'I think most people do.' Jack followed her example. 'It's a simple case of the old NIMBY syndrome.'

Audrey nodded. 'I suppose we're all a little guilty of that at times.'

'Yes, but the shame is that these young people have so much to offer the community. By restoring Resolve, they're giving back a real bit of history to Broadland. Anyway, once she's operational, the wherry's going to be cruising most of the time and mooring in different locations. My only worry is that word of all the bad feeling here is bound to spread, so they could well find themselves regarded with suspicion wherever they go.'

'What you need,' explained Audrey, pouring her husband his second cup, 'is something to bring commune and community together.'

Jack nodded. 'A great idea, Aud, but it would have to be something pretty spectacular to win over Harvey Laydock and this Councillor Wanstead's support. They'll be dead against anything even remotely related to Resolve.'

Audrey shrugged. 'How about a fete of some sort? You remember all that disagreement we had between our two parishes. Then someone came up with the bright idea of combining the two parish fetes. Everyone had a great time and since then the animosity has disappeared to the point of being forgotten.'

'Hmm.' Jack slowly stirred his tea while churning this idea over in his head. 'What about something like the old water frolics that they had a century ago?'

'Rowing and sailing races, boats all dressed in bright flags, various stalls on the staithe.' Audrey was letting her own imagination play over the possibilities. 'It could be a real fun time for everybody, Jack, and even organising it would involve bringing the opposing sides together.'

'The trick would be to circumvent the Brothers Grimm until we've got the thing off the ground.' Jack blew between gritted teeth. 'If Laydock and

Wanstead got so much as a whiff of any plans, they'd do all they could to put a spanner in the works.'

'Then form a joint committee between the Trust and selected members of the village to organise it.'

'That wouldn't be a problem as far as Gloria Vale is concerned. She's up for anything to improve public relations, but I don't know anyone in the village to represent their side.' Jack stroked his chin before suddenly slapping the table in mock triumph. 'Yes I do. Of course, Greg Kennard is from the village as well as being connected to Resolve. I bet he'd know the right people in the parish to support the idea.'

'Especially if it got one over on that chairman of the council,' said Audrey. 'From what you've told me, I should think there are several villagers happy to have him put in his place. And what about Harvey Laydock's son? You liked him, and I bet he'd support the idea.'

'You mean Damien. You're right, Aud, and, with a foot in each camp like Greg, he'd be a perfect choice.' Jack mulled this thought over before voicing his concerns. 'The only trouble could be his father, who'd be furious if he found his son was going behind his back.'

'Well, why don't you have a chat with this Gloria Vale and Greg Kennard first and run the whole idea by them,' suggested Audrey, getting up and beginning preparations for the evening meal.

Between laying cutlery, she paused to give Jack's shoulder a gentle rub. 'You know, love, if the only thing you achieved during this spell on the southern rivers was to reconcile these two warring factions, that in itself would make it all worthwhile.'

Jack nodded and stroked his wife's hand. 'You're right. I'll try and see Greg and Gloria tomorrow.' He could see the merit in Audrey's idea, but playing on his mind was the extent of the bitterness between the two groups. He felt it went deeper than simple social conflict and could sense some personal animosity between Harvey Laydock and Gloria Vale.

He didn't tell Audrey, but that was something else he'd be checking out just as soon as he could.

*   *   *

Atop Resolve's cuddy roof, Gloria sat entranced as the sun set before her, its beauty reflected in the river ahead, where the mirror-like surface was disturbed only by a pair of passing swans. Determined that nothing should break the spell of this magic, Gloria cast aside thoughts of the obnoxious likes of Harvey Laydock and allowed herself a little inward sigh of contentment. This morning's visit by the authorities had been disturbing, but was surely only to be expected. Soon the sun would make its final dip below the horizon before rising again tomorrow, bringing with it renewed hope and optimism.

She glanced up to the foredeck where Greg was teaching Freddie Catlin how to splice a rope. Sitting on the main cargo hatch, Rita and Jenny chatted happily between chords played by the latter on her guitar. Just beyond the entrance to the dyke, the River Yare flowed swiftly to the sea on the last of the evening's ebb. Gloria glanced at her watch. The state of the tide would be almost the same twelve hours hence and shortly after, its flood would carry them upriver for their new mast.

How lovely it would be, she mused, to see Resolve rigged for the first time in nearly eight decades, sailing along the rivers well away from the meddling of Harvey Laydock and his minions, crewed by capable, trustworthy young people who were once destitute. With the public's backing and her restoration complete, Resolve could well accommodate twice the number she had onboard now: four more youngsters off the streets sharing a new life afloat.

These young people were Gloria's life now as she had no family of her own, her mother having died suddenly at the time her restaurant chain had been forced into bankruptcy. How she wished her mum could be with her now to share this new-found peace and happiness in her life.

As always at these times, her thoughts strayed to her father. She had hardly known him, of course, but her few hazy memories were of a loving, generous man. It was his inability to say "no" that had been his downfall – that and being with the wrong people in the wrong place at the wrong time. Gloria shook her head, determined that painful memories would not break the magic of the evening stillness. Peace and privacy, however, with a boatload of youngsters, was always something of a compromise and now a figure was emerging from the main cabin and slouching back to join her. It was John Flint.

'Hello, Flinty.' Gloria nodded towards Resolve's big tiller, curving above the cuddy and glistening with its new coat of white gloss. 'You made a lovely job of that. Well done.'

'Thanks.' He glanced down at the boats floating in their own reflections just off the wherry's quarter. 'Mind if I take one of the canoes, Gloria?'

'No, of course not, Flinty – but what for?'

'Just want to go for a paddle.'

Gloria knew she should be pleased at this troubled young lad finally finding pleasure in wholesome pursuits, but her sense of progress was edged with caution. Flinty had been slower than the rest to adapt to this waterborne life and, in spite of being given shelter and purpose in Resolve, he seemed to fight against showing any signs of rehabilitation or gratitude for any of the opportunities being offered to him. Instead he appeared to harbour unnatural resentment towards those who had succeeded in life. Was this simply jealousy or was there an underlying bitterness? Whichever, he hoped his sister, Jenny, might change his outlook, but there was still an issue she needed to clear up.

'You're doing quite a lot of paddling these days, Flinty.'

'How d'you mean?' There was suspicion, even challenge, in his voice.

'I mean like Saturday night.'

'Don't know what you're talking about.'

'I'm talking about you taking a canoe at midnight on Saturday. I was asleep in the cabin when a thud woke me. I heard a couple more, so I got up to investigate in time to see you paddling off upriver in the moonlight. Where were you going?'

Flinty shrugged. 'Couldn't sleep, so I decided to get myself some fresh air.' He raised his head to look at his inquisitor through narrowed eyes. 'Anything wrong with that?'

'No, as long as that's all you were doing.'

'Do you mean was I nicking engines?' He jerked his head forward. 'Go on ... say it.'

'Well, were you?'

'No, but I expect the police won't believe me anyway, if that's what you told them.'

'Against my better judgement, I didn't tell the authorities anything, Flinty. We have problems enough with local opinion.' Gloria closed her eyes and shook her head. 'Alright, Flinty, if you tell me you've done nothing wrong, I believe you, but please don't let me down.'

'Don't worry, I won't.'

As Gloria watched this dejected, spotty-faced teenager paddle away upriver, she tried to calm her thoughts and enjoy the now-clear starlit night sky with its almost-complete lunar orb silhouetting the encircling reedbeds.

But the magic had been broken. Very soon she threw the rest of the coffee overboard and disappeared down into her cabin. How she hoped Flinty was true to his word – whatever that was worth.

*　　*　　*

Being summer, darkness came late and certainly not soon enough for Amanda Laydock. Her work aboard Great Taste complete, she was now engaging Phase Three of her endeavours to expand distribution and sales.

After leaving the boat, she'd set off on foot into the village as she always did, cursing the almost full moon that shone down from a cloudless night sky. There was no street lighting and normally she could rely on darkness for her deliveries, but tonight moonlight bathed the narrow street with its row of timbered houses and rustic cottages. With her rucksack slung over her shoulder, Amanda had already visited three of her "clients" and made the usual sales. Now, heading for the edge of the village and the fourth delivery, she still worried about being spotted.

33

Although no longer intimidated by her father's bullying ways, Amanda knew he would go mad if he discovered what she was up to behind his back. The dreaded press would have a field day if the story leaked out and, with the family reputation teetering on the brink of collapse anyway, it could well spell the end of his television career.

She was reaching the edge of the village now where the last few houses gave way to open country, stark and ethereal. Fatherly repercussions being firmly put aside, Amanda concentrated on the task in hand, pausing only to scan the surrounding habitation and adjacent countryside. First priorities were to ensure that there were no witnesses to this nocturnal dealing. Satisfied there was not a soul to be seen, she headed for the last house and, at its front door, gave a surreptitious knock. Footsteps came from within and the door opened. This was the third supply she had made to the person standing there waiting expectantly.

'I've brought you some more.' She slid the rucksack from her shoulder, took out a small package, and handed it across. 'This should keep you going for another week.'

'That's great,' was the reply as money changed hands.

'Remember, not a word to anyone.'

'My lips are sealed, don't you worry yourself about that.'

The door closed and Amanda made her way back down the path, closing the squeaking gate behind her. Back on the road, she paused to count the money, added it to the rest of the night's takings and allowed herself just a little sigh of satisfaction. She had a regular client base now and a steady income.

Swinging the rucksack back onto her shoulder, she strode off towards the staithe where her next customer should just be arriving.

*　　*　　*

Chapter Four

The wind next morning was south-easterly and fresh enough in the straighter reaches of the Yare to produce little overfalls in the still-ebbing tide. Heading downriver at the start of his day's patrol, Jack watched them break into showers of protesting spray against the bows of craft plying the waterway in the glorious sunshine. The air had that invigorating lift to it, with just the faintest whiff of the North Sea.

A perfect day to be on the river, though perhaps not-so-perfect for the small lugsail dinghy tacking ahead of the launch in a laborious attempt to beat against the wind. Drawing closer, Jack read the name Once Bittern on her transom and recognised young Damien at the helm. They were past the dyke to the village now and Jack surmised he must be en route to Resolve for the move to Brundall. In spite of the tide, it was going to be a slow haul. Jack brought the launch almost to a stop between the dinghy's tacks.

'Sailing well, Damien, but can I offer you a tow?'

'Yes please,' was the prompt response, and another minute had Damien onboard and securing his little boat to one of the launch's stern cleats. As they picked up speed again he joined Jack in the wheelhouse. 'I do appreciate your help, Mr Fellows.' He glanced back to assure himself that Once Bittern was indeed bobbing along happily in the launch's wake. 'Resolve's getting under way just as soon as the tide turns, and I promised Greg I'd be there to man the tender.'

'You will be.' Jack increased their speed very slightly. 'I should think you'll all be glad to get some water past Resolve's hull again.'

'Too right, and she'll be sailing just as soon as we get her fully rigged and ready to go.' Damien was obviously inquisitive to know how the previous day's visit had gone. 'Did you get to see all over her, Mr Fellows?'

'Yep, and a great job you've all done on her restoration.' Jack described his meeting with Gloria Vale and the rest of her team. 'They're a good bunch.'

'Yes they are,' agreed Damien, 'even Flinty when he's in the right mood.'

'Ah, yes, a slightly angry young man, that one,' agreed Jack.

'Oh, he's not so bad really. Just got a chip on his shoulder, that's all,' said Damien. 'Reckons public school types like me are all upper class twits out to exploit the underprivileged.'

'I can't see how he can think that of you. Not after all the work you've done on Resolve.'

'Probably more than him, if the truth be known.' There was a glimmer of pride in the teenager's voice as he added, 'Greg has let me do some of the work unsupervised.'

'Yes, he obviously thinks a lot of you and said you'd like to be a boatbuilder yourself?'

'That's my dream,' said Damien, shaking his head sadly, 'but not much chance, I'm afraid.'

Jack frowned. 'No reason why you shouldn't is there?'

'There is if you have a dad who wants you to be a lawyer.'

'Ah.' Jack nodded sympathetically. 'How old are you, Damien?'

'Seventeen.'

'Still at school, I presume?'

'Yes, worse luck. Dad's absolutely adamant I should go on to university and then law school.'

'Well, my advice is to finish your A-levels and then see how you feel about careers.'

'Which means another wasted year away when I could be enrolled on a boatbuilders' course.' Damien gave a small sigh of frustration, 'And for a fraction of what Dad would be paying in school fees.'

'I expect he just wants the best for you,' said Jack, diplomatically.

'He wants the best for himself, more like, and says it will be an embarrassment to explain his son's taken up a trade.' The lad looked despondent. 'He won't admit it, Mr Fellows, but I know he's a bit strapped for cash at the moment, so I'd be doing him a favour if he'd only see sense.'

'How about your sister?'

'Amanda? Well, she excelled at school, which pleased Dad, as he wants her to be a doctor.'

'And does she?'

'I'm not sure. She's clever at science and all that, and she'd make a good doctor, but, secretly, I think Mandy just rebels against anything Dad suggests, on principle. She thinks he's a control freak.'

Jack smiled. 'You're both at that awkward age of still being dependent on your parents, but already having ideas of your own. It's a difficult time.'

'Even more difficult in our case because it's parent rather than parents.' Realising he was being a bit obscure, Damien turned and faced the ranger. 'I'm afraid Mum's an alcoholic.'

'Sorry to hear that, Damien,' said Jack, with genuine feeling. 'That's a horrible thing for you and your sister to have to deal with.'

'And for Dad.'

Damien didn't say any more and Resolve was coming into sight now, just visible in the dyke with the tide almost at its lowest. There were further questions Jack would liked to have asked, but now wasn't the time so he simply handed across one of his cards and said, 'If you ever need to talk to someone, Damien, you can call me any time.'

'Thanks, Mr Fellows.' He put the card in his shirt pocket. 'I appreciate that ... and the tow.'

'You're welcome.' They were turning into the dyke now and Jack could see Resolve was all ready for her trip downriver, with the canoes pulled clear onto the farm bank and the tender with a large outboard clamped to its transom, secured to the wherry's port quarter. As they came alongside, Damien threw the launch's lines to figures already on deck and quickly followed them across the gap. Freddie Catlin expertly tied the sternline and Rita Wakefield was trying to secure the bow, but seamanship obviously wasn't yet on a par with her artistic talents and, seeing what a hash she was making, Damien ran to help. The line was soon secure, but not before Jack had noted a more-than-eager willingness on Damien's part to help this elfin blonde with sparkling eyes and ready smile.

As Jack climbed aboard himself, the small doors of the aft cabin opened and Gloria and Greg emerged.

'Morning, Jack.' Gloria, in spite of the slightly-cool breeze, was dressed in jeans and striped tee-shirt, and looked genuinely pleased to see the ranger again, though she did glance over his shoulder to confirm that this morning's visit was without the law. She nodded in the direction of the cuddy. 'Come and have a coffee, if you've got the time.'

'I have, but have you?' questioned Jack. 'You'll want to be off shortly.'

'Not until the tide turns,' said Greg, pushing back a sliding hatch in the roof and leading them below, 'and it always seems to take its time when you're keen to get going.'

The cuddy, or "men's cabin" as it was sometimes called, was only six feet in length, and Jack could imagine its cosiness in winter months when it would be heated by the coal-burning ship's stove which, surrounded by built-in cupboards and lockers, stood cold against the for'ard bulkhead. In Resolve's trading days, this would have been the domain of both skipper and mate, but only one bunk remained, built-in to the starboard side. In place of the mate's bunk to port, there stood a narrow table littered with books and partly filled-in forms. A single wooden chair took up the remaining space, though it too was covered with miscellaneous paperwork. Gloria swept the clutter off and ushered the ranger into its place. 'Sorry for the mess, Jack, but this cuddy doubles as home and office and, like any registered charity, there's a never-ending mountain of forms to complete and submit. We get some funding but, in the end, I rather think the paperwork outweighs the money.'

'Rather you than me.'

Jack waited while Jenny brought in mugs of coffee. As the young woman turned to leave, Gloria asked, 'Is Flinty up yet?'

'Just.' Jenny gave a disapproving frown. 'I'm sorry about that, Gloria. He did stay out late last night.'

'Too late.' Gloria nodded towards the brass bulkhead clock. 'It was two o'clock this morning when your brother finally came stumbling back on board.'

Jenny nodded apologetically. 'I know. I will talk to him, Gloria.'

'Please do, Jenny.' After the young woman had disappeared back on deck, Gloria sat down next to Greg on the bunk, rolled her eyes and said, 'Slight team problem.'

Jack smiled. 'That's okay. I'm glad I've got the chance to chat to you two together because I have something I'd like you to consider.' As they sipped their coffees, he explained Audrey's idea of a joint water frolic as a means of breaking down barriers between commune and community.

'It sounds a lovely idea,' acknowledged Gloria, when he'd finished, 'but would they want it.'

'If by "they", you mean Laydock and Wanstead, then probably not, which is why I propose we organise it over their heads.' Jack nodded at Greg. 'That's where you'd come in.'

'Me?'

'Yes, because you're the bridge between the two factions. You live and have a business in the village and, I'm sure, know a few friends who you could call on.'

Greg nodded. 'Several, actually, who'd be glad to stick their fingers up at both Laydock and Wanstead.' He glanced sideways at Gloria. 'I'll be going to the workshop tonight because I have a customer coming in the morning.' He turned back to Jack. 'If you like, I could pop and see a few people and sound them out.'

'And, in the meantime, I'll have a good think about what we could contribute,' said Gloria, obviously enthusiastic about the scheme. 'When do you think we should hold this, Jack?'

'About two week's time. I know that's not long, but it's important we get things under way before anyone has a chance to oppose the idea and while we've got the benefit of this summer weather.' He stood up to leave. 'For my part, I'll see what other support I can drum up from the Broads Authority and the police.'

'The police?' Greg seemed more surprised than alarmed. 'Why them?'

'Because BroadsBeat like to be involved in any organised activity based on the river and open to the general public. It'll also add credence to your own project if it's shown to have their support.'

'Yes, I can see that,' agreed Gloria, getting to her feet.

Greg excused himself and went back out on deck, leaving the tiny cabin at least a little less congested. Jack scanned its cramped interior with its open deadlights and brass oil lamps mounted on woodwork with a strangely artificial finish.

'It's comb-grained ochre,' explained Gloria. 'It's how the old wherrymen always used to paint the inside, so we've done the same.'

'And very nice it looks.' Jack was also taking in the little touches of homeliness that only a woman could bring. These included two framed photos attached to the bulkhead, both in black and white. One was a turn-of-the-century image of Resolve in her old trading days. The other was of a young couple, arm-in-arm, he fresh-faced and smiling, she somewhat nervous and holding a bouquet of flowers. Jack bent forwards to examine it closer. 'Your mum and dad?'

'Yes, on their wedding day.' Gloria smiled sadly. 'They didn't have many years of wedded bliss, bless them. Dad was killed when I was two. Mum brought me up as well as she could, but I was quite headstrong and could have very easily gone off the rails. As it was, I managed to achieve some success and give her a bit of support back.'

'Didn't she ever re-marry?'

Gloria shook her head. 'No, she never stopped loving my dad and really spent the rest of her life mourning him.'

Greg's shout came from up on deck. 'Tide's turning, Gloria.'

'And time for me to get patrolling again,' said Jack, mounting the short steps and leaving them to it.

Damien was already down in the tender warming its engine while Greg stood on the afterdeck directing the novice crew in letting go the lines. Even Flinty was taking a part, be it somewhat unenthusiastically. Damien had already moored Once Bittern to the rhond and, once Jack had started the launch's engine, Gloria handed down his lines. 'I'll chat to the rest of the team about your idea, Jack. We try and keep things on board as democratic as we can.' She indicated upriver. 'We'll be stepping the mast as soon as we get there. Stop by and see how it's all going.'

'Thanks, I'll do that.'

Continuing his patrol downriver, Jack mused over things observed and deliberated on this morning's encounters. They'd raised questions which he knew would be turning over in his head until he found the answers.

Why did a successful TV personality like Harvey Laydock have "some money worries of late" and why did Gloria Vale's father's face seem somehow vaguely familiar?

*　　*　　*

'It's not the time you got home, Amanda, it's that we had no idea where you were.' Back at Fayre View, Harvey Laydock sat in a white towelling robe beside the pool, refreshed by his morning swim, but angered at the seemingly evasive nature of his daughter. 'It must've been two in the morning when we finally heard you come home. Your mum and I were worried sick.'

'Yes, I'm sure you were.' Amanda cast a dismissive glance at her mother, wrapped in her own robe and sipping some exotic cocktail that probably constituted this morning's breakfast. She'd seen many photos of her mother in her modelling days and grieved that such natural beauty should so easily evaporate in the never-ceasing flow of booze. 'I'm home now, though, so what are you worrying about?'

'It's just that it's been all the time, this holiday, Amanda.' Lucy put down her drink and tried to at least sound the concerned parent. 'You've become so secretive lately, sneaking into the house in the early hours and obviously hoping we won't hear you. Who are you seeing?'

'Oh, just a boy.' If her parents chose to think that, Amanda was happy to nurture their suspicions. At least it deflected from the true nature of her activities. Besides, it wasn't a total lie.

'A boy? What boy?' Harvey had big plans for his only daughter and they didn't include liaisons with the locals.

'Oh, just someone I met hereabouts.' It was time to put the brakes on her father's rapidly-forming alarm. She poured herself a coffee from the pot and sat down. 'It's nothing serious, Dad. We're just friends, that's all.'

'Friendly enough to keep you out till the early hours.' Harvey pointed a warning finger. 'But that's the last time. In by eleven in future for you, my girl.'

'And what if I don't want to? I'm over eighteen, so you can't make me.'

'No, but I can slow you down.' Harvey nodded in the direction of the drive and Amanda's sports car. 'I can pull that off the road quicker than you can say "on your bike".'

Amanda sighed. She loved her little car and the freedom it gave her and, more than ever, she longed for financial independence to run her life as she wanted. Already her venture was showing the promise of just that, so the less conflict with her parents right now, the better. It would just be a case of temporarily changing her business arrangements. Standing up, Amanda slipped off her robe, ran an agitated hand through long hair and said simply, 'Eleven it will be, Dad.' Then she went to the side of the pool and dived in.

It was good to feel that water cleansing both her skin and thoughts. As she leisurely swam the first of her morning twenty lengths, she was already calculating a new modus operandi. There was no way she was going to give up her money-spinner now. Besides, her father would be away for the next few days.

*   *   *

Nearing Hardley Cross, Jack was at the limit of his patrol. Standing here on the southern bank for four and a half centuries, this ancient stone landmark marked the boundary of jurisdiction between Norwich and Yarmouth. It also marked the entrance to the River Chet, that narrow tributary of the Yare, up which Jack now turned his launch. Halfway to the small town of Loddon and as Hardley Flood came in sight, the waterway was made even narrower by the working presence of the dredging team.

Here, the mighty grab crane sat atop its floating pontoon, its clanking bucket dragging great scoops of oozing mud from the river bed, to then swing and deposit it into the mud wherry lying beside. When full, this modern steel version of the old black-sailed traders would take the dredged sediment to some site needing filling. Now though, it sat high in the water, its diesel rumbling at tickover and nowhere near its forty ton capacity. Jack brought the launch alongside the crane-pontoon and threw his lines to the operator, who seemed glad of a break from his noisy task.

'Morning Charlie.' Jack and Charlie Wendlove's paths had crossed often on the northern rivers, where extensive dredging projects were on-going. 'Almost done here?'

'Just about.' The round-faced jovial lead-operator looked out over the marshes towards the distant and unseen River Waveney. 'Should have been going there for the next job, but I understand you've got a little dredge of your own you want doing first.'

'That's right. Has Tom given you the details?'

'More or less.' The crane operator unscrewed the cup from the top of his flask and poured himself a tea. 'We'll get shifting there in the next hour, so if you've got a specific location, it will certainly help.'

'Right.' Jack produced a large-scale map and showed where water depths had been particularly low.

'Hmm, right in the channel.' Charlie knocked back the dregs of his tea and screwed his cup back on the flask. 'We may need help keeping boats clear while we lay our mud-anchors, Jack. Any chance of helping us with that?'

'Shouldn't be a problem. When do you think you'll be starting?'

The lead-operator glanced at his watch. 'A few hours to get everything there, so how about later this afternoon? That way we can get started first thing tomorrow.'

Jack checked the time. 'I'll be there at three.' He climbed down into his launch. 'The boat owners will really appreciate this, Charlie. Some are already having difficulty getting out at low water.'

Charlie Wendlove let go the lines and threw them across. 'No problem, Jack. We'll soon have it sorted for them.'

*   *   *

Appreciation for the dredging was not something that would be shared by Councillor Wanstead who, right now, was off to see his "friend", Harvey Laydock, to get it stopped completely.

It was the last-ditch act of a desperate man. By daylight, exhausted from lack of sleep and mental turmoil, Henry knew he had to do something, but taking direct action on his own could well trigger the suspicion he was so keen to avoid. Big guns had to be brought to bear on his behalf and the biggest he knew was Harvey Laydock.

Even so, it was with some trepidation that he walked the mile from his village home to Fayre View. In spite of his desire to be admitted into that coveted sanctum, he still shied away from appearing "pushy" and irritating the great man. So, approaching the big oak front door, wiping beads of sweat from his bald head and gingerly about to ring the bell, Henry was startled to have the door suddenly flung open by the rather up-tight figure of Amanda. Pushing past him without so much as a word, she strode to her sports car and was soon backing away with a rebellious burst of revs and so close that she almost hit both Henry and the angry figure of her father who had just appeared at the councillor's side.

'Just you remember what I told you!' shouted Harvey, but his words were lost in the noise and dust of his daughter fast-disappearing down Fayre View 's long drive. He turned to Henry. 'Teenagers! What can you do with them?' Before the councillor could reply, it suddenly dawned on Harvey just who was standing on his doorstep. 'What do you want, Wanstead?'

'I'd just like to talk to you, Harvey. Could I come in?'

'Can't it wait?' The celebrity nodded towards his Jag. 'I'm just leaving for a very important meeting. I'll only be gone a couple of days. Call me when I get back.'

Before the door slammed in his face, Henry decided to push his luck just that bit further. 'It really is important, Harvey. It won't take long. Could you just spare me a few minutes?'

The last thing Harvey wanted right now was another boring discussion with this most tedious of local officials. Just because he expected the chairman of the council to be at his beck and call, didn't mean he had to reciprocate any favours and he wanted the man gone. But, looking into Wanstead's eyes, he did detect a definite element of desperation. By nature Harvey wasn't a compassionate man, but he was intuitive and knew only too well that desperate men would do a lot in return for favours. Begrudgingly he said, 'All right, I suppose you'd better come in.'

Any elation that Henry felt at achieving this long-sought goal was lost in his uncertainty as to how broach the subject. Besides, he noticed he was not being ushered into the inner house, but left standing, somewhat self-consciously, in the entrance hall.

'Well, what is it that's so important?' Harvey snapped, indicating his bags ready by the front door. 'I need to get off.'

'It ... it's this proposed dredging ...' began the councillor.

But he was cut short by Harvey's impatient response. 'Yes, and about time. Should've been done years ago.

'Yes ... yes ... quite ...' Henry hesitated before summoning inner courage to persist, '... but personally, Harvey, I'm against it, as you know.'

'Whatever for? Great Taste's ploughing the bottom every time we go out and even the smaller boats stir up the mud.'

'Yes, but dredging causes untold damage to plant life and ...'

'Sod the plant life,' said Harvey before placing his hand back on the front door handle, 'so if you've nothing else to waste my time about ...'

'But, Harvey, I'd do anything to stop them.' Henry wasn't even attempting to hide the desperation in his voice now. 'Can't you support me on just this issue?'

Harvey Laydock removed his hand from the door, raised his head and viewed the agitated figure before with a frown. 'Why this desperation, Wanstead? What do you need to tell me?'

'Nothing, Harvey – absolutely nothing – I just need your help, that's all.'

The look in Harvey's eyes said, I don't believe you, but he kept his silence for another agonised few seconds before indicating the small armchair by the hall telephone. 'Sit down.'

Henry sat down with all the relief of a condemned man sensing reprieve.

'I could telephone the Broads Authority, I suppose, and request them to hold off.' Harvey drew himself up slightly. 'I don't think there's any doubt my name would have them reconsidering.'

'Yes ... yes ... that would be wonderful, Harvey.' Henry went to stand up, but the celebrity's eyes forced him back down.

'I said "could", Wanstead. The question is, what could you do for me in return?'

The councillor frowned. 'I'm doing all I can for you already, Harvey. I know how much you want that Resolve Trust out of the area and I'm working on that, but ...'

'Yes, but you haven't managed it yet, have you?' interrupted Harvey. He paused a second to let this failure sink in before continuing, 'So, if you want my immediate help, there is something I need urgently dealing with in return.'

'Well, if I can help you further in any way, Harvey,' stammered Henry,' you know I will.'

'Excellent.' Harvey rubbed his hands gently together. 'That boatbuilder who has his workshop in the village ...'

'Greg Kennard? What about him, Harvey?'

'I want him thrown out.'

'Thrown out!' Henry's voice echoed his startled look. 'Why?'

'Because he's exerting a detrimental influence on my son,' explained Harvey calmly. 'Damien had a wonderful career in law charted out for him, and now that damned Kennard has talked him into wanting to be a bloody boatbuilder of all things.'

This was a step too far even for Henry. 'But Damien loves working on boats and helping out on the wherry, Harvey. Is it so bad that he has ambitions of his own?'

'It is when you've spent a fortune on private education. But I'm not asking you for advice, Wanstead. Do you want me to stop this dredging or don't you?'

'Yes ... oh yes ...' the councillor was almost on his feet again before sinking back with dismay, '... but I can't just go in and close down Kennard's business. He's well-thought of in the village for helping local young people, so I'd need a good reason.'

'There must be something you can pin on him.' Harvey thought for a second. 'That building he uses as a workshop – it used to be the village garage didn't it? Did he ever apply for permission to change its use?'

'Well, no, not specifically.' Henry cast his mind back to Greg Kennard starting his small business two years previously. 'We were just pleased that someone had turned what was a bit of an eyesore into something far more in keeping with the village.'

'Yes, well, if he didn't apply as he should, you have reason to shut him down, so see what you can do while I'm away.' Harvey glanced impatiently at his waiting bags.

Henry took the hint and stood up. 'And in return, you promise you'll get this dredging stopped?'

'I'll try and call the Authority and see what I can do.' Harvey held out his hand. 'Do we have a deal, Henry?' Knowing he had run out of any other options, Wanstead found himself taking the hand in return as he was being ushered to the door, where Harvey managed a reassuring smile. 'Now, off you go, Henry, and stop worrying.' He nodded again down the road. 'Just go and get the paperwork rolling to get shot of Kennard and his workshop.'

With the chairman of the council successfully ejected, it was time for Harvey to be on his way too. Picking up his bags, he shouted a hurried 'I'm off,' to his wife somewhere in the house and was actually out of the front door before her faint, 'Bye, darling,' could reach him in return. In less than a minute, his Jag was roaring off in the opposite direction to Councillor Wanstead, and Harvey was congratulating himself that, hopefully, he had engineered the removal of at least one divisive element influencing his family.

From Fayre View's upstairs landing window, Lucy Laydock watched her husband depart. For the last five minutes she had been quietly standing there listening to every word of his conversation with that insufferable Councillor Wanstead.

Now she sauntered back into the bedroom, sat at her dressing table and wondered what she should do with this new-found knowledge.

*   *   *

Chapter Five

A speeding cruiser and an angler trolling under power delayed Jack on the return leg of his morning's patrol, so it was past midday when he arrived back at Brundall. That was all part of the job, but keeping abreast of other river projects was another and he now turned into the main marina to check on progress with the wherry's rig.

He found Resolve at the far end, where a large mobile crane was just swinging the new mast over her foredeck. Although suspended close to its lower end, the lead counterbalance already attached to its foot was allowing the near-fifty foot length of timber to hang horizontally. Aided by signals from Greg Kennard, the crane operator was skilfully edging the whole assembly into position.

Jack came to a stop a fair distance off, not wishing to interrupt proceedings or distract the other team members whose lines were guiding and steadying in the still-fresh wind. A sudden thumbs-up from Greg, and the easing stopped. Six feet from the mast's foot, a two-inch thick pin, projecting from either side and on which the mast would eventually pivot, sat poised above iron-reinforced slots in the top of the tabernacle. While Damien hurriedly gave the pin a quick coating of grease, Greg made a final check that the team were holding it true. Then the crane was easing down the last few inches until the pin sat squarely in its slot. With the masthead crane iron resting on the metal horse that spanned the roof of the cuddy, there were cheers from the whole team as the lifting strop was unshackled and craned back onto the quay.

'That looks better,' said Jack, breathing in the sweet scent of Canadian pine.

'It will do once we've treated it,' replied Greg, walking aft and wiping surplus grease from his hands with a cotton rag.

'With what?'

'Mainly teak oil, a bit of varnish just to harden it, and a drop of white spirit to help it soak in.' The boatbuilder gave the mast a hearty slap. 'Can't say it's not a relief to have that lot safely installed. One and a quarter tons of pitch-pine there, and the same in lead to counterbalance it. If we've got it right, it should only take the pull of one hand to bring it down.' Greg was appearing nonchalant, but, in the craftsman's eyes, Jack could detect the gleam of satisfaction of a job well done.

Gloria Vale seemed equally delighted to see this vital stage of the project nearer completion. She'd just emerged from below with a tray of glasses filled with sparkling drink. 'I think this calls for a celebration.'

'I thought this was a dry ship?' observed Jack, with a mock frown.

'Just fizzy grape juice.' She looked proud of the small group gathered together on the main hatch, chatting happily. 'You've all done well this morning.'

Indeed, even the surly Flinty was showing a sliver of enthusiasm, taking one of the glasses and giving his mentor a quick smile of thanks before disappearing for'ard to join the others. Jack directed a questioning glance towards Gloria. 'Finally got up then?'

'Yes, eventually, after a lot of nagging.' She gave a tolerant shrug. 'He's a strange lad. I asked him where he'd been so late last night and his only explanation was "private reasons".'

'Hmm.' Jack helped himself to a glass of grape juice, cleared his mind of cynical thoughts and nodded towards the mast. 'So, when will you have her sailing?'

'Very soon, we hope.' Gloria glanced at the quayside and the large spar lying close by. 'We'll be getting the gaff on next and the sail should be delivered later this afternoon.'

'Rigging will be one big learning curve,' said Greg, placing his empty glass on the cabin roof, 'but sailing her will be the real challenge.'

'You mean none of you have actually handled a wherry before?'

'Well, we've crewed on a couple and even done stints at the helm,' answered Gloria, 'but those few hours won't seem much when we sail Resolve out for the first time.'

Jack nodded. 'Then you'll need an experienced skipper with you to begin with.'

'I agree, but all the present skippers are busy sailing their own wherries,' explained Greg.

'And, I think there's also a bit of reluctance to become involved with a controversial project still in its infancy,' added Gloria.

'That's a pity.' Jack thought for a few seconds. 'You know, there's an old boy called Alf Rumball in my village, and he used to skipper wherries way back. He's in his eighties now, but what he doesn't know about these old traders isn't worth knowing. Why don't I ask him if he'd help?' Jack noticed a shadow cloud Gloria's previously smiling face. 'What's wrong with that, Gloria?'

She shook her head. 'It's just the thought of an octogenarian handling this huge rig, Jack. Would he be up to it?'

'Oh yes, Alfie's still pretty active for his age.'

'And the old boy wouldn't have to do any physical work,' added Greg, with more eagerness than his employer. 'We could do all the heaving and hauling and all we'd need from him would be his experience and advice.'

Gloria shrugged and smiled. 'If you think he'd be okay, then it's a wonderful suggestion, Jack, but do you think he really would be prepared to help us?'

'No harm in asking. I see him most days on my evening walks. He'd probably jump at the chance. When would you need him?'

'Day after tomorrow,' answered Greg. 'Rigging the gaff and then bending on the sail will be new territory for me, so if he could give us pointers on that, it would be invaluable.'

'Except we can't afford to pay him much, Jack,' warned Gloria. 'We're close to our budget as it is.'

'Well, if there's the chance of sailing a wherry again at the end of it, I should think his expenses plus some baccy for his pipe and the odd bottle of rum will do him fine. Hopefully, I'll see him tonight when I'm out with Spike.' Jack turned back to Gloria. 'Have you given any more thought to my other suggestion?'

'The water frolic? Yes, we all talked it over on the way here and everyone thinks it's a great idea.' She nodded towards her charges, chatting and laughing atop the main hatch. 'In fact, they're very enthusiastic.'

This group of youngsters certainly appeared contented in their new life. Damien and Rita seemed to be particularly companionable, whispering and laughing together while the young artist kept running a hand, slightly self-consciously through her spiky hair.

Greg's voice brought Jack back to the business in hand. 'So, I'll have a chat in the village tonight and see what support I can drum up there. If you'd like to stop by the workshop tomorrow morning, I'll let you know how I got on.' He gave a mischievous laugh. 'We'll certainly upset Wanstead's applecart when he finds out what's going on right under his nose. He's got just what he deserves coming his way.'

'Starting today,' said Jack, glancing at his watch and giving a chuckle of his own. 'The works crew arrive in an hour to start dredging his precious broad.'

*   *   *

The Ranger was certainly correct on that point, for Henry Wanstead was already standing by the broad, worried out of his mind.

It was the councillor's custom to take a short walk every afternoon, ostensibly, as a period of healthy exercise but, in reality, to check no unauthorised building or other goings-on were occurring in what he considered very much his parish. During this afternoon's stroll he'd been going over his strained chat with Harvey Laydock and the celebrity's assurance that he would try and get the threatened dredging halted. Any hope this had given him, however, was instantly dashed as he arrived at the broad in time to witness the arrival of Charlie Wendlove and his fleet.

The first harbinger of doom had been the crane-pontoon, its raised boom gliding above the treeline like the neck and head of some prehistoric creature. For Henry Wanstead, it was just as threatening. By the time it had been manoeuvred down the narrow dyke and into the broad by its pusher-tug, a couple of mud-wherries had already appeared and stopped in the channel fairway. Wanstead groaned inwardly, fumbled for his mobile phone, selected a much-coveted number and dialled.

'What do you want, Henry? I'm just going in to a meeting.' Harvey Laydock wasn't pleased at this call.

'Harvey, the dredgers ... they're here and about to start.'

'Right, well it's too late to do anything about it now then, isn't it?' Harvey sounded almost relieved.

'But ... but you promised to stop them.'

'I didn't promise anything, Henry. I said I'd try and call.'

'And did you?'

'No, I didn't have time.'

'Well, can you call them now? You might still be able ...'

'I've just told you, I'm going into a meeting.' Harvey gave his most exasperated sigh. 'I'll try and talk to them later.'

'Please, Harvey. This is important.'

'Yes, well so are the jobs I asked you to do for me,' grumbled Harvey. 'Have you done anything about Kennard's workshop yet, or getting that damned Resolve Trust outfit drummed out of the county?'

'No, not yet, but I'm working ...'

'Then you'd better pull your finger out and work harder or I might let slip just how much you want to avoid this dredging.' Harvey allowed a few seconds for that to sink in before adding, 'If you have some dark little secret you want keeping, then you'd better do as I ask and pronto.' He gave a meaningful sigh. 'I'm running out of patience, Wanstead, just like you're running out of time.'

And with that, Harvey Laydock rang off leaving his parish councillor feeling more desolate than he'd felt for eight long years.

*   *   *

'Looks like the water frolic might be a goer, Aud.' Jack had just finished his evening meal and was feeling the contentment of any man blessed with a warm home, loving wife and good food. He stretched his legs under the kitchen table and sighed. 'Perhaps we'll get some equanimity between those two groups yet.'

'Yes, well let's see if Greg Kennard manages to get others in his village feeling likewise,' said Audrey, with wifely caution. 'If he doesn't, we're back to square one.'

'He will. He's a popular chap hereabouts and there must be plenty of locals just ready to get one over on Laydock and Wanstead.' Jack gave a little chuckle. 'Actually, our councillor's got even more to worry about now they've started dredging. You should have seen his face this afternoon. I stopped at the staithe to put up a notice about the temporary channel and he attacked me as soon as my feet touched shore. Yelled that we had "no right to go against the wishes of the parish", when of course, it's only him who doesn't want the channel dredged.'

'But why ever not?' Audrey frowned. 'You'd think he'd be delighted at work to improve water access to the village.'

'I know, it puzzles me. In fact, it's beginning to make me downright suspicious.'

'Now Jack,' said Audrey, putting a placatory hand on her husband's, 'that's enough of that. You're not a detective anymore and just you remember it. Do your job as a ranger and be happy with that. No investigations.'

'Yep, you're right, love. Okay, Spike,' said Jack, sliding back his chair and patting the head of his border collie, sitting close and looking expectantly towards the door, 'let's get you walked by the river and we might see Alfie Rumball.'

'That's more like it,' agreed Audrey. 'I'm sure old Alfie will jump at the chance to be aboard a wherry again. He's always looked so down since he lost his wife a couple of years ago.'

'Well, this could certainly be just the tonic he needs.' Jack went to the kitchen door and took Spike's lead from its hook. 'I'm off to see Greg tomorrow morning about the frolic, and it would be great if I could tell him I've found a willing skipper.'

'Just which weekend are you planning to hold the frolic on?' asked Audrey, with another concern just surfacing.

'Two weeks time.'

'Have you forgotten Jo's baby is due about then?'

'No, don't worry, I haven't,' Jack reassured her, 'but first babies generally arrive late, don't they, so all being well, we'll be free.'

'"We'll"?' queried Audrey, raising her head.

'Well, there's going to be a lot of catering needed, love, and the more stalls the better, so I was hoping ...'

'… I could do some baking, I suppose.' Audrey shook her head. 'I knew I'd end up being cajoled into giving something more than advice if this went ahead.'

'Well, it was your idea, love, and it will keep your mind off Jo in those days before the birth.' Jack gave his wife an encouraging smile. 'And then we can head for London to do the grandparenting thing, contented with a job well done.'

'I think we'll both need a break after all the "frolicking",' said Audrey, opening the kitchen door and ushering out her husband and Spike, whose tail was now wagging uncontrollably. 'Go on, off with the pair of you and have a nice walk.'

It was one of those idyllic summer evenings, a blessed stillness enveloping their small village while the fast-setting sun threw into vivid relief the endless marshes that stretched beyond it. The sky was reddening now, its huge arcing expanse all set to darken after another glorious Broadland day. Red sky at night – sailors' delight. Jack hoped the events of the morrow would be as calm as the weather if the old lore was correct.

He was at the edge of the village now, picking out the familiar landmarks of abandoned windpumps and distant church towers peering above the otherwise-unbroken horizon. Close by, the river, so much narrower and lazier than the Yare, ebbed its languid way south.

Jack was thinking back to his post-supper chat with Audrey and, in particular, her last firm advice. He had always valued her thoughts and opinions and certainly never consciously went against her wishes, but this evening, with Spike now off his lead and running excitedly ahead, he couldn't help mentally doing just that. For his thoughts were still on Councillor Henry Wanstead's extraordinary aversion to having the broad dredged. His opposition had been strenuous from the start and this afternoon, on finding it was actually happening and far sooner than he thought, his reaction had bordered on hysterical. People didn't behave like that without some underlying reason and Jack made a mental note to learn a little more about this unpopular man.

The sudden flight of a pair of startled mallards from the riverbank brought Jack's thoughts back to the present. The cause of the disturbance was a lone figure making his slow way back along the riverbank. He was an old man wearing a faded seamen's cap which barely contained the mop of unruly white hair beneath. Hunched shoulders accentuated an air of sadness, but when the old boatman looked up and recognised the ranger walking towards him, a spontaneous smile broke through his unkempt whiskers.

Jack gave a cheerful wave in return and quickened his step, pleased at this happy meeting with old Alfie Rumball.

'Hi Mum.'

'Hi, Darling. Come and tell me what you've been doing today.'

Damien threw his old rucksack into the corner of the hall and went on through to the lounge. His mother was just pouring herself another drink at the well-stocked bar, but she turned and smiled warmly as her son joined her. 'Drink, love?'

'No thanks, Mum,' said Damien, hiding his disapproval, 'but a cup of tea would go down well.' He didn't really want a cuppa and was quite capable of making his own if he did, but giving his mother a task was a trick he often used to prise her away from the booze. 'Care to make me one?'

Damien followed his mum into the kitchen. This imposing room, fitted out in oak with state-of-the-art equipment to beat all states, was highly appropriate for one of the country's most well-known chefs, and where Harvey spent much of his time when at home. To maintain public interest, he had to keep coming up with new cooking ideas, if only to fill the Christmas book which his publishers and eager public demanded annually. So, this was where Harvey concocted, experimented with, practised and, finally, perfected his new, innovative recipes. There was even the suggestion of one programme being made right here at Fayre View with Harvey cooking at home in his own kitchen.

They'd have to get it cleaned up first, thought Damien, as he glanced around at work surfaces littered with the results of just one day's attempt by his mother to feed herself. Sadly, marriage to Harvey had brought none of his culinary talents to the decidedly undomesticated Lucy. When her husband was away, she would potter and dabble in this temple of cuisine, but eventually the only food she produced was out of a packet and the only equipment used was the microwave. Damien watched her now as she managed to get a kettle boiling on the Aga, but then struggled to remember where the tea was kept. He pretended not to notice.

'Ah, here it is!' exclaimed Lucy, triumphantly, as she located the earthen pot, removed a bag and was about to drop it into a mug.

'Hang on, Mum, why don't you make a pot and join me?'

'Oh no, I don't think ...'

But Damien was already getting out the white teapot and placing cups, saucers, sugar and milk on the big farmhouse table that filled the central space. He guided her into one of the big carving chairs. 'Sit yourself down, and I'll brew up.' Soon, he was sitting down opposite and pouring a cup for his mum before filling his own. 'When's Dad back?'

'Tomorrow night ... hopefully.'

Damien wasn't sure if his mother really was "hopeful". It was an undeniable fact that Harvey's absence produced an altogether happier atmosphere in the family home and also one of the few times he could chat to his mum one-to-one. He leaned forward and said. 'Well, Resolve's got her new mast now.'

'Oh good.' Lucy spooned sugar into her tea, added milk, took a token sip and smiled. 'Did you do much of the work?'

'Quite a bit. Greg was in charge, but he let me do most of the hands-on stuff.'

'You really enjoy working with that man, don't you?' Lucy was viewing her son over the top of her cup. Having heard this morning's conversation between her husband and Councillor Wanstead, she needed to know if what she was planning to do was for the best.

'I'm learning all I can about traditional boatbuilding, Mum, and there's no better teacher than Greg.' Damien paused to take a swig of tea before looking his mother straight in the eye. 'That's what I want to do for a living, Mum – be a boatbuilder.'

'I know.' Lucy placed her cup back into its saucer, unsure on how to proceed with this recurring conversation. Finally, she just said, 'But that's not what your dad wants, Damien.'

'Why not?'

'Oh, he just wants you to be a success in life without the struggles he had.' Lucy was aware she was using oft-repeated reasoning, but it was a subject she found difficult to handle.

'But surely "success" in life is doing what you want to do.' Damien looked abstractedly into his teacup. 'Just working on Resolve, seeing her coming back to life with me having played a part, has been so satisfying.'

Lucy stretched a hand across the table and laid it on her son's, something she did very rarely these days. 'You really do want to do this, don't you?'

'More than anything else, Mum.' He had never wanted to create any added tensions between his parents, but this was one of those times when he had to push things all the way. He looked his mother straight in the eye and asked, 'Would you talk to Dad about it, Mum?'

'Well... I don't know.' Lucy would have liked something stronger right now, but instead took a gulp of her tea. 'He's so keen for you to be a lawyer, Damien.'

'But, Mum, I can't imagine anything worse than being stuck in an office all day. I want to work with my hands as well as my brain.'

Lucy stretched her once-pretty mouth into a grimace before allowing it to relax into a smile of surrender. 'All right, Damien, I'll see what I can do.'

'Brilliant!' Damien jumped up, went around the table and gave his mother a big hug.

This was another sign of affection she hadn't experienced for a long time, but she raised a finger of caution. 'I'm not promising anything, Damien. You know how stubborn your father can be.'

'Don't I just.' Damien sat down again and poured fresh cups of tea for both of them. 'I wish I could just get him to come and look around Resolve. If he saw how beautiful she's looking, I'm sure he'd realise what rewarding work boatbuilding is.'

'I don't think there's much chance of that, Damien.' Lucy pulled a face. 'You know how much he hates your Gloria Vale.'

'Goodness knows why.' Damien scowled. 'All this animosity. Why can't people just get on?'

'Because that's the way of the world,' explained Lucy, wearily.

'Not my world, Mum.' Damien suddenly brightened with a thought. 'But you could come. I'd love to show you all the work I've done. You could meet all the gang. They're a great bunch really, in spite of all that Dad says about them.'

'But I couldn't do that, Damien – I can't be seen to be disloyal to your father.' Lucy shook her head firmly. 'He'd be furious.'

'How much loyalty does he show you?' Even as he said it, Damien saw a shadow of pain cross his mother's face. Quickly smiling again, he leaned conspiratorially closer and said, 'But would he have to know? We could wait until he's away again and then I'd take you in Just Bittern.'

'What, that tippy little thing,' laughed Lucy. 'Damien, you know I don't like boats. I only go on Great Taste because your father wants me to.'

Damien crinkled his nose with mock disdain. 'I don't blame you.' It was good seeing his mother laugh again and somehow he wanted this simple evening of maternal warmth to go on forever. 'Come and see Resolve, Mum, and then you'll see what a real boat should look like.'

'I'll think about it Damien.' Then, seeing a good-humoured down-turn of his mouth, she just as quickly relented. 'Oh, alright, I'd love to see this wonderful boat of yours and meet all those strange ... enthusiastic ... young people you're always telling me about.'

'I'll keep you to that, Mum. At least that way you'll get to meet Greg.'

'Mmm,' replied Lucy, thinking she would probably be meeting the man far sooner than that. Keen to change the subject, she glanced at her watch. 'It's gone ten o'clock. Where is that sister of yours? What does she do with herself these evenings?'

'Oh, Amanda's okay, Mum. Don't worry about her.' Damien knew exactly what his sister was doing on board his father's cruiser, but now was not the time to come clean and spoil such a rare, homely evening with his mum. He picked up the teapot. 'How about another cup?'

'Hmm, yes please.' Lucy couldn't believe she was drinking tea and actually enjoying it. But neither could she remember when she had last felt so contented and relaxed. Jumping up, she refilled the kettle and placed it back on the Aga. 'I'll make a fresh pot. It's just so lovely sharing this with you, Damien.'

Her son nodded agreement and wondered if it really was so bad to wish his father would never come back and spoil it.

*   *   *

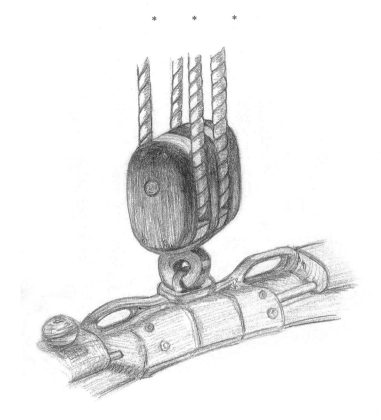

Chapter Six

Long before Jack glided onto the broad next morning, he could hear the rumble of diesels and clank of the crane. Charlie Wendlove and his team had begun their dredging and he could imagine Councillor Wanstead hearing the same noise and cursing the day Jack Fellows ever came on to his broad.

Where the dyke entered the broad, the crane was hard at work, its clamshell bucket scooping a cubic metre of sediment with each drag of its hungry jaws and dumping it into a mud-wherry moored alongside. Yellow marker buoys kept other river traffic well clear of this area of activity. A hire cruiser that had obviously spent the night at the staithe was already negotiating around them as Jack slid his launch alongside the steel hull of the mud wherry. He threw across his lines and climbed aboard. It wasn't a high climb as, almost fully laden, its gunwale was close to the waterline. The skipper, who'd been watching the loading from the steering well aft, came for'ard and joined him, the cigarette in the corner of his mouth a seemingly fixed object that showed not the slightest chance of slipping even as he spoke. 'Almost our first load, Jack.'

'Great, you'll soon have this channel deepened.' The ranger looked at the great mound of sediment filling the hold. 'Where are you going to dump this stuff?'

The skipper indicated eastwards with his cigarette. ''bout three miles downriver. They're working on the flood defences there and glad to have it to fill the setback area.'

Flood defence work was a long-term project being carried out by the Environment Agency, involving a secondary dyke being dug behind the main river and creating a new reed-rhond. The sediment being dug here would be perfect for that purpose and Jack was glad there was going to be a double benefit to this work. Once again the crane swung its great boom and emptied a final bucketful of mud into the hold, causing the big hull to rock only slightly. The skipper glanced over the side at his freeboard and gave a thumbs-up to Charlie at the dragline's controls. The crane wouldn't be idle for long: already another mud-wherry was entering the broad and a third would be having its load craned out as this one made ready to slip its lines. Charlie came out of his cab and shouted, 'Time for a coffee, Jack?'

'No thanks, I've got to go and see someone in the village.' As Jack's temporary mooring began to move off, he slipped his own lines, jumped down into the launch and motored away. Before he reached the staithe, the other mud-wherry was securing alongside the dredger, all ready to have her empty hold filled with another load of bottom mud. It was certainly a disruptive process in an area that normally basked in peace and tranquillity, but the long-term benefit far outweighed a week of inconvenience and, anyway, most holidaymakers enjoyed seeing the working side of life on the Broads. If the water frolic went ahead as planned, it could double as a celebration of this broad's rebirth. But that all depended on whether the villagers supported the idea, and Jack hoped Greg Kennard's testing of that particular water had been a fruitful one. He'd soon find out.

Unfortunately, his meeting with Greg might be slightly delayed because already standing on the staithe was Councillor Wanstead, watching the dredging work with almost hypnotic obsession. The last thing Jack wanted this morning was another battle of words with this man.

As it was he had the perfect excuse for ignoring him because, once alongside, he saw a police vehicle parked on the road and two men standing by the parish moorings talking, one of whom was the unmistakable figure of PC Stan Meadows. The other man moved off as Jack approached.

'Morning Stan. Seems like you can't stay away from this place.'

'You could say that, Jack.' The PC gave a groan. 'More thefts, I'm afraid. Another outboard, same as last time.'

Jack nodded towards the figure just disappearing back into the village. 'Is he the victim?'

'Yep. Keeps a small fishing dinghy on the parish mooring. Used it over the weekend, locked the engine like he always did, but came to check it last night and found it gone. He has to go to work so I drove out to see him first thing.'

'Presumably another one without a cover?'

'Right, but this one was locked, not that that put off our thief. He cut right through it.' PC Meadows shook his head. 'Whoever he is, he's getting a bit more determined ... or just greedy.'

'So, from what you tell me, it could've been stolen last night?'

'Yep.' PC Meadows was reading the ranger's thoughtful expression. 'Do you know something, Jack?'

'Only that Flinty from Resolve went off in a canoe last night and didn't return until after midnight.'

'I didn't trust that one from the start.' PC Meadows placed his notebook and pen back into the breast pocket of his uniform shirt. 'I think I'll pay Mister Flint another visit.'

'And I'm just off into the village to chat with Greg Kennard. I'll see if he can shed any more light on the subject.' Jack looked the constable in the eye. 'But, do me a favour, Stan, and keep the Resolve side low key for now. I'm trying to build some bridges between parish and wherry and there's enough suspicion between the two already without blue lights flashing everywhere.'

'I'll do what I can, but you know how quickly rumour spreads.'

Jack agreed, before indicating the distant figure of Councillor Wanstead. 'He's the last person we want involved. I'm surprised he isn't here now demanding to know what's going on.'

'Oh, he's already spoken to me. As soon as I drew up, he came rushing over wanting to know what the problem was.'

Jack rolled his eyes. 'I can believe that. Nothing much gets past him regarding village matters.'

'Yeah, but that's the strange thing,' said the PC, looking bemused. 'When I told him about the new theft he seemed almost relieved.'

'Interesting,' was Jack's only comment as he wished Stan farewell and set off for the village, but with thoughts that remained on the staithe with a man whose past definitely called for more investigation.

*   *   *

Greg's workshop was in the centre of the village. Old petrol pumps, unused and rusting, stood outside like sentinels of its previous incarnation. The street itself was so narrow that Jack was amazed anyone had ever managed to get a car here in the first place. As it was, the couple of wooden dinghies standing on the forecourt looked much more in keeping with their surroundings.

It was another fine summer's day and the main doors to the workshop stood open, allowing the unmistakable smell of oak shavings and varnish to come wafting outside. Greg didn't seem to be around, so Jack paused to admire the two boats.

One was a simple rowing boat, but the other had a mast and spars lying across her thwarts and a rudder hanging from the transom. On each, the wood was varnished to the smoothness of glass and the bronze fittings and painted sheerstrakes gleamed in the morning sunshine. Jack had never been much of a handyman and always felt in awe of those who had the technical know-how and practical ability to produce such perfection. He could well understand Damien's ambition to be a boatbuilder.

'Hello, Jack.' The deep voice made Jack jump, as Greg Kennard emerged from his workshop, a bacon sandwich in one hand and mug of coffee in the other. 'I just stopped for a quick brekki.' He glanced up to his studio flat above. 'Care for some?'

'Thanks for asking, Greg, but I ate earlier and have to watch the old waist-line.' Jack gave the dinghy they were standing by a gentle stroke. 'I've just been admiring the quality of your craftsmanship.'

'Well, I always feel wooden boats should be an extension of your soul.' The boatbuilder shrugged broad shoulders. 'Unfortunately, attention to detail means time and money. The result is a beautiful boat that few people can afford.' He indicated over his shoulder to the workshop. 'Come and look around.'

The inside of Greg's premises were much as Jack had imagined, with the bare ribs of a new dinghy occupying most of the floor space and tools, blocks, oars, paddles, ropes, spars and even old sails hanging from every spare inch of wall or ceiling. Along one side, two striking new Indian canoes sat above the shop floor on a purpose-built rack. One was beautifully varnished while the other was bright red with imaginative designs in yellow painted along the gunwale. 'Young Rita Wakefield did that artwork,' explained Greg, noticing Jack's interest.

'Clever girl. Do many of the Resolve's team, other than Damien, come and help out here?'

The boatbuilder shook his head. 'Not yet, and Rita tends to only come when she knows Damien will be here.'

'Ahh.' Jack gave a knowing wink.

'But I'm hoping they'll all become involved eventually,' continued Greg. He reached up to a shelf, pulled down a large roll of paper and spread it out across the bench. It was plans for a rowing boat. 'A rowing skiff, actually,' explained Greg with suppressed enthusiasm. 'They've been designed as a cheap alternative to the vastly more expensive gigs. The idea came from Scotland where they hope to encourage groups of young people to build and race their own.' He tapped the outline of the sleek boat depicted. 'It's the sort of project I'd love the Resolve group to take on, to build the boat and then race it competitively. Of course, something like that would cost money.'

'Sounds a terrific scheme though. How much?'

'The boat itself would cost about three grand to build.'

'Surely not an unrealistic goal. Couldn't Gloria fund it herself?'

Greg shook his head. 'Resolve's restoration has just about cleaned her out and I work for next to nothing just for the love of it.' He let go of the plans which sprang back into their roll with symbolic finality. 'No, for this it's sponsorship or nothing, I'm afraid.'

'Which makes the water frolic even more important,' said Jack. 'How did you get on drumming up support last night?'

'Very well.' Greg visibly brightened. 'Everyone I spoke to is absolutely for it. They're forming a committee to work out what we can all do and want Gloria and her team to come along for a first meeting at our local, The Ferryman, tomorrow night. I'll be telling Gloria when I do my stint on Resolve this afternoon. Can I tell her you'll be there as well, Jack?'

'Wouldn't miss it.' Jack indicated the rolled up plans. 'A bit of publicity at the frolic might well get you that sponsorship and help Gloria at the same time. With Resolve's restoration complete she'll be able to increase numbers. Presumably she qualifies for grants from social services?'

'Some, but Resolve's also a registered charity and public awareness might increase donations, which will be good all round. The restoration of another trading wherry, set to sail the Broads once more must surely be a plus for tourism, so, hopefully, some local businesses might also cough up a bit of support.'

'Which brings me to more good news,' said Jack. 'Alfie Rumball says he'll be happy to help in any way he can.'

'Oh, that's great!' exclaimed Greg. 'Working with Resolve has fulfilled a lifetime dream of mine, but I must admit getting her sailing without expert help was a bit of a daunting prospect.'

'Well, Alfie will set you straight,' said Jack. 'He's thrilled to be able to contribute something again. I've got a day off tomorrow so, if I bring him to Brundall, can one of you pick us up in the tender?'

'No problem, and why don't you suggest he stays on board with us for a few days. Gloria will be glad to have him and it'll save a lot of time.'

'Good idea.' Jack's thoughts returned to the proposed meeting. 'Are any members of the parish council going to be there?'

'No, we'll be a totally independent body and you wouldn't find any of the council prepared to go against the chairman anyway. He intimidates them too much for that.'

'If he's so unapproachable, how did he get made chairman?'

Greg gave a humourless laugh. 'By default. He'd been on the council for years and I think they all felt sorry for him when his wife left him.'

'When was that?'

'About eight years ago. Ran off with another man ... and who can blame her?'

'Quite. What was Mrs Wanstead's first name?'

The boatbuilder scratched his head. 'She's been gone so long now, but let's think ... Alice ... yes, that's right ... Alice.'

'So, where is she now?'

'Canada with her fancy man, according to Wanstead.'

'Doesn't anyone keep in touch with her? She must have relations or friends hereabouts.'

'Nope, no-one heard from her again after she left. We all just assumed she felt guilty and wanted to cut all ties.'

'Interesting,' muttered Jack, to himself, but it was a reaction picked up by Greg who looked at him quizzically.

'What are you thinking?'

'Oh, just possibilities,' said Jack while making his way back outside. 'Time to find out how the dredging's coming along. Hello ... looks like you've got a visitor.'

The middle-aged woman who had just appeared on the forecourt must have been quite stunning in her younger days, but her approach now was surprisingly nervous, and the ranger's presence seemed to have her thinking twice about continuing at all. It was only Greg's quick response that stayed her retreat and confirmed Jack's suspicions as to her identity.

'It's Mrs Laydock, isn't it?'

'Yes ... yes, that's right ...' she turned and smiled weakly and her voice held just a hint of shyness, '... and you must be Greg?'

The boatbuilder nodded, shook her hand and introduced her to the ranger. 'Jack, this is Damien's mum.'

She shook Jack's hand. 'The name's Lucy, actually.' She turned back to Greg. 'But how do you know my name?'

'Damien showed me photos of all his family. He hoped one day I'd get to meet you and here you are.' He nodded back towards the workshop. 'If you're looking for Damien, I'm afraid he's not in this morning.'

Lucy smiled and nodded. 'No, I know. Actually, it's you I want to have a chat with, Greg.'

Jack took his cue, said his goodbyes and was walking away when Lucy Laydock unexpectedly caught up with him. 'Mr Fellows, just one minute.' She paused as though unsure how to continue. Taking a deep gulp, she asked, 'I believe you've already had some dealings with my husband?'

'Indeed. We met when he reported the theft of his outboard motor.'

'So, you might meet him again?'

'Probably.'

'Then, can I ask a favour? Will you please not mention you met me ...' she nodded back towards Greg's workshop, '... here?' Seeing the look in Jack's eyes, she quickly added, 'Harvey doesn't like Damien doing what he considers menial work and he'd be furious if he thought I was here behind his back.' Her own eyes spoke more than her final word. 'Please?'

'Of course not,' Jack gave her hand a squeeze of reassurance, 'if that's what you want.'

*   *   *

Back at the staithe, Councillor Wanstead had ended his vigil on the dredger, which had already moved another few metres further into the broad. Jack gave Charlie Wendlove a cheerful wave as he motored by, heading for the main river and resumption of his patrol.

The water frolic idea seemed to be working out well but, as invariably happened, solutions seemed to be raising ever more questions than answers.

Just why was Lucy Laydock so keen to talk to Greg Kennard? And why had no one heard from Mrs Wanstead since she left her husband?

*   *   *

'She's not in her bedroom either.'

Amanda Laydock was shouting down the stairs to her brother after they'd both been surprised to find their mother missing from her recliner by the pool. Usually, when their mother failed to come for breakfast, it was because she was hungover.

'Where can she be?' asked a concerned Amanda, as she joined Damien in the lounge.

'I can't think. We had a lovely chat together last night and when we went to bed she seemed really cheerful, so I don't think ...' Damien drew short of putting into words the fear that both he and his sister secretly shared for a mother whose drink-fuelled mood swings were sometimes to the point of morbid. '... unless ...'

'Hi darlings.' A cheerful call from the front door had them both turning in surprise at the sight of Lucy entering, her face flushed, but with a smile of genuine satisfaction. 'Goodness, you both look like you've seen a ghost.'

'I ... it's just that we couldn't find you,' stammered Amanda, following her mum into the kitchen. 'Where have you been?'

'The village.'

'The village?' A very public conviction for DWI had long ago lost their mother her driving licence and the alternative of walking or cycling was something she never even considered. Consequently, although the village was only a mile away, it remained almost unknown territory for Lucy unless driven there by either their father or Amanda.

'Yes, the village,' emphasised Lucy. 'It was a lovely morning so I decided to walk in and do a bit of shopping.' She dropped a bag of assorted groceries onto the kitchen table with all the pride of a war trophy.

This was even more astounding as their weekly shop was usually an extravagant delivery, ordered online by their father.

Amanda wasn't sure whether to laugh or cry. After all, it must have been almost as big a shock for the staff at the village store as it was for her and

Damien. 'Was that the only reason you went in?' she asked. 'Just to get some shopping, or had you run out of drink?'

'Not at all, I just noticed we were a bit short of teabags.' Lucy leaned against a kitchen unit. 'Phew, two miles. A long time since I did that!' She glanced about her. 'I could do with a drink.' As looks of disappointment clouded her children's faces, she reached for the kettle and smiled. 'So let's have a cup of coffee together.'

As Amanda prepared the cafetiere, Damien laid out cups and saucers. Words couldn't express his joy at this seeming transformation, but it left him equally mystified. How could one short walk to the village work such a startling change? What could have happened there? The answer came in his mother's next few sentences.

'Oh, I met your Greg Kennard while I was there,' she said over her shoulder, with a nonchalance so affected, it was almost comical. 'He told me all about this water frolic thing and said there was a meeting at the pub tomorrow night. Perhaps I can come with you?'

While Amanda and Damien gave each other bewildered glances across the kitchen, their mother added, 'And, while I was walking, I gave some thought to your invitation to look at this big boat you work on, Damien.' She poured herself a cup of coffee. 'Yes, I think I'd love to see Resolve.'

*   *   *

Back on the main river, Jack keyed in a number on his mobile phone. In his years in the Met, he'd made many useful contacts, not least the Fleet Street journalists whose own intelligence gathering was usually on a par with the Yard. For just the odd titbit of discreet information passed to the paper in question, huge savings in investigative time could be made when they needed personal data in a hurry. These days, Jack rarely had use for this invaluable arrangement, but he was still owed a few favours and now was the time to claim one of them. The receptionist at a well-known popular daily answered his call and put him through to the extension requested.

'Bill Whitely.'

'Hi Bill. Jack Fellows. Still dishing the dirt then?'

'Jack, good to hear from you. You must need a favour.'

'Just a small one, Bill. I need some information on TV celebrity chef, Harvey Laydock.'

The journalist gave a chuckle. 'Good old Harvey. His little indiscretions keep us going in scandal from one edition to the next.'

'Well, I need to know if he's been involved with a woman.'

'A woman?' The voice at the other end gave a laugh. 'Jack, if you want me to go through the list, you'll run out of phone credit before I'm halfway.'

'Yeah, I can imagine. But just one, Bill - Gloria Vale.'

'The name doesn't immediately ring a bell, but I'll check and call you back.'

'Thanks, Bill, I appreciate it.'

Jack rang off and continued downriver. In some ways he felt a little two-faced to be checking the backgrounds of newfound acquaintances, but he was trying to help them all and needed to know why there was such unreasonable animosity between Gloria and Harvey.

He was passing Resolve, now back in her dyke and with her team already busy rubbing down the new mast, still horizontal along the wherry's length. Gloria and Flinty weren't in sight, but the other youngsters, recognising his launch, gave a friendly wave. He would be seeing Gloria tomorrow when he brought Alfie, so he didn't stop, but waved back in return as he motored past.

The thought occurred that Gloria and Flinty might well be below being interviewed again by Stan Meadows, so he gave it a few more miles further downriver before ringing the number stored in his mobile phone.

'Stan ... Jack ... you finished with Flinty?'

'Yep, but says he didn't go anywhere near the parish moorings last night.'

'Yeah, well we probably guessed he'd say that, but I need you to check something else, Stan.'

'What's that, Jack?'

'Just a check in Missing Persons.'

'Sure, what's the name?'

'Wanstead ... Mrs Alice Wanstead.'

*   *   *

'Hi, I'm home.'

Harvey threw his bag into the corner of the hallway and wandered through to Fayre View's swimming pool. This was where he invariably found his wife, ensconced in her recliner, semi-lucid and oblivious to most of life around her. To Harvey, this was almost a plus these days – at least it deflected any awkward questions as to his movements or sleeping arrangements while he'd been away.

Lucy looked up at her husband's entrance and, unusually, pushed reading glasses onto her forehead. 'Oh, hi there. Good trip?'

'Yes, very productive.' Harvey sat down on the recliner beside her, a little unsure how to handle this newfound sobriety. 'The new series is all set to run. I signed the deal, which should at least put us back in the black, financially.'

'Thank goodness for that,' said a Lucy, whose normal concern for their liquidity only ran to the bar stock. 'When will you start filming?'

'As soon as possible.' Harvey pointed to the book on his wife's lap. 'You're reading.'

'Yes.' She held it up. 'It's a book on boatbuilding which Damien loaned me. Very interesting it is too.'

'Boatbuilding?' Harvey spat out the word as though it was some appalling disease. 'Since when have you had the slightest interest in boats? You won't even come on Great Taste unless there's a party.'

'Yes, well, it's our son's abiding interest, so I thought I should learn more about it. It keeps me out of trouble. Speaking of which,' she looked enquiringly over her specs, 'where did you stay last night?'

'In the flat of course.' Harvey wasn't sure whether he liked this lucidity or the cross-examination it was producing. He glanced around quickly and asked, 'Where are the children?'

'Amanda's out on one of her walking expeditions and Damien's gone off to the wherry.'

'To learn more bad ways from that bunch of delinquents, I suppose.'

'No, to learn more about a skill he loves, Harvey, and which we should encourage.'

'Oh, I see it now.' Harvey tutted. 'He's been buttering you up to support his cause. To get me to pay for that course he so badly wants.'

'And why not?' Lucy laid down her book. 'It would cost you far less than law studies and our son would at least be fulfilling his dreams, not yours. Greg Kennard says he's got natural talent and it should be developed.'

Even as the words left her lips, Lucy realised she'd said too much, and her husband wasn't slow to zero in on her slip.

'Kennard? The boatbuilder? When did you meet him?'

'I ... I didn't,' stammered Lucy. 'I'm only repeating what he told Damien.'

'Yeah, well Kennard won't be in business in the village much longer any-way,' declared Harvey with almost-gleeful honesty. 'I've taken steps to have him evicted.'

'Yes, I know. I overheard your conniving conversation with that hideous little Councillor Wanstead yesterday morning,' admitted Lucy, feeling it was time to show at least a few of her own cards. 'How could you do such a thing? After all Greg's done to help our son.'

'Because he's a bad influence, that's why.' Harvey made a chopping motion with his hand, as though he were butchering meat for one of his dishes. 'When something's a problem, you get rid of it. That's my way.'

Lucy turned on her recliner and looked her husband straight in the eyes. 'You really are a bastard, aren't you, Harvey?'

She felt better finally saying that. Nevertheless, she wondered if there might be some merit in her husband's last appalling sentiment. Perhaps it was one she might yet follow herself.

*   *   *

'Well, that's a revelation,' said Jack, coming back into the kitchen and slumping down into his chair.

Arriving home that evening, he'd only just started telling Audrey of the morning's enquiries when the telephone rang. It was journalist Bill Whitely. Audrey listened to several exclamations of "Crikey" and "Blimey" before her husband thanked his contact and rang off.

'Why, what did he say?' Audrey always tried to keep some distance between Jack's work and home life, but a bit of scandal between people living locally was always – well – interesting. She took off her apron and sat down opposite. 'So, did Laydock and this Gloria Vale have something going between them as you suspected?'

'Far from it. From what Bill tells me, they've always been arch enemies.'

'Good heavens. Why?'

Jack leaned across the table and poured himself another cup of tea. 'Do you remember the series that Laydock did on TV a few years back, the one where he visited different restaurants around the country and then often tore them to shreds for public entertainment.'

'DIRE DINES ... yes, what of it?'

'Well,' said Jack, adding sugar, 'Gloria Vale's was one of those restaurants.'

'Ah,' sighed Audrey, seeing where this was now leading. 'Presumably, the report wasn't good?'

Jack shook his head. 'A pure hatchet job, apparently. So bad, in fact, that it drove Gloria's whole chain into insolvency. She was left with nothing to show for all she'd built up through the years, thanks to our Mr Laydock and his malicious tongue.'

'How awful.' Audrey shook her head. 'That does explain why she hates him so, but not why he reciprocates. Surely he should be doing all he can now to make amends.'

'Oh, he's made amends all right,' explained Jack, with a chuckle. 'Our gutsy Gloria wasn't prepared to roll over that easily, took him to court and proved that some of his criticisms were manufactured simply to make good viewing. The court awarded her a million pounds in compensation against Harvey.'

Audrey almost clapped. 'Good for her. It was time someone brought that man down to size.'

'Almost down to a size that broke him. Word on the block is that our Harvey is well in the red and only hanging on by the prospect of another series.'

'Well, let's hope he's learned his lesson and thinks a bit more of the consequences before ruining someone's life.' Audrey poured a cup for herself. 'Presumably, that million is what's financing Gloria's Resolve project?'

'Yep, which must be really galling for Harvey, knowing he's financed a commune he hates right here on his doorstep.' Jack's smile though quickly faded to concern. 'But losing her business was a dreadful period for Gloria that left her penniless at a time her own mother was very ill and needing care. She died soon afterwards, and it was that which drove Gloria to seek justice and compensation through the courts. When Harvey had to cough up, Gloria remembered her own troubled early years and vowed to help kids with the same problems. Hence the Resolve Trust.'

Audrey gave a heartfelt sigh. 'What an amazing coincidence that their paths would cross again, and how cruel that poor Gloria's new venture should run into opposition from the very man who'd ruined her life once before.'

'I agree,' said Jack, 'but presumably, Harvey now feels he has a score to settle with Gloria for almost bankrupting him. The whole thing has turned into a vicious circle, with those homeless youngsters caught in the middle. But, blow Harvey, because the frolic's going ahead and he'll just have to lump it.' Jack told his wife of the morning's good news and the proposed meeting at The Ferryman. 'It'll be good if you can be there, Aud. It'll be a chance to meet some of the people your clever idea is meant to help. I'll get you to run Alfie and me to Brundall in the morning and then you've got the car for the evening.'

Audrey nodded. It did indeed all seem to be working out, but she couldn't help worrying that this whole project was rapidly turning into a drama. How easily it could all end in tears.

*　　*　　*

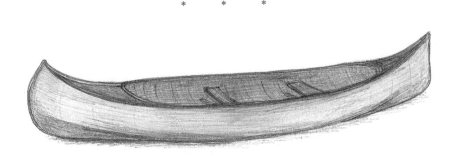

Chapter Seven

'Is it far to go now, Mr Fellows?'

Hunched in the bow of Resolve's tender, Alfie Rumball had pulled his cap tighter over his head and glanced only briefly back from his fixation on the river ahead.

'Round the next bend, Alfie.' Jack smiled to himself. The old wherryman had been showing almost boyish excitement since being picked up first thing this sunny morning. Minutes after Audrey had dropped them both at Brundall, Freddie Catlin had arrived with the tender and they'd motored off downriver. There was a slight chop and many cruisers, but Alfie seemed to positively revel in the occasional showers of spray coming onboard as they bounced through the wakes. Jack leaned a little closer from his seat on the centre thwart and shouted above the noise of the outboard, 'How does it feel to be afloat again, Alfie?'

The old man's toothless grin only confirmed his words. 'Real good, I tell yer. Some ways, seems like I never left orf.'

'So, how long is it since you last sailed a wherry?'

Alfie scratched his head through the cap. 'I was thinkin' 'bout that misself las' night, Mr Fellows. Must be nigh on fifty years since I las' sailed one a them ole gals but, a course, I done more 'an twenty years on motor wherries af'er that.'

'So, do you think you'll remember how to rig this one?'

'Yer, I reckon so. They's all the same an' you never forget what you learns as a boy.'

Jack looked over the wherryman's rounded shoulders. 'Well, you'll soon be proving that because here she is.'

Resolve's mast, still horizontal, was just visible above the riverbank, but shining now with a fresh coat of oil and varnish. Kneeling on the cabin roof in paint-smudged dungarees, Rita Wakefield paused from putting the finishing touches to a new bright colour design on the masthead, waved to the dinghy turning into the dyke and climbed down to meet it. Jack could well imagine the old man's thoughts as they glided down the wherry's sixty foot clinkered length, the likes of which Alfie Rumball doubtless never expected to see again. Soon they were moored alongside the aft end, where Rita eagerly took Alfie's small kitbag, while Flinty helped Jack heave the old man out of the boat and onto the wherry's deck. The former wherryman stood gazing about him in awe and his voice trembled slightly with emotion. 'Never thought I'd be standin' on one of these old darlin's agin.'

'We're so glad you are.' Gloria Vale came up on deck from her cabin, smiling and seeking the old man's hand with earnest gratitude. 'Welcome aboard Resolve, Alfie.' Then she introduced all the youngsters and Greg Kennard, who had just emerged from the for'ard hatch. Jack thought the boatbuilder seemed a little careworn. Perhaps he was just anxious that his work should meet with the old skipper's approval.

'We've tried to keep her as original as possible, Alfie,' he explained, indicating all the renovation work they'd done on the vessel.

'Well, she looks a real good'un to me.' Alfie looked down at the flush deck of the stern area where the absence of a well into the cabin required the big tiller to curve level with its roof. 'She's a high-sternsheeter.'

Greg nodded. 'The only one afloat now.'

'Which makes her jus' right for these southern rivers 'cos that's where they used 'em.' Alfie pointed towards the bow. 'But not with a white snout like you've given her.'

'But, I thought all wherries had those,' said Greg, a little dismayed.

'Not high sternsheet ones on the southern rivers, they din't.' He glanced now at Rita's masthead colour scheme and then to the young woman herself. 'You done that?'

'I got the design from an old print, but ...' Rita paused, apprehensive that yet another part of the restoration wasn't totally authentic, '... we chose the colours between us.'

'And a lovely job you done too, gal,' reassured Alfie with a smile. 'You have whatever colours you want 'cos the idea of them designs was so each wherry could be identified sailing over the marshes.' He nodded towards the hold. 'Don't forgit the cuddy roof an' dead hatch were always done in red.'

'Enough of the technical talk,' declared Gloria, picking up the wherryman's kit, taking the old man's arm and leading him gently for'ard. 'Come on Alfie, let's get you a cup of tea.'

Before following them, Jack had just enough time to buttonhole Greg. 'Is everything all right, Greg? You seem to have a load on your mind.'

The boatbuilder smiled and nodded. 'You're right, Jack. Big problems.'

'Want to share them?'

Greg closed his eyes for just a moment and gave a deep sigh. 'It's just those bastards, Laydock and Wanstead.'

'What about them? What are they up to now?'

'They're trying to run me out, that's what.' Only undisguised bitterness in Greg's voice kept the pent-up emotion in control. He breathed out noisily with frustrated disbelief. 'Apparently, I should have applied for change-of-use permission when I took on the lease of the garage for boatbuilding. Or, at least, that's the excuse they're going to use for closing me down.'

'Surely no-one has immediate power in this day and age. Have you actually received official notice of this, Greg?'

'No, just a tip-off.' He looked about him to ensure there were no ears close enough to overhear them. 'You remember Laydock's wife, Lucy, coming to the workshop while you were there?'

'Yes, seemed a lovely lady.'

'The best,' agreed Greg. 'You see, the reason she'd come was to tell me she'd overheard her bastard of a husband persuading Councillor Wanstead to do a hatchet job on my business.'

It was Jack's turn to shake his head. 'But your business is such an asset to the village, Greg. Why would Laydock be so intent on closing you down and why would his wife, Lucy, be prepared to spill the beans to someone she'd never met?'

The boatbuilder shrugged. 'I think, like us, she's just about had enough of him, added to which, she's grateful for all the help and guidance I've given Damien.'

'Perhaps that's the very reason he hates you.' Jack fixed Kennard with a meaningful look. 'Jealousy's a terrible emotion, Greg. You and Lucy need to tread carefully. By all accounts that man's used to getting his own way.'

'Yeah, I know, but she's wasted on him, Jack, and ... talking of which ...'

Jack followed Greg's excited gaze to where a small sailing dinghy was broad-reaching down the main river towards them. It was Once Bittern, Damien Laydock's little boat, sailing well, but low in the water with the weight of two passengers.

With the fresh wind, Damien sailed in at quite a speed before swinging his dinghy around in the width of the dyke and, with a great slapping of sails, stopping dead beside the wherry's quarter. The young girl in the bow threw a line and Jack caught it. Seconds later, she had jumped up onto the deck, a slim girl in shorts and lightweight waterproof, her fair hair tied back in a ponytail that hung through the vent of a yellow baseball cap. Damien quickly followed her onto the deck.

'Mr Fellows, this is my sister, Amanda.'

'I've heard a lot about you, Mr Fellows,' she said, giving him a friendly smile, 'and all the help you've been giving our family.'

'All part of the job,' Jack assured her, before turning to the other passenger in the boat, someone he had met for the first time the previous day. 'Good to see you again, Mrs Laydock.'

Lucy was looking slightly shaken and out of place in little Once Bittern, but cheerful for all that, laughingly shaking spray off her fleece and running a nervous hand through wet, straggly hair. 'Wow, what a ride! Come on you lot, help me out.'

Jack went to take her hand, but got beaten to it by Greg. A good heave by the boatbuilder soon had Lucy up beside him and, seemingly, in no hurry to let him go.

'My goodness, this is more my size of boat,' admitted Lucy, looking about her. She turned to her son. 'Well, come on Damien, show me all this work you've been doing.'

Before her son could comply, however, Rita Wakefield had joined them, wiping a paint-stained hand on her teeshirt and grinning widely. 'Damien, I painted that locker down below last night, but I can't seem to refit the door. Can you help me?'

'Of course ... but ...' Damien dithered between two fervent females.

It was Greg who solved the dilemma. 'I'll show your mum around, Damien. You go and help Rita.'

Both mother and son seemed equally content with this solution. While Lucy wandered for'ard with Greg, making brave attempts to seem genuinely interested in all he was proudly pointing out, Jack turned to the somewhat abandoned Amanda. 'Is this the first time you've been on board Resolve?'

'No, I've been a few times with Damien when Dad's been away.'

'Your father isn't one of Resolve's greatest supporters is he?' said Jack, dryly.

Amanda rolled big hazel eyes. 'You could say that. In fact, given his way, he'd can the whole project.'

'So, presumably, he's away at present?'

The young girl shook her head. 'No, he's home now, but Mum told him straight this morning that she was going to come and see what Damien was doing, and so here we are.'

'That can't have pleased your dad?'

'Bloody well infuriated him, actually,' admitted Amanda, with a mischievous giggle. 'He doesn't like being ignored.'

'Well, it's good to see your mum taking an interest in Damien's work.' Jack's eyes turned towards Resolve's bow, where Greg and Lucy seemed to be in quiet discussion.

'Yes,' agreed Amanda. 'Funny really, because Mum's never had much interest in boats before, but suddenly seems fascinated with this whole project.'

Jack couldn't decide whether Amanda was being sarcastic or was genuinely

71

puzzled, but further discussion was interrupted by Gloria and Alfie reappearing from below. 'So, Alfie, do you think you're going to fit in here?'

The wherryman paused to light his well-chewed pipe. 'Sure I do,' he finally answered, before turning to acknowledge Resolve's youngsters smiling behind him. 'A right good crew.' The only exception was Flinty, who had managed to slide away from the main group and linger alone beside the tabernacle, prompting Greg and Lucy to return aft and join the rest. Alfie took another contented puff. 'And I'm right lookin' forward to workin' with you all.'

'Great!' Somewhat reluctantly, Greg broke away from Lucy. 'We'll have some lunch, Alfie, and then perhaps ...' he paused to slap the huge spar lying along the main hatch, 'you can tell me the best way to get this gaff rigged.'

'Love to.' The wherryman removed the pipe and gave another toothless grin. 'The sooner we get this ole gal sailin' agin, the better.'

'Amen to that,' agreed Gloria.

'I suppose it's time we were getting back.' Lucy glanced about. 'Where is my son?'

The answer came from the for'ard hatchway from which Damien and Rita were just emerging, chattering intimately. Jack glanced briefly at Amanda and received an amused knowing smile in return before she moved off herself to somewhere up for'ard. Jack turned to Gloria. 'So, all set for your meeting at The Ferryman tonight?'

'You bet. It'll be good to meet the other side and exchange ideas.' She gave Jack an encouraging smile. 'Between us we'll put on the best frolic seen for years.'

'By which time the channel will be dredged and Resolve will be able to sail in and be the star of the show.' Jack smiled at the crewmembers still gathered around. 'There's going to be a lot of work involving all of you, but I know it's going to be fun.' Most of them smiled agreeably back, but he noticed that Jenny Flint was looking for'ard towards her brother. He wasn't alone now because, quietly talking to this surly youngster was Amanda. Even as Jack followed Jenny's concerned gaze, he saw something secretly being pressed into Flinty's hand, a small but indistinguishable package that he quickly dropped into his pocket.

'Right, let's get going,' ordered the still upbeat Lucy. She turned and climbed down into Once Bittern assisted by the attentive Greg. 'I'll see you all tonight at The Ferryman.'

Jack couldn't help notice this was directed more to Greg than the rest, but it was still news that surprised him. 'Are you going to be there, Lucy?'

'Of course, we'll all be there – well, not Harvey of course – but we wouldn't miss it.'

Amanda was with them now and being helped into the dinghy by Damien. 'Until tonight then,' said Jack.

Soon, Once Bittern was tacking away with the flood tide under her, Amanda helming this time, Damien tensioning the halyard and his mum giving a slightly nervous, but cheerful wave. Jack waved back, genuinely pleased to see this good-natured woman somehow finding her own escape from the downward-spiral of alcohol addiction. It took strength and life-changing events to achieve that and Jack had little doubt from where it came. He wished her well, but felt there'd be stormy waters ahead for them both to ride.

The good thing was that the relationship between Lucy and her children seemed to be improving. Jack was sure the youngsters would be keen to encourage their mother to keep off the drink and start to live life again. Daughter Amanda was an immediately likeable girl - high-spirited, intelligent and with much to offer the world. Odd then, that she should appear close to the likes of John Flint. And what was that mysterious package he had seen her secretly passing to this morose and troubled young man?

'Jack, can you give us a hand with the gaff?'

Greg Kennard's hail meant these were questions to be answered at some later time. Perhaps this evening at the frolic's first meeting.

*　　*　　*

Henry Wanstead had been watching the dredger work its relentless way further into the broad. To the councillor's jaded eyes, that mud-spewing bucket seemed to be digging into his own soul, scooping away the future with its every hungry lunge. Then his morbid thoughts were distracted as he caught sight of Lucy Laydock and her two children sailing off in their little dinghy and knew there was at least something he could do to divert his troubled mind.

Henry knew Harvey had returned from his business trip away and, now, while the celeb was home alone, it seemed a good opportunity to visit and talk. Henry set off through the village and strode the mile-long walk to Fayre View. Fifteen minutes found him at the top of the Laydock drive and ringing their front-door bell. Harvey's open-topped Jag was parked outside, so the great man himself must be in.

He was, but in a wrathful mood, made all the worse by his uninvited visitor. 'Yes, Wanstead. What the blazes do you want now?'

'The dredging, Harvey ... they're still at it and you promised me you'd get it stopped.' Invited no further than the doorstep, Henry glanced about him distractedly. 'We had an agreement ... remember?'

'I said I'd try,' reminded Harvey. 'I made no promises.'

'Well, did you?'

'Look, I'm not going to be cross-examined by the likes of you.' Harvey made a point of looking at his watch. 'How many times do I have to tell you, I'm a busy man and your blasted dredging worries are pretty low on my list of priorities so ...'

'But couldn't you call them again and still get it stopped?' There was an edge of panic back in the councillor's voice now.

Harvey was sick and tired of this reoccurring discussion. 'For God's sake, just give it a rest, Wanstead. Now, before you clear off, how about the favours I asked you to do for me? I don't see much progress being made.'

'No, well ...' Henry shook his head, regretfully, and tried to explain, '... I've taken steps to get Kennard evicted, but these things take time. As for the Trust, so far I haven't been able to come up with any reason to discredit it and, anyway, I've no jurisdiction on river matters, so what else can I do?'

'Well, you'd better come up with something pretty damn quick. If not, I may feel it's my duty to start investigations into why you're so keen to have this dredging stopped.' Harvey raised his eyebrows slightly. 'I wonder what dark little secret you're harbouring?'

'Harvey, you wouldn't ...' But Henry's protest was cut short by Fayre View's solid front door slamming straight into his face and the realisation that Harvey Laydock certainly would.

Henry slouched his way back down the drive feeling more dispirited than ever. Far from achieving any improvement in the situation, it had now degenerated into something far, far worse. Facing loss of his authority, reputation and even freedom, he had now been duped by a man he'd hoped would help and who could now well be the trigger to all the disgrace to come. What a fool he'd been. Henry's expression hardened. Perhaps it was time to teach Harvey-thinks-he's-so-bloody-great-Laydock a lesson.

After all, thought Henry with just a sliver of smugness, he'd handled worse situations before and this time he'd got nothing to lose.

*   *   *

After slamming the door on the insufferable councillor, Harvey had returned to his study and the planning of his next TV series. This was important because, after all, he needed to get some cash coming in as soon as possible. If he could regain his former popularity with the viewing public, it would assuredly restore his ailing finances. The trouble was, his success on screen was based on arrogance and rudeness and he was finally realising that same persona was having the reverse effect on his personal life. Deep down, Harvey knew, he was becoming a pure and total arse.

Ah well, he went back to an idea he'd been mulling for a while – a series in which he'd conjure up meals in extreme and unusual settings. There were several possibilities – a trans-Atlantic flight, in a submarine, up a mountain with an expedition, on a round-the-world yacht race and even one in a hot-air balloon. This would surely widen his audience to include viewers interested in travel and adventure. He'd got those five episodes sorted, but he still needed a good pilot to lead into the series. Harvey tried again to put ideas down and realised just as quickly that it was impossible with his thoughts so far elsewhere. The truth was, he couldn't stop thinking of Lucy.

He dropped his pencil, put his head in his hands, and wondered how he could have gone so far wrong as a husband and parent. He'd married Lucy because he loved her and had every intention of remaining true and faithful. Inevitably though, increasing celebrity status had made him fair game for any star-struck fan, and it wasn't long before he succumbed to temptation during his weeks away from home. What he hadn't reckoned on was the destructive effect this would have on Lucy. While he'd convinced himself that she was far too involved in caring for their new young family to bother about his own amorous adventures, the sad fact was that his wife's only way of coping had been to dull the pain with drink. By the time that realisation hit home, it was too late.

Lucy had become an alcoholic and, despite his spending a fortune on rehab, only stayed off the bottle until his next of many scandalous affairs hit the headlines. So, throughout their marriage, he'd never remained faithful and his wife was seldom sober – that was until now. Suddenly, the drunken wife he had treated so shabbily through all those years had changed beyond recognition and he had a pretty good idea why.

Harvey had never liked Kennard, primarily because Damien idolised and respected the man. Why hadn't he ever enjoyed that sort of relationship with his son? Boatbuilding! What sort of career was that for a lad destined for the bar? Now, it seemed, even dear Lucy had fallen under the spell of this tedious, but charismatic, artisan. Getting Greg Kennard evicted from his workshop would, hopefully, get rid of both problems.

Of course, he had no proof that Lucy was smitten with the boatbuilder, but he recognised all the signs of a woman falling in love – and she'd given up drink. He'd forgotten how lovely his wife was when she was sober, and felt stirrings of jealousy.

And now both Lucy and Amanda, like Damien, were blatantly defying him by going off to visit that bloody wherry. Clearly, it was time to eliminate that problem once and for all.

How? He'd already taken some steps this very morning, but that mealy-mouthed councillor was far too preoccupied with his own current dilemma to be relied on for decisive action. No, if he wanted quick results, it was time to take matters very much into his own hands.

He went back to his desk and started jotting ideas, but this was no list of recipes or proposals for a TV series. What Harvey was seeking now were ideas to cement the demise of the Resolve project and all it stood for.

*　　*　　*

Chapter Eight

'There's Audrey.' As Resolve's tender brought the wherry team to the village staithe and their meeting at The Ferryman, Jack looked ahead and saw his wife already waiting at the water's edge.

It was another of those blissful summer evenings, the hubbub of river life once more stilled with that indefinable peace now settling over broad and marsh. Out there, the dredging fleet was at rest, the great crane and attendant mud-wherries lying in silent anchorage near the middle of the broad. The workboat which had taken their crews ashore was moored alongside the staithe together with two hire boats and a traditional sailing cruiser whose crew were busy mopping decks and covering sails and outboard motor. Greg managed to slot the tender in just astern of this boat and soon they were securing lines and jumping ashore.

With introductions to Gloria, Greg, Rita Wakefield and John Flint, Audrey was pleased to put faces to some of the characters Jack had been telling her about. 'You have a sister with you as well, I believe,' she said to Flinty.

'Yeah, but Jenny's stayed behind with Freddie Catlin to look after the old boy,' explained Flinty, rather disapprovingly.

'... and Resolve,' added Greg before glancing at his watch. 'Right, ten to seven, just time for us all to meet the village committee and have a quick half before the meeting starts proper.'

'I'll stay here an' keep an eye on the tender,' said Flinty. It was more a statement than an offer.

Gloria raised questioning eyebrows. 'I thought you, of all people, would enjoy a run ashore. Surely the tender will be okay left here?'

Greg nodded in agreement. 'Of course it will. Come and have a change of scene and unwind a bit, Flinty.'

But the youngster was seemingly unenthused. 'I don't have much time for meetings and the like, especially on a lovely evening like this and, besides, with all this pinching from boats, someone ought to be keeping an eye on things.'

Jack detected just a hint of sarcasm in Flinty's excuse, but he could well understand anyone preferring the outdoors on such a perfect evening. 'Please yourself, Flinty. If you feel like a drink later, you know where we are.'

Inside The Ferryman, the atmosphere was one of jovial charm. A couple of families, probably from the two hire cruisers moored at the staithe, were eating at tables just off the bar. There were several other strange faces who Greg quickly introduced as the village committee, plus Damien Laydock and, much to Audrey's delight, his mother Lucy.

'I was rather hoping I'd get to see your husband,' Audrey admitted. 'Will he be coming?'

Lucy shook her head and took another sip of orange juice. 'No, and all the better for it as far as I'm concerned.'

'Oh dear.' Audrey took the martini just being handed to her and glanced about. 'I believe you also have a daughter?'

'Yes, Amanda, but she's not here either, I'm afraid.'

'Other commitments,' joined in Damien, though Jack couldn't help feel there was a more ominous reason behind his sister's absence.

'Here's one to see you through the meeting,' said Greg, handing Lucy another orange juice and edging in between her and Audrey. They were simple words for a simple act, but the look in this couple's eyes told Audrey of feelings far more intimate. 'Right, let's go through shall we.' Greg gestured towards the private room provided for the meeting. It was seven o'clock and the crew of the sailing-cruiser were just arriving – four vibrant young men all set to complete a perfect day's sailing by downing a few jars of local brew.

Greg sat himself down at the head of a long table in the meeting room and Audrey noticed him nod Lucy into the seat to his right. Everyone else sat where they wanted, though, inevitably, it ended up with the village committee on one side and Resolve Trust on the other. Jack chose the other end as the most neutral seat remaining.

'As you know, we're here to start organising a village water frolic,' began Greg, 'but the primary aim of this whole event is to bring a new understanding between two very different communities ...' he paused and nodded to each side of the table before opening his file and taking out a pen, '... so, let's see what ideas we can come up with between us.'

There were plenty of them, beginning with a firm date for the event that would give them only two weeks in which to prepare. All agreed on the frolic being open to everyone and that catering arrangements should be on a scale that could feed, possibly, many hundreds of people. A group of volunteers happily accepted this responsibility and made an arrangement to get together later to decide what form it should take. Greg suggested rowing races and free canoe trials, and offered to supply the boats. Gloria explained how Resolve would be open for public viewing with team-members on hand to show people around.

It was a positive start to this first meeting and, as it progressed, Jack and Audrey could sense the enthusiasm building on both sides. From others there were ideas for alternative attractions and side-stalls where local craftsmen and women could market their wares. Rita said she'd like to try selling some of her paintings and received an admiring smile from Damien. Finally, Jack explained the tourist board's keenness for such events and the availability of a small grant towards this one.

How should such money be spent? Insurance was one demanding requirement, but Jack felt the remainder should be spent on something everyone could enjoy. 'How about a firework display to conclude the day?' he suggested. Everyone agreed.

All this discussion had taken three hours and as Greg started to wind up, one villager, a Mrs Willows, the postmistress, had one final point. 'This is going to be such a wonderful day,' she said in her slightly squeaky, but quite forceful voice, 'so shouldn't we ask someone to open it?'

There was much nodding of heads before the inevitable question, 'Who?'

'It's got to be somebody famous,' said one.

'Yes, a celebrity,' said another.

'Well, we already have one living right here in our village,' squeaked Mrs Willows, as though this was what she had been leading up to all the time. She leaned forward and looked directly at Lucy. 'How about your husband, Mrs Laydock? Would he open the frolic for us?'

'Oh ... I'm not sure about that ... he's so busy,' Lucy glanced sideways at Greg.

The boatbuilder was already shaking his head. 'I really don't think Harvey Laydock would be the right person to ask.'

'Especially as he's the one who has stirred up the most trouble for Resolve in the first place,' agreed Gloria with conviction. 'I should've thought he'd be the last person we'd ask.' She seemed to have almost forgotten that Lucy was the wife of the man in question. Biting her lip, she looked across and said, 'Sorry Lucy ... forgot, but ...'

'It's all right. I know exactly what you mean.' Lucy tossed back the dregs of her orange juice. 'He is the most arrogant thing in creation.'

'I can't believe we'd even consider him,' said Greg, shaking his head in despair. 'The whole idea of this frolic is to hit the right note, and involving Harvey Laydock would be just too high risk.'

'But, surely, he's the person to ask,' interjected a rather scholarly-looking villager introduced as Mr Denby, a retired headmaster, known locally for his fair-minded, common-sense approach to life. 'I thought the whole idea of this frolic was to bring people together and that, surely, must include those who are the most bigoted. If we merely sideline them, we'll only alienate that faction even more. Let's at least ask Laydock to open the thing and show the right spirit.'

Jack could certainly see the merit of the suggestion. 'I think Mr Denby's right. We have to take the risk and ask Harvey.'

It was difficult for Greg to refute this logic, no matter how much he would have liked to do so. 'All right – if you have to have him.' He turned lamely to Lucy by his side and asked, 'Would you…?'

'I can try,' replied Lucy, without enthusiasm, 'but I'm not promising.'

'We'll both try,' said Damien, speaking for the first time. 'We have to. It would be good all round.'

It was a sentiment not wholly shared by everyone present, but no-one felt inclined to labour the point further. 'Time for one last pint then,' concluded Greg, closing his file after agreeing a second meeting in one week's time.

*   *   *

It was ten o'clock when they all filed back into the bar area. It was quieter now with the families from the hire-cruisers already gone and the slightly-merry sailors from the yacht just leaving. A last drink and then the frolic committee followed them. It was still a beautiful evening and all decided to stroll down to the staithe to wave the Resolve contingent off. Gloria, particularly, was in good spirits.

'I really feel we've achieved something positive tonight,' she whispered to Jack as they wandered through the narrow street between quaint timbered cottages.

'Let's hope so.'

Back at the staithe, the broad lay black and brooding, with just the anchor lights of the dredging fleet floating like some waterborne oasis out there in the darkness. From the hire-cruisers alongside came the sound of laughter and soft music, but, around the traditional yacht, flashing torches and muttered oaths spoke of rather less harmony. Keeping public moorings peaceful and holidaymakers happy was part of Jack's job and he strode over to the yacht to source the problem.

'Someone's nicked the bloody engine, that's the problem!' exclaimed the stocky chap who seemed to own the boat. An angry finger pointed at the transom where, true enough, the lifting-bracket that just a few hours ago had supported the yacht's auxiliary power, now sat decidedly engine-free.

Jack didn't waste time asking if it had been locked, and the well-oiled crew certainly weren't in the mood for having any blame shifted their way. 'You should be able to leave the bloody boat for one evening,' said one, and Jack could only agree. The mystery was that such a theft could have occurred with watch being kept on Resolve's own tender, except …

'Where's Flinty?' asked Greg as the rest of the group caught up and added to the disturbance.

It was a good question, for the troubled young man was nowhere to be seen.

'He said he was going to keep watch,' stated Gloria, with mounting concern.

'Yes, well a pity he didn't keep watch on ours as well.' The yacht's owner was now aiming his torch into Resolve's tender. 'Is this your boat?'

'Yes, why?' threw back Gloria, a little defensively.

'Because I'm wondering what that is lying in the bottom?' Sure enough, wrapped in the dinghy's cover beneath the centre thwart was a bulky object of suspicious size and shape.

'I don't know,' offered Greg, lamely. 'It wasn't there when we left the boat.'

'Can I have a look then?'

Gloria glanced at Jack and the ranger nodded back, but it was Greg who jumped down into the tender and pulled aside the cover.

'That's my bloody engine all right!' exclaimed the owner, gazing angrily at the gleaming outboard now revealed.

It was an eight-horsepower four-stroke and light enough to be lifted by one man, as Greg demonstrated by heaving it back onto the staithe. 'I have no idea how that got there,' was all he could say.

'No, but perhaps the police will have.' The owner was already pulling a mobile phone from his pocket and tapping three nines.

'Can we just hold off on that?' requested Jack, producing his Authority ID. 'I agree this has to be sorted, but you have got your motor back and I can vouch for everyone here.'

'Some sort of problem?' The voice came from the back of the group where a well-dressed man had joined them unnoticed.

'Harvey!' Lucy Laydock seemed equally surprised and dismayed to see her husband. 'What are you doing here?'

'Oh, it was late and I didn't like to think of you and the children walking home in the dark.' Harvey, somewhat pointedly, put his arm around his wife's shoulder and nodded back to where his Jag lay parked just by the staithe. 'So I thought I'd drive down to meet you.'

Neither action seemed to be appreciated by Greg, who growled, 'Very considerate of you.'

Harvey ignored the sarcasm and nodded down to the outboard motor lying like some slaughtered creature on the quay-heading. 'Another one going walk-about, I see.' He transferred his glance now to the tender. 'And not much doubt where to.'

'What are you implying?' Even in the darkness, Gloria Vale's red hair seemed to be bristling.

'I don't think I need to imply anything, dear lady,' responded Harvey condescendingly. 'We've all had suspicions as to who's responsible for all the thieving we've been suffering, and now the culprit's been caught red-handed, so to speak.'

'What culprit?' challenged Greg. 'We were all at The Ferryman for the whole evening, but how come you just so-conveniently happen to be hanging around?' He leapt ashore threateningly, only to be met by Harvey's shaking finger.

'Don't you go trying to intimidate me, Kennard. For someone only too ready to take what belongs to others ...' Harvey glanced briefly at Lucy, '... you should be the last to be playing the innocent.'

'You bastard.' Greg was toe-to-toe with the celebrity now, his big fists clenching with suppressed anger.

It was Jack who stepped between them. 'Okay you two, that's enough. We have bigger problems here than personal grudges.'

'Like where's Flinty, who was supposed to keeping an eye on everything?' intervened Lucy, keen to raise any aspect that would deflect attention away from this very-public washing of dirty linen.

The answer came immediately in the slouching footfall of the lad himself. 'Hello, what trouble's this then?'

'Where have you been?' asked Gloria, angrily swinging round. 'I thought you were going to keep an eye on things here?'

'Went for a little stroll,' explained the scruffy young man scratching his tousled hair and scanning the large group of very agitated onlookers. 'Why, what's been going on?'

'You tell us,' said Greg.

'Theft, that's what's been "going on",' smirked Harvey Laydock.

'Is there anyone who can account for your time away from the staithe, Flinty?' asked Jack, trying to keep this potentially-damaging situation as low-key as possible.

Flinty shook his head. 'Nope.'

'That's not true. He was with me.' It was a new voice joining the gathering, the smooth sweet feminine voice of Amanda Laydock. Edging through the now-silent throng, she put a reassuring hand on John Flint's shoulder. 'It's all right, Flinty. You don't have to cover for me. I can take care of myself.'

She would soon have to, judging by the colour of her father's face. 'You ...?' he transferred his stare from his daughter to the shuffling youngster beside her, '... with him?'

Amanda remained unfazed. 'Yes. Why not?'

Harvey seemed unable to answer, so he simply asked, 'Where?'

'The cruiser.'

'Great Taste!' Harvey's ire seemed on the point of peaking. 'You had this moron on my boat? Who let you ...?' His voice trailed away as he glanced at his son. Damien simply shrugged sadly in return. 'I'll deal with you later,' promised Harvey before turning back to his daughter. 'So, you've been using the boat behind my back as some sort of knocking shop.'

'No, Dad. It's not what you think,' answered Amanda evenly. 'We haven't all got your one-track mind.' She nodded beyond the village. 'Shall we go home and continue this domestic squabble somewhere less public.'

'Too true we will,' promised Harvey, guiding his wife in the direction of the Jag before turning finally to his children. 'You two can walk. It's something you,' he pointed at Amanda, 'need to get used to because you can kiss that car of yours goodbye.'

From the yacht, there came a clunk as its crew lifted their engine back onboard.

* * *

'Oh dear,' Audrey sighed as she and Jack drove homeward through country lanes. 'Tonight's little attempt at bridge-building seems to have demolished more than we've constructed.'

'You could say that,' agreed her husband, thumping the steering wheel in exasperation. 'Finding that motor in the Trust's own boat was bad enough, but it had to be in front of the very villagers we're hoping to work with.'

'I just hope they found the whole thing as phoney as we did. It all seemed so – well – contrived.' She turned to Jack. 'I know that Flint lad has a host of hang-ups, but surely he wouldn't be so stupid as to steal an engine and then hide it right where it's sure to be found?'

'No, of course not, Aud.' Jack frowned. 'That whole scenario had to be some sort of set-up. I've been dealing with human nature long enough now to recognise acting when I see it, and Flinty's reaction, when he found out what had happened, was genuine surprise. No, our poor Flinty was what the Americans call, "the patsy".'

'So, if Flinty didn't take that motor, who did?'

'One candidate springs immediately to mind.'

'Harvey Laydock?'

Jack nodded. 'Strange why he should just turn up like that. That story about wanting to see his wife home had to be a load of baloney.'

'I'm not so sure.' There was caution in Audrey's voice now. 'We both know Harvey Laydock had a very good reason for coming down to the staithe to meet his wife.'

'Jealousy over Lucy's new-found friendship with Greg, you mean.' Jack knew from past experience that, when it came to emotional matters, women were far more astute than men and his own wife was a master on the subject. 'You could be right.'

'I know I'm right and it's more than just friendship, Jack Fellows. I was watching those two and the looks they were giving each other. I'm convinced that what you have there is the makings of a full-blown love affair.'

'Laydock's jealous enough of Greg's influence over Damien,' explained

Jack, before relating all the boatbuilder had told him that morning about eviction from his workshop. 'If he thinks the man he so resents is also having an affair with his wife, his bitterness will know no bounds.'

'We know Harvey Laydock has a definite capacity for dirty tricks,' surmised Audrey, 'but trying to get rid of Resolve seems a very roundabout way of going about it.'

'Not if you remember that it's actually Gloria Vale he's got his knives out for. She's the one who's almost broken him with that court case, and bringing the Resolve Trust into disrepute is Harvey's way of getting back.'

'Yes, but after he bankrupted her,' pointed out Audrey. 'What a mess, but all his shenanigans don't seem to be bringing our celebrity much luck on the family front. Now, as well as alienating his son and losing his wife to another man, his daughter seems to be having a relationship with a boy who's the most disturbed one of the lot.'

'John Flint? Yeah, not exactly the most eligible of bachelors is he?' Jack gave a humourless chuckle. 'I must admit that was a real shocker for me. Amanda Laydock was a girl I had down as having a bit more savvy than to get involved with the likes of Flinty.' He gave a sigh and shook his head. 'But, somehow, I don't think they're an item. There's more to it than that, something I can't quite put my finger on.' Jack told his wife of the strange passing of the mysterious package, that afternoon, on Resolve.

'Drugs?'

'Could be, but I don't see that bright young girl getting involved with those either.'

'A lot have, Jack.'

'Well, let's just suppose Amanda is dabbling with dope, which I very much doubt, where would a forsaken soul like Flinty get the money for it?'

'By stealing and selling outboard motors?'

'I know it looks that way, love, but why would Amanda need to get involved with anything like that? That sports car of hers alone is worth fifty outboards.'

'Perhaps it's not for the money. Perhaps it's just to get back at her unreasonable father who, as of tonight, has even confiscated her car.' Audrey gave a gasp of frustration. 'We must be mad to even consider Harvey Laydock opening the frolic.'

'I know it seems bizarre,' admitted Jack, 'but Mr Denby made a good point. If the whole idea of this frolic is to break down prejudices, we can't start by being prejudicial ourselves.' Feeling it was time to return to a more positive note, he continued, 'but at least we've achieved something, Aud. Village and Trust have sat down together for the first time and agreed a common goal. There's a lot of work to do in the next two weeks, but some good people sharing it.'

'Which, I hope, will include us on the big day,' said Audrey, 'but don't forget we have a daughter about to give birth. If our first grandchild decides to be a few days early, we'll be in London helping Jo instead of being at the frolic.'

Jack realised he'd clean forgotten Jo's imminent motherhood, but knew better than to admit that to his wife. Instead, as they motored the last few miles home, he lapsed into contemplative silence which inevitably led into darker channels. They'd made huge strides in getting the opposing factions together, but there was still such a gulf between the main participants. Running through this evolving situation were the heart-warming threads of enthusiasm, initiative, excitement and the romantic companionship of shared endeavour. He just hoped it wouldn't all end in tears.

These diverse thoughts were cut short by their arrival home and, even more abruptly, by the ringing of Jack's mobile.

'Jack – Stan Meadows – been trying to get you all evening.'

'Sorry, Stan. At a meeting, so I had it switched off.'

'You asked me to check with Missing Persons about old Wanstead's wife, Alice.'

'Yep. What did you find?'

'Nothing.'

'Nothing?'

'Nope. Not even registered as missing so, obviously, no-one reported her as such.'

'Right, thanks for trying, Stan. Another twist in the stolen-outboards case tonight, but I'll brief you when I see you.'

'I'll look forward to that,' said the PC, sarcastically.

They rang off leaving Jack wondering where all this was really leading.

*　　*　　*

Chapter Nine

It was three days before Jack could return to Resolve. One had been spent calling various organisations, enlisting help and support for the frolic, and the rest back on duty in Norwich dealing with problems of late-night riverside safety. It was a relief to find himself finally heading back downriver, early morning radiation fog hanging over all, but the sun all set to burn it off by mid-morning. For the moment though, visibility on the Yare was down to a few hundred metres and the river surface unusually calm in the still morning air.

Not good conditions for sailing, but perfect for hoisting sails for the first time. Jack wondered how Alfie Rumball's help with rigging the old wherry had been progressing. The generation gap between the old wherryman and Resolves's young crew was like a yawning chasm and bridging it would take a lot of patience and understanding on both sides. It would be interesting to see how things were working out. He continued downriver, the encircling stillness only broken by the soft purr of the launch's engine.

Soon though, another sound began to penetrate the blanket of precipitation as the rumble and clunk of Charlie Wendlove's dredging operation passed by, but the broad and most of the dyke leading to it were still cloaked in eerie invisibility. Jack continued on along the main river, the shallow fog over the marshes creating a sea of white that ended only at the higher ground beyond, rising island-like above. Very wisely, few boats were moving on the river, giving a peaceful air of unreality to this normally busy waterway.

In this obscured world, Jack peered ahead, knowing that senses of time and distance are always distorted in reduced visibility, and wondering if he really was as close to Resolve as he thought. And then the old wherry's newly oiled mast and gaff suddenly emerged from the fog like some spectre from the underworld. More exciting still, hanging from the angled gaff was the huge black expanse of new sail.

'I see you've all been busy,' Jack shouted as he slid into the dyke and came alongside. Most of the wherry's crew were on deck, coiling lines or simply gazing up at this great spread of black synthetic canvas hanging limp and formless in the dead-calm.

Gloria flashed Jack a welcoming grin and then whispered something to Jenny Flint, who scampered down the main accommodation hatch, to emerge seconds later with a steaming mug of coffee. She handed it over as Jack arrived on deck, its delectable aroma all the more welcome in the slight morning chill.

'Thought you'd be ready for that,' smiled Gloria. 'We're going to have ours now as well.' She gazed up again at Resolve's source of power, as yet untamed and with its clew still free and unattached to the mighty sheeting blocks lying on top of the cuddy. 'Just wanted to get the sail hoisted for the first time while the air was still.'

'It's a wonderful sight,' observed Jack.

'Got it bent on yesterday, with Alfie's good advice,' explained Greg. He gestured towards the old wherryman, standing toothlessly smiling amidst a cloud of pipe-smoke up for'ard by the main winch. Under his direction, Freddie and Flinty were unshipping the heavy winch handles and stowing them close by, satisfied grins on their faces despite being breathless from winding the three hundred-weight of gaff and canvas aloft. Alfie gave them encouraging slaps on the back.

'Well done, lads. Yer know yer done some work gettin' that up there.' The skipper indicated the main winch with the stem of his pipe. 'But don't forgit one man used to hoist it one-handed in them old days.'

Freddie and Flinty could only shake their heads in disbelief, as Alfie made his way sternwards to join the others.

'I think you've earned your cuppa, Alfie,' said Gloria, smiling.

'Tha's right good to see that up there.' The wherryman pushed his cap to the back of his head and took a steaming mug off the tray just brought by Jenny. He nodded towards Freddie and Flinty, now recovering full-length on the main hatch. 'Them youngsters did a real good job.' He gave a wry smile. 'They'll soon be findin' muscles they never knew they had.'

'Well, it doesn't seem to be doing them any harm.' Jack was particularly pleased to see Flinty actually smiling. 'He seems to be finally enjoying honest shipboard life.'

Greg agreed. 'Quite a remarkable change of attitude generally over the last few days.'

'Good for him. After all the accusations levelled at him at the staithe the other night, I expected to find him more bitter than ever.' Jack turned to Gloria. 'Any repercussions from our yachting friends since then?'

She shook her head. 'No, I think even they realised it was all a bit too blatant to be true.'

'As did the village committee,' added Greg. 'I spoke to them all the next day and they agreed the whole thing had been orchestrated by someone out to stir up trouble.'

'... and I think we all know by whom,' completed Gloria. She paused to sip her coffee and lower her voice. 'I don't think there's anything that man wouldn't stoop to, to bugger up the whole project.'

'I know there's been a lot of agro between you and Harvey,' sympathised Jack, feeling it was time to lay cards on tables, 'but, isn't it time to put all that behind you.'

'It is as far as I'm concerned,' shrugged Gloria, 'but, the fact is, Harvey Laydock could well save himself a load of money if he managed to have us discredited.'

Jack took a swig of coffee. 'How come? I thought he'd already parted with a cool million in the damages awarded you?'

'Not all of it.' Gloria glanced about to check none of the youngsters were within earshot. 'Harvey pleaded those damages would break him, so the court allowed him to pay in four instalments of a quarter of a million with the last due in a month's time. I'm suspecting he wants to get me and the trust discredited so he can go back to court and appeal against that last payment. If he did, it would be disastrous for the Resolve Trust. We really need that money.'

'Accusing him of faking thefts, so you get the blame, is pretty serious stuff,' cautioned Jack. 'My advice, Gloria, is to keep that theory to yourself until you've got more proof.'

'I will,' she promised. The sun was climbing now, its radiated heat starting to disperse fog and calm alike. A small slap of canvas caused her to look up to where the leech of the sail was just starting to float and curl in the imperceptible first eddies of moving air. 'Breeze getting up.' It was a good time to end a painful conversation.

Alfie pulled his cap back over his forehead and glanced aloft. 'We'll drop it now,' he said with a wrinkling of his nose. 'Flaggin' sails don't do 'em no good, 'specially new uns.' He nodded to the huge blocks, as yet without the rope, that would eventually control this huge area of canvas. 'We'll get the mainsheet on 'er now an' pr'aps get the old girl sailin' this af'ernoon.'

'Really?' Both Gloria and Greg looked at each other like children just told school was ending.

'Don't see why not,' said Alfie, clambering onto the hatch-covers. In spite of his age, just being on one of his beloved wherries again seemed to have triggered a new-found agility. 'Right, you lads, let's see if yer can lower that thing as smoothly as yer got it up.'

'Time for me to be off,' said Jack, reluctantly putting his empty mug back on the tray brought by Jenny. Seeing this girl made him think of the other female crewmember. 'Where's Rita?'

'Off to the village to try and buy more paints, but secretly hoping to see Damien,' smiled Gloria, climbing on the cuddy roof and getting ready to receive the sail as the winch crew let go.

It gave Jack the excuse he needed to edge Greg just to one side. 'I'd have thought Damien would have wanted to see this?'

'He called me on my mobile earlier,' explained Greg. 'He's hoping to make it this afternoon, but at the moment things are a bit too fraught at home.'

'Ah, poor lad,' sympathised Jack. He checked they were alone and lowered his voice. 'Greg, perhaps this is none of my business, but are you aware of all the heartbreak you might be making for yourself there?'

The boatbuilder nodded. 'Yes, I am Jack, but you can't help who you fall in love with.'

'It's as serious as that already, is it?'

'Yes, for both of us.' Greg gave a lopsided smile. 'I know what a rocky road we're both heading up, Jack, but Lucy's a lovely woman who's been drowning in the depths of despair for years because of that cheating husband of hers. If we can find happiness together, it'll all be worthwhile.'

Jack gave him a slap on the back. 'Well, don't let it distract you from other things ...' he nodded up to where the gaff peak was beginning its steady descent, '... like sailing old wherries.'

Greg smiled. 'No, it'll be good to have Resolve taking my mind off other things for a while.' He brightened at a sudden thought. 'Jack, if trials go well this afternoon and the next few days, we plan on taking her for an extended shakedown cruise at the weekend. Why don't you and Audrey join us?'

'We'd love to,' smiled the ranger, knowing how much his wife would also welcome such an opportunity. He climbed back down into the launch, paused and gave the boatbuilder a reassuring grin. 'Perhaps things are finally beginning to go the right way, Greg.'

Any further pleasantries were cut short by the launch's VHF radio blaring to life.

'Yeah, go ahead.'

'Jack,' said the familiar voice of Tom Maynard, 'we need you at the dredger ASAP. They've got big problems.'

*　　*　　*

So had the family at Fayre View.

'But you can't leave me, Lucy. Not you as well.'

Harvey Laydock shook his head in disbelief as his usually-servile wife sat poised to hammer this last nail in his domestic coffin. There had been a series of bitter confrontations since that night at the broad. Harvey had laid down the law to Amanda and carried out his threat to ground her beloved sports car. Lucy had pleaded for her daughter and Harvey had thrown it back in her face, accusing her of cheating with Greg Kennard. Damien had told his father he was a hypocrite and Harvey had chastised his son for allowing Amanda to use Great Taste, following through with the promise that he would "never ever" get the boatbuilding course he so badly wanted. The result was a family in tears, despair and, finally, estrangement. Damien had gone first, throwing his few things in a kitbag and saying he was off to Resolve. Amanda had followed soon after, ignoring her father's warnings and assuring her mother she would "stay close". Now, with the children gone and the repossession of the house probably soon to follow, Lucy had made her own tearful declaration.

That had shaken Harvey more than anything. For years now he'd regarded his wife as the proverbial millstone. But, despite Lucy's alcoholism giving him ample grounds for divorce, he had always held back, telling himself that such an action would demand a settlement way beyond anything he regarded reasonable. Now, on the verge of bankruptcy and faced with Lucy leaving him for another man, he realised it had been ties far deeper than financial that made him persevere with such a crap marriage. After years fantasising about all he would do if he ever found himself a free man again, Harvey realised he didn't really want it after all.

It was a realisation too late. All his past infidelities had been enjoyed, secure in the knowledge that his wife wouldn't have the guts or rational state of mind to do a thing about it. Now, this very different Lucy was telling him that she was about to make another life for herself and it wasn't hard to guess with whom.

'Think what you're giving up, Lucy. What can that bloody boatbuilder offer you?'

'Love,' said Lucy, wiping her eyes with an already-wet tissue, 'and a life based on real values and not that phoney world of TV and drama that you seem to revel in.'

'That world has provided us with some of the best things in life, which you have enjoyed more than any of us.'

'I'd rather have had a dependable, trustworthy husband,' threw back Lucy.

Harvey decided not to pursue that aspect. Instead, he chose to try the path of practicality. 'But how would you cope without me, Lucy? You can't even buy a postage stamp without a family conference and ten hours of training.'

'I'm useless because that's how you've made me.' Lucy took a deep sniff. This was painful beyond words, but she knew she had to follow it through. 'Perhaps getting out of your life will be the best thing I've ever done, Harvey. And, anyway,' she concluded, 'we're due to lose everything in a month when you have to pay off Gloria Vale.'

'I haven't paid her yet and I don't intend to!' Deciding not to pursue that one either, Harvey made an effort to calm his voice and said, 'Lucy, it's not too late for me to change. Give me another chance.'

'You won't change, Harvey. You might act the attentive husband for a while, but you won't be able to keep it up.' Lucy gave a little scoff. 'A few weeks and you'll be the bastard you've always been.'

Her husband gulped. It was a long time since anyone had spoken that bluntly to Harvey Laydock. 'I can change, Lucy. I'll prove it. I'll even open that bloody fete thing you're organising.'

Lucy, as promised, had at least gone through the motions of asking her husband and received the derision-filled response she'd expected. This sudden change of mind, under duress, meant nothing. 'Do you really think you could save our marriage by making that one concession, Harvey, when you've driven our children from their home and me to the point of alcoholic suicide?' She stood up. 'You've got a nerve – and perhaps I have a bit more myself now, because I'm off to pack.'

'All right, sod your frolic-thing and clear off if that's what you want,' fired Harvey as his last shot to the slamming door.

He sat for a few minutes contemplating the domestic destruction he'd wrought and all its ramifications for his future. He was still determined to avoid paying that Vale woman, keep Fayre View and, hopefully, restore his fortunes with the new series. Getting stuck into that would soon take his mind off all his domestic troubles – that and the women he'd now be free to indulge at will.

Thoughts of the series and his still-lacking pilot episode somehow suddenly gelled with those of the stupid event he'd been asked to open. Could he just possibly ...?

Harvey went to the phone and dialled the number of his production director. 'Jim, I've just had a great idea for the opening of the series.'

*   *   *

The fog had dispersed by the time Jack entered the village dyke and the sound of dredging had disappeared with it. At the broad, the crane lay idle, a mud wherry alongside her only half-filled and with her skipper and Charlie Wendlove peering down at something lying on the vessel's sidedeck. The ranger quickly secured his launch alongside the crane-pontoon and stepped across, giving a questioning look at the lead-operator who had come over to meet him.

'What's the problem, Charlie?'

'Something we just dragged up from the bottom.' He led Jack across to the mud-wherry and pointed at an object lying at the skipper's feet. 'Knowing what's been going on here, I thought you'd be interested.'

Jack bent down and took a closer look. 'You're right, Charlie, that's very interesting indeed.'

'And it aint the only one,' said the operator, pointing into the wherry's gaping hold. 'We picked them up at the same time.' Sure enough, two similar objects lay amongst the spoil from the broad's bottom. 'Haven't fished them out yet,' he added.

'Right.' Jack straightened up, pulled out his mobile phone and keyed the selected name.

PC Meadows answered immediately. 'Yes Jack, what can I do for you now?'

'Get to the broad as quick as you can, Stan,' replied the ranger. 'You won't believe what's just been dredged up.'

*   *   *

Amanda Laydock leant her bicycle against a tree, wiped away a tear with the back of her hand and sat down on an old fallen trunk.

It wasn't the loss of her sports car that was causing her to uncharacteristically break down. She had loved her little car, but having to use her bike now to get around was really no great hardship for a girl who relished fresh air and all the sights and fragrances that the countryside offered. Leisurely peddling down tree-lined lanes to her favourite wood and well away from Fayre View, she'd actually felt a sense of freedom and oneness with nature.

No, it was all the trouble at home that was wearying Amanda. As she and Damien had grown up, they'd been well aware that their parents' marriage was anything but idyllic. In her early teens she had found the nerve to sit down and talk to her mother and begun to understand all the pain her father's infidelity caused. Thereafter, although their relationship was often strained, Amanda's sympathy was always with her mother, regardless of the drink problem. Now, Lucy was miraculously on the wagon and her daughter was well aware of the reason why.

Amanda's reaction to her mother having an affair had at first been a simple "Good for you, Mum", but all the confrontation resulting from her own revelations at the staithe had brought things to a head far faster than intended. This was bad enough, but added to the family's sudden estrangement was their probable homelessness. Amanda couldn't believe it when the recriminations had disclosed her father's legal wrangle with Gloria Vale. Now, she and Damien both realised for the first time why their father and Gloria hated each other so vehemently. At the time of the court case, both she and her brother were away at boarding school and totally unaware that their father's television programme had caused such dire repercussions. With their mum on the brink of leaving and their father on the verge of financial ruin, Amanda knew she and her brother were best moving out.

Damien would cope. He had met Rita in the village that morning and gone off with her in the canoe to Resolve, where he planned to stay. He'd promised to ask if his sister could also have a bunk until things settled down at home. The Trust, after all, had been set up for homeless youngsters and that was exactly what they had become. She gave a fleeting smirk. How ironic if they both ended up living with their dad's arch-enemy.

Even more important was that she continued building up her own little business. Doubtless, her allowance would soon be going the way of the car, and carrying out her undercover activity would be more difficult with Damien's keys to Great Taste now confiscated. Amanda's eyes filled with tears again as she thought of all she'd lost but, determined not to cry, she stood up, took the basket from the front of her bike and wandered into the wood, forcing her mind to concentrate on the task in hand.

It wasn't easy as her thoughts continuously returned to Fayre View and the affluent life she'd taken so much for granted. How she despised her father for all the unhappiness he'd caused so many people. Was she the only person to secretly wish him dead? Amanda tried to clear her mind of such unforgivably dark thoughts, but they kept creeping back as she imagined how much easier life would be for everyone without him.

'I must be stark raving mad to even contemplate such a thing,' she admonished herself, determined to bury such horrific ideas and concentrate on her quest.

Fate, however, had other plans. Was it pure chance or perhaps some sub-conscious instinct that had drawn her back to the very spot she'd made that previous discovery? Was it even still there?

It was, and this time she wouldn't leave it. Amanda put on her rubber gloves.

*   *   *

'In the broad ... outboard motors ... I can't believe it.' PC Stan Meadows pushed his uniform cap to the back of his head and wiped some sweat from his forehead, pleased at this turn of events, but mystified as to its meaning. 'Are you sure they're our stolen ones, Jack?'

'Same makes and models,' confirmed the ranger as he led the constable along the mud-wherry's deck.

PC Meadows had arrived in the police RIB within fifteen minutes of Jack's call. He and a fellow constable from BroadsBeat had already been out on a training exercise close by and the orange inflatable's powerful engine made short work of the two miles between. Jack pointed to the three muddy motors lying on deck. 'A check of your serial numbers will tell us for sure though.'

The other two motors had been recovered from the hold and their manufacturer's plates cleaned while they were waiting. Now, they all gathered around as PC Meadows compared their numbers with those in his pocket book. After just a minute, he stood up, returning the notebook to his pocket. 'They're the ones all right – Harvey Laydock's and the two stolen before that at the beginning of the month, but not the one nicked a few days ago.'

'Because that was stolen after the dredging started,' explained Jack. 'Our thief wasn't going to chuck it where he knew it might be found within days.'

'But why dump them in the first place?' The policeman glanced into the broad. 'We still ought to check if anything else is down there. What do you reckon, Charlie? Any chance?'

'That's all we pulled out with that bucketload,' said the operator, 'but it aint to say there's not others down there.'

The PC turned to Jack. 'We could get the diving team to go down and look?'

Jack shook his head, nodding towards the huge crane and bucket. 'After all the disturbance of the dredging, you'd stand a better chance by taking a few more careful scoops around the same area.'

'Okay, let's try that.'

A few minutes later and the crane boom was swinging once more over the placid waters of the broad, carefully dropping the bucket into the hidden depths and bringing all to an agitated maelstrom as it hauled a fresh load of water-spewing sediment up and over the awaiting mud-wherry. All wearing safety hats and expectant looks, policemen, ranger and skipper peered into the hold as the grab disgorged its new load like the retchings of some megalithic creature.

'Nothing this time,' observed PC Meadows, shaking his head with disappointment.

'Not an engine, but it's brought something.' Jack pointed to the edge of the new mound of mud where something protruded from the watery glutinous mass. 'There, Stan, just sticking out. Is that what I think it is?'

PC Meadows shielded his eyes against the midday sun and followed the ranger's outstretched arm. 'By God, it is.' The constable took off the safety helmet, ran a hand through stubbly hair, and pulled out his mobile. 'Now we really do have to call in the big boys.'

*   *   *

All this activity on the broad had not gone unnoticed by the lone figure on the staithe. Councillor Wanstead had watched the morning's dredging, seen all operations cease and the arrival of the ranger, but hopes that this had just been some technical hitch were dashed by the arrival of the police RIB. From that point on, the chairman of the council knew the worst had happened.

But, strangely, after all these days of anguish and fear, Wanstead suddenly felt a strange peace descending upon him. He'd protested and connived to avoid this, but fate had irrevocably worked its relentless and inevitable way. He'd dreaded this moment but, now it was here, there was a sense of anti-climax, an acceptance that the waiting was over and there was nothing else he could do. He turned away and slowly made his way home to enjoy the peace of his garden while he still could.

He was already making a cup of tea when the first police vehicles arrived at the staithe.

*   *   *

Jack watched the RIB come speeding back, full of Crime Scene Investigators. He would know most of them, but not the CID officer because this section of the southern rivers came within Norwich CID and not North Walsham, where his friend Phil Hengrove ruled the roost. The RIB was alongside now, and he helped the CSI team and their kit onboard. He was about to do the same for the remaining officer when he recognised a face, and a familiar voice said, 'Hello, Mr Fellows, how are you?'

'It's DC Bailey!' Jack exclaimed, shaking the hand of DCI Hengrove's previous young partner. 'What are you doing here?'

'Transferred to Norwich last month,' answered the still fresh-faced young detective, 'but it's DS Bailey now, sir. Got my promotion at the same time.'

'Congratulations then, Detective Sergeant Bailey.' Jack liked Bailey, but knew his own old rank of Detective Superintendent would always deter this keen young copper from over-familiarity. Now seemed a good time to put things on a friendlier footing. 'Great to see you here ... and call me Jack.'

'It's good to be here, sir ... Jack,' acknowledged the DS before glancing into the wherry hold where white-suited figures were already squelching through glutinous mud to reach something protruding from its edge, 'even if this does promise to be the messiest job I've had for a long time.' His expression hardened. 'Bones, you say?'

'Yes, a skull and ribcage and assorted other bits that look pretty human to me.'

'Well, we'll soon know.' Bailey glanced again into the hold. A figure who Jack recognised as the police pathologist, was bending over the mud-splattered remains. A few seconds examination and then he straightened up, looked in their direction and simply nodded. Bailey gave a thumbs up and the rest of the CSI team began their task of photographing, cataloguing and examining the surrounding mud for any remains still hidden. By this time the pathologist had joined them on deck. He glanced down at his once-white coveralls, now liberally caked in black ooze. 'I hope all your jobs won't be as filthy as this one, Bailey.'

The DS wrinkled up his nose. 'No, sorry about that, Doc.' He nodded towards the activity in the hold. 'Anything you can tell me at this stage?'

'Only that there's massive damage to the cranium consistent with a heavy blow delivered by something pretty substantial, so it looks like murder. I'll need to get the remains back to the lab before I can give you more details like sex and age, but, in the meantime, we need to check if there's any more down there.'

'Right, I'll contact the diving team.' As the pathologist left, Bailey made his call. After a quick explanation, he turned back to the ranger still beside him. 'They'll be here in about an hour.'

'I doubt they'll find any more bones. What you've got there was dredged from feet under the mud,' explained Jack. 'They won't find more motors either.'

Bailey raised his eyebrows questioningly and Jack explained about the outboard thefts, the three being found and how their search for a fourth had resulted in the discovery of the bones.

'Bit of a coincidence, isn't it, sir?' puzzled Bailey, scratching his head, '... these motors being found in just the same place as the skeleton.'

'Yes, if you believe in coincidence which I don't,' replied Jack without offering an alternative. Instead, he smiled and asked, 'What's your next move?'

Bailey wasn't sure if this vastly experienced ex-Scotland Yard detective was quietly checking him or simply curious. 'Run through all local missing persons I expect, sir. After that, it will depend on what the pathologist tells us.'

'Well, there's one name you won't find in Missing Persons, but well worth a check.' Jack filled Bailey in on Councillor Wanstead's missing wife, Alice, and his opposition to the broad being dredged.

'Thanks for the tip, sir,' said the DS tapping the data he'd just copied into his notebook. He smiled just a little self-consciously. 'First case of my own, so I'll be glad of any help ... Jack.'

'You're doing just fine,' reassured the ranger, 'but never forget the value of local knowledge.' The ranger waved to a passing hire cruiser, its crew obviously fascinated by all the police activity. 'We've already got marker buoys out for the dredging, but I think I'd better put some more further out before your diving team arrive.'

'And I'll head back to HQ for a check of other missing persons before I go and interview your Councillor Wanstead.' He nodded towards the dredger and its crew standing idle. 'Sorry Jack, but this is going to delay your mud digging for a few hours yet. If the divers don't find anything though, you can start again as soon as they're through.'

'Thanks, Bailey. We've got a water frolic here in just over a week and we need to have it dredged by then.'

'Sounds fun.' The DS was obviously glad of a lighter subject on which to conclude. 'If work permits, I might well come and join you. I could do with a day away from crime and transgression.'

'Be good to see you,' said Jack.

Minutes later and he was watching the RIB speed the young detective back to the staithe, some old instinct telling him that he'd be seeing Bailey again much sooner than that. He took a deep breath of river air. It was as invigorating as ever, but there was just the hint of something else now tainting its nectar-like purity. It was the scent of villainy.

The afternoon sun was way past its zenith as Jack eased his launch from the village dyke and back onto the main river. The diving team had finished their search with predictable negative results and, just astern, the renewed crash and bang of the working clamshell bucket heralded a return to normal operation. But Jack knew that the dramatic events of the morning were only the start of what could well be a long and disturbing process.

Turning downriver for a final patrol leg before heading back, Jack found himself admitting that the discovery of those skeletal remains was something he'd been expecting for a week. Was it Councillor Wanstead's vociferous opposition or just plain copper's nose that had told him something secret lurked beneath the placid waters of that broad? Probably a combination of both, but however disruptive the ensuing investigation might be, it would certainly be less worrying to him than it undoubtedly was to Henry Wanstead. Bailey had said he would be paying a visit to the chairman of the council very soon. The sooner the better, thought Jack. Knowing how Wanstead had been keeping an almost-obsessive eye on the dredging from the start, he would now be all too well aware that something significant had been discovered.

And those outboard motors – the diving team had predictably failed to find the last one stolen, but why had the others been dumped there? Second-hand outboards were worth a lot of money, so why go to the trouble of thieving them in the first place, only to jettison them later? Pure vandalism might be one motive, but Jack had a shrewd idea of the real reason. He'd already told Bailey he didn't believe in coincidence, but perhaps it was just that which had led them to the discovery of the skeletal remains – that or fate.

A few miles further downriver, Jack was brought out of his musings by the sight of a hire cruiser dead ahead. It had slowed to a stop and its occupants were obviously keen to speak with the ranger.

'Hello,' they shouted cheerfully, 'sorry to bother you.' They were a young couple with two children, a boy and a girl, all looking tanned and healthy from their holiday afloat.

'No problem, that's what we're here for,' assured Jack, coming out into the launch's open cockpit. 'How can I help you?'

'We'd like to moor in Norwich tonight, but we're afraid we might not find a space and then it'll be too late to turn back.' The man looked a little embarrassed. 'Phone's out of credit, I'm afraid, so I was wondering if you have contact.'

'I'll try.' Jack called base on his VHF and, within minutes had the results. 'Yep, there's a space at the Yacht Station and they're going to hold it for you.'

'That's great. Thanks so much.'

'No problem.' Jack was about to let go, but paused to ask the children, 'Are you having a good holiday?'

'Yes, brilliant,' replied the boy, 'and we even saw a wherry this afternoon.'

'A really long boat,' added the little girl, excitedly, 'and it had a big black sail.'

'Ah, and was it called Resolve?' asked Jack.

Their double nods told him that at least one happy event had occurred this ominous day.

*   *   *

'So, whose remains do you think they are?'

Audrey had waited until the evening meal was finished before delving deeper into the less savoury aspects of her husband's day. During Jack's career in the Met, she had always respected his rule not to discuss cases. These days, however, although drawing the line at gruesome, she was prepared to talk about bare skeletons.

'I'd put money on it being Alice Wanstead,' said Jack, without preamble.

'The Councillor's ex-wife?'

'Late-wife, if my suspicions hold good. Hopefully, DNA should confirm it one way or the other. In the meantime, I expect Bailey will be going to put the frights up our good councillor.' Jack allowed himself a little chuckle. 'Explaining that at the next Parish Council meeting will take a bit of doing.'

'If he really is connected,' replied Audrey, always ready to see the best in others. 'But these dumped outboards, what do you make of them?'

'Strange business,' acknowledged Jack, 'but if the motive wasn't theft or vandalism, then my thoughts are that it was sheer vindictiveness.'

'What against Harvey Laydock and the other owners?'

'No, against the Resolve Trust,' explained Jack. 'To discredit them by instigating a series of thefts right on their doorstep.'

'Do you think Henry Wanstead's responsible?'

'He's the likely candidate,' conceded Jack, 'but difficult to think of him jeopardising his council position by indulging in common theft.'

'Sounds like he might have indulged in worse than that,' said Audrey.

'Yes, but that's not for general discussion, Aud. And, remember, Harvey Laydock is another factor in the equation.'

'Talking of which, I have some startling news of my own,' announced Audrey, leaving the kitchen table and leading them into the lounge.

'Go on,' urged Jack, pleased to get off suppositions, but worried daughter Jo might be having twins or something.

'Well, Mrs Willows, the postmistress rang me today, all excited, and – guess what – Harvey Laydock had just rung her personally and agreed to open the frolic.'

'Good grief!' exclaimed Jack, genuinely astounded. 'He must be hard up. How much is he charging?'

'Nothing. Says he's glad to help the village. In fact,' continued Audrey, pleased to be the bearer of such a revelation, 'he says he wants to contribute further by providing a barbecue for everyone at the end of the day.'

'Our bridge-building seems to have exceeded even our wildest dreams,' declared Jack. 'Harvey Laydock, philanthropist – who ever would have thought it.' Jack hoped he didn't sound as cynical as he felt when he asked, 'What's the catch?'

Audrey smiled her most disarming smile and admitted, quietly. 'Well, he did have one proviso.'

Jack raised his eyebrows. 'Right – which is?'

'That a film-crew be allowed to record the whole event.'

'Film crew ... recording ... what the heck for?'

'For television,' explained Audrey, with suppressed excitement. 'Apparently he's making a new series in which he knocks up meals in unusual places, and he wants our frolic to feature in the opening programme.'

'Does he now.' Jack shook his head, 'I'm not sure about this, Aud. People might feel inhibited in front of cameras. We want them to be enjoying themselves, not feeling self-conscious.'

'Oh, don't be such an old spoilsport,' scolded Audrey. 'People will love a chance to be part of a television production and the publicity will be wonderful, not just for the frolic and the village, but also for the Resolve Trust. This is a great opportunity, Jack.'

'Hmm, perhaps, but why would Harvey Laydock put himself out to help the Resolve Trust when he has such a grudge against Gloria?'

'Because he might actually be having a change of heart.' Audrey put on her confidential tone. 'Mrs Willows did say that Lucy really has left him to be with Greg Kennard, and the children are staying on the wherry.'

'Blimey! In that case, you'd think he'd be more against the Trust than ever.' Jack paused to consider this news. 'No, Aud, this TV thing is just plain opportunism. Laydock needs a programme and we happen to be a useful frame on which to hang it.'

'Well, what's wrong with that?' Audrey threw up her hands in mock despair. 'Jack, we started this whole thing to bring people together, we've done just that, and now you're grumbling.'

'I know – sorry, love.' The need to change the subject again, reminded Jack of something else he'd meant to tell his wife. 'And talking of good things, we're invited on Resolve this weekend, for her first day-cruise.'

'How wonderful! Dear old Alfie must have worked his magic already. Gloria must be thrilled.'

'I'm sure she is.' Jack stood up and Spike, knowing it was walk-time, leapt up and came to his master's side, tail-wagging. 'Right, the river-bank for you, old chap.'

'It's such a beautiful evening, I think I'll join you,' said Audrey, springing to her feet. There was so much going right and this would be a perfect way to end the day.

Five minutes later and they were strolling the rhond, Spike chasing a dragonfly that flitted in the last uplifts of sun-warmed air and Audrey with thoughts on the coming frolic and all the good it would do.

Jack's were a few miles away in the Norwich mortuary, where a collection of old bones cried out for recognition and long-overdue justice.

*   *   *

Chapter Ten

'A skeleton ... in the broad ... crikey.' Greg Kennard wiped his brow and contemplated this latest turn of events. 'Have they any idea who it might be?'

'None as yet,' answered Jack, 'but the police are, as the saying goes, "pursuing enquiries".'

'And I can imagine who with.' Greg gave an undisguised scoff. 'That will give our good councillor something else to think about instead of how to evict me. Just as well now.'

'Yes, I did hear that Lucy had moved in with you,' admitted Jack, who'd stopped by Resolve to check on Alfie's progress and also acquaint them all with what was transpiring on the broad. He'd guessed the boatbuilder had spent the previous night ashore and must have been too preoccupied to pick up what must already be common village gossip. 'I'd no idea things were that serious between you two.'

'Our feelings are serious, but things happened much quicker than either of us planned,' explained Greg. 'Apparently the scene at the staithe the other night led to a general family bust-up and Lucy decided that if she was going to make her break, then was the time to do it. So, now she's living above the workshop with me.'

'How is she?'

Greg shrugged. 'Emotionally confused, as you can imagine, but really just glad to be out of it.' He nodded towards the village. 'I can imagine everyone there thinking that I stole her, but it's not like that. Lucy's been desperate to leave Harvey for years, but didn't have the opportunity until we met.' There was concern in his eyes, but relief in his voice as he added, 'Thankfully though, she's kept off the bottle.'

'Let's hope she keeps it up, as she'll have a lot to deal with in the months ahead.' As Jack spoke, Damien and Amanda emerged from the main cabin and gave him a friendly wave. 'Can't be easy for them. How are they taking it?'

'Pretty well, considering. They're good kids and totally support their mum.' He glanced towards Damien, coiling away ropes on the foredeck with the help of his sister. Rita had now joined them from below and gave Damien a quick peck on the cheek before joining in the work. 'She'll help him and I'll keep him busy while Amanda's engrossed in her own little research project.'

'Oh really. What's that?' There was a lot more to Amanda Laydock than met the eye and Jack was keen to put his finger on just what. That information, however, would not be coming from Greg Kennard.

'I don't know, Jack.' He sounded genuinely ignorant. 'Some sort of science thing, I think but, whatever it is, Gloria seems happy for her to continue it on-board Resolve.' Flinty had also emerged from the main cabin now, joining the Laydocks on the foredeck where Amanda put a caring hand on his shoulder and her face close to his. 'I can't believe how that lad's changed recently,' said Greg watching with apparent disbelief. 'Even his spots have cleared up. He's like a different lad.'

'Yes, and a lucky one too in more ways than one.' Jack lowered his voice slightly as he explained the finding of the outboard motors in the same location as the skeleton.

'This whole business gets weirder by the day.' Greg ran a hand through his mop of hair. 'Why would anyone go to that effort and then dump them?'

'Just stirring up trouble for The Trust seems the likeliest motive at this stage.' Jack nodded towards John Flint. 'At least that lets him off the hook as far as I'm concerned.'

'Yep,' agreed Greg, 'Flinty stealing them for money was hard enough to comprehend, but vandalism just isn't in his nature.' The boatbuilder turned towards the ranger. 'So, if it wasn't any of us, who was it?'

'Too soon to say, but remember it was Harvey Laydock who arrived very quickly on the scene that night at the staithe.'

Further discussion was ended by the cuddy doors opening and Gloria joining them on the small afterdeck. Jack quickly briefed her on recent events on the broad.

'My goodness, how terrible. What happens now?'

Jack explained procedures, with assurances that it shouldn't affect the frolic or delay the dredging. 'The broad will soon be deep enough to sail Resolve across. Speaking of which, how does she sail?'

The pair's beaming faces gave the answer, but it was Gloria who put it into words. 'Poetry in motion, Jack. To feel sixty tons of wherry gliding along on only the breeze, is a dream come true for me.'

'And one you could be sampling yourself in a couple of days, Jack,' added Greg. 'Are you and Audrey still on for our shake-down trip?'

'Try and stop us.' The ranger nodded to the bent, but lithe figure of Alfie Rumball ascending the gangway steps from below. 'And there's a man who already looks ten years younger.' He turned back to Gloria. 'Your wherry seems to be working its magic on all who touch her.'

'I hope so,' said Gloria. 'Alfie has certainly put his heart and soul into this project, and we'd never be where we are now without him.'

The old man in question made his way aft and joined them at the stern. 'So, how do she look, Mr Fellows?'

'She looks great Alfie and I can't wait to see her sailing.'

The wherryman smiled and gave Resolve's tiller an affectionate slap. 'Yep, for two old-uns, we're not doin' too bad are we?'

Jenny had joined them at the stern with a mug of coffee for Jack, but he'd only taken a few welcome sips when his mobile rang. It was DS Bailey.

'Morning, sergeant. How's it going?'

'I've just finished having a chat with your Councillor Wanstead,' explained the young detective. 'Thought you'd like to know how it went. Any chance of meeting up before I go back?'

'Yep, I can be at the staithe in about twenty minutes.'

'See you there then, sir.'

Jack swigged the remains of his coffee, wished the wherry crew farewell and set off back upriver.

*　　*　　*

'Right, give us the gen.'

On board the ranger's launch, Jack had just finished pouring Bailey a coffee from his own flask. It was the start of an investigation, that blank-case sheet facing them and the thrill of the hunt to come. Jack realised he was merely an outsider with certain connective privileges, but it didn't prevent him feeling that old tingle of excitement, even if the DS's report wasn't particularly illuminating.

'Nothing much really, sir, or at least nothing that takes us any further forward.'

'Sometimes it's what people don't actually say that's revealing. What was his reaction when you arrived at his front door?'

'Pretty twitchy, but he had an air of resignation as well.' Bailey shrugged. 'It was as if he'd been expecting me and seemed almost glad to talk. He made me a cuppa and we went into his lounge, but I could hear his cup shaking in its saucer when he sat facing me. I came straight to the point and said I was investigating the discovery of unknown human remains in the broad.'

'And what was his reaction?'

The DS shook his head. 'That's the really strange thing, sir – his whole demeanour changed from then on.'

'Changed? In what way?' Jack had to remind himself that he wasn't a Detective Superintendent anymore, grilling a young subordinate on his first case. He forced a smile, sat back a little and asked, 'How did he change, Bailey?'

'It was strange, sir, almost as though he was – well – relieved.'

'Relieved!' Jack quietened his voice and repeated, 'Relieved?'

Bailey nodded. 'Yep, became a little haughty and asked how on earth he could help with any skeletons. I reminded him his wife, Alice Wanstead, had disappeared and he corrected me, pretty forcibly, saying she hadn't "disappeared", but just moved abroad to Canada. I asked if he could give me an address, but he insisted he'd lost all contact with her and honestly didn't know if she was alive or dead.'

'Hmm, interesting,' murmured Jack. 'Did you enquire if Alice had any living relations, particularly brothers or sisters?'

The DS smiled and nodded. 'For DNA, you mean? Yes, I did ask, but according to Wanstead, she was an only child.' Bailey glanced down at his notebook. 'They do have children though – a girl married in New Zealand and a son in Australia, but Wanstead reckons they never contact him and he's lost track of them too.' He flipped shut his notebook. 'Seems like no-one wants to know our chairman of the council and, frankly, having met the man, I'm beginning to see why.'

'I know what you mean,' agreed Jack. 'So, what's your opinion?'

'Hard to say, sir. In some ways I wanted to believe him, but perhaps he's just a good actor. Either way, there's something about the man that gives me the creeps.'

'It's called intuition,' smiled Jack. 'How about the pathology report? Any help there?'

'Some. The pathologist reckons we're dealing with a female aged between thirty-five and forty-five who died as a result of a huge blow to the head.'

'That all fits Alice Wanstead,' confirmed Jack. 'Have they got DNA?'

'He's sent samples off for that, but it appears there are other aspects he's not happy with, which need checking.'

'Such as?'

Bailey shook his head. 'Didn't want to say until he had hard facts.' The DS shrugged. 'Typical.' He nodded towards the broad where the clank and groan of renewed dredging contrasted with the gentle rippling of water sparkling in the midday sun. The warning buoys had been moved in again now, and some cruisers were lying peacefully at anchor mid-broad. 'Hard to think a place like this has been harbouring such a secret for so many years.'

'It'll recover,' said Jack philosophically, 'in more ways than one.' He noticed the work had made good progress again after yesterday's disruption. Another few days should see the dredge complete and larger boats back onto the broad.

'Time I was off,' said the DS, standing up and handing back the mug. 'Thanks for the coffee, sir.'

'You're welcome. I appreciate the update, Bailey.' Jack looked towards the staithe. 'Hopefully, I'll see you at the frolic but, in the meantime, keep me in touch with events.'

After promising to do just that, the DS was gone, leaving Jack to reassess all his previous suspicions and wonder what Henry Wanstead was thinking right now as he sat alone in his bungalow.

In fact, Henry Wanstead was not the only man in the village sitting alone contemplating his future. A mile up the road at Fayre View, Harvey Laydock slouched beside his pool trying to appreciate his freedom and failing miserably. For, much as he would have liked to be cavalier about his predicament, Harvey was shocked to realise just how much he missed Lucy.

He glanced again at the recliner beside his own, devoid now of a wife who, for good or bad, had put up with him for nearly twenty years. True, Lucy was pretty weak when it came to the responsibilities of life, but would any other girl have put up with his philandering and bad tempered ways and still been there when he came grumbling back through the front door? And the children - how empty the house seemed without them. It had almost become a family tradition that breakfast should start the day with recriminations and petty squabbles, something at least preferable to this morning's black coffee at a table silent in its desolate emptiness.

At one point he'd actually considered going to Kennard's workshop, finding Lucy and begging her to return. But that would be one humiliating step too far for Harvey's over-developed pride. No, he would be subtler than that in his attempts to woo her back, and years in the media had at least made him well practised at regaining people's loyalty.

Agreeing to open and participate in the frolic had been a shrewd start in that direction. The production company had gone along with his idea for the first programme and a camera team would be there to film the event. With a bit of clever editing, it would show Harvey Laydock as a very popular local figure generously supporting his village community by cooking top quality food using only local produce.

He had, he realised, given himself a gargantuan task, with less than a fortnight in which to organise and prepare everything before the big day. If all went to plan though, this idea should provide all the ingredients to present a perfect first episode to what could well be his most successful series so far. Harvey suddenly felt more positive about his future. Surely, with his finances back on track and the promise of rave-reviews, he'd soon win back the love and respect of his family. In the meantime, however, the important thing was that the media didn't get wind of his current domestic situation.

Harvey was still working on his plan when his mobile rang. It was a national tabloid.

'Mr Laydock? Care to comment on the latest rumours that your wife has finally left you?'

'Piss off,' said Harvey, resisting the temptation to throw the phone into the pool. Instead, he went and poured a stiff Scotch and slumped down again in his recliner.

To one side of the pool were large patio doors leading into the garden. Harvey could see his reflection in those doors and what he saw was a middle-aged man with a noticeable paunch and forlorn looks. How often he'd seen that same image in his wife and how quickly those tables had turned, he thought miserably.

Groaning, he turned his gaze the other way. Life could be so bloody mean. Perhaps he really should go and have it out with his estranged wife.

*　　*　　*

'Your father would go mad if he knew we were here.'

'Well he doesn't, Mum, so just relax.' Amanda stretched herself in Great Taste's main saloon. She and Damien had paddled back to the staithe that afternoon to meet with their mother after she had accepted their reluctance to meet in Greg Kennard's flat. Both children were steadfastly behind their mother in her new relationship, but they both felt it wrong to bring old Laydock family business into Greg's domain.

Great Taste, however, provided the perfect solution. Damien might have had his key to the cruiser confiscated, but Amanda still had her illicit one, so stealing aboard this forbidden territory carried just a sliver of satisfaction at yet another moral victory over their father. Besides, as yet Amanda hadn't told her mother her biggest secret, or recovered her precious kit still hidden on board. First though, she needed to know her mum was okay.

'I'm fine, darlings,' Lucy assured her children, 'but I do miss you both terribly.'

'And we miss you, Mum,' returned Damien. 'We know Greg will make you happy, but we're just a bit worried you'll get ... well ... bored, up in that flat with nothing to do all day.' He hoped he'd managed to hint at what he meant without mentioning his and Amanda's greatest fear.

'Yes, I confess the days do seem to drag until Greg comes home.' Lucy gave a rather dreamy sigh. 'I went to the Post Office this morning and Mrs Willows told me there'd already been a reporter asking if it was true I'd walked out on your father. The last thing I want is to get cornered by the paparazzi, so I'm staying inside for most of the day, but there are only so many hours you can spend reading.' As she spoke, Lucy's eyes were inextricably straying towards Great Taste's well-stocked drinks cabinet.

'You need something fulfilling to occupy your day, Mum. Isn't there some work you could do towards the frolic?'

'I've been making lists of things, but that's about as much as I can do at present.' Lucy took another glance towards the cabinet. 'The final meeting's next week, so perhaps I'll be able to do something more constructive in Greg's workshop after that.'

'Hmm.' Amanda didn't want to change the subject, but they'd brought Rita with them to shop in the village, so time was limited. 'Mum, there's something I need to collect from the boat here.'

'Of course dear, but what could you possibly have on board?'

'It's been a secret, Mum, but I guess we're all sharing confidences these days, so I'm going to tell you all about the little business I'm running here in the village.'

Amanda told her mother how she was putting her talent for chemistry to good use to make welcome extra cash. She went and retrieved her metal case.

'Good heavens! Is it legal, Amanda?' Lucy was as shocked by the secrecy of this revelation as the contents of the case. She turned to her son. 'And did you know about this, Damien?'

'Yes, Mum.'

Lucy nervously ran her fingers through her hair. 'Well thank goodness the press hasn't picked up on this yet. If they ever did, it would be yet another nail in your father's professional coffin.'

'I should think he's got a drawerful of those already, Mum,' joked Amanda, with a smirk. 'When does he have to make this final payment to Gloria Vale?'

'Soon, unfortunately, and I guess when that's been paid, there'll be precious little left for divorce settlements for me or allowances for you two.'

'None of which matters to us, Mum,' assured Damien. 'It's you we worry about.'

'And I can make a few pennies with my business.' Amanda removed some of her equipment from the case, including reference books and a sealed plastic container. 'Now I'm involved with Resolve, the problem is finding time for collecting my raw materials.' Even as she contemplated the problem, the solution struck her. 'But you could, Mum.'

'Me?' Lucy laughed at the suggestion. 'I know nothing about things like that, Amanda. I'd be useless.'

'No you wouldn't, and I can teach you. We'll go through a few right now. You can use Damien's bike to get out into the countryside and it'll keep you well away from any news-types who might be lurking in the village.'

'Well, if you think I could ...'

'Of course, you could, Mum,' assured Damien. 'Apart from helping Mandy, it would be good therapy for you.'

'Well, I suppose at least we'll all go to gaol together.' Lucy smiled and took her children's hands. 'A real family business, heh?'

'We'll make a great team,' smiled a relieved Amanda, giving her Mum a heartfelt hug before opening one of her books, a large one with coloured illustrations. 'Now, let me show you what I need.'

'But first I think we could all do with a drink,' declared Lucy. Smiling at the dismayed look on her children's faces, she nodded towards the galley. 'Damien, pop the kettle on.'

*　　*　　*

'Jack, where are you?' The voice on the other end of the mobile was PC Meadows'.

'I'm on the dredger, Stan. What can I do for you?'

'I'll be at the staithe in fifteen minutes. Meet me there.'

The police four-wheel drive drew up just as Jack finished securing the launch. 'Not more thefts I hope, Stan?'

'No, returning some, actually. Hop in.'

As they drove off through the village, Jack glanced in the back at the three outboard motors dredged from the broad the previous day. They were very different to how he'd last seen them, cleaned of mud and smelling of WD40. 'Obviously forensics have finished with them?'

The constable nodded. 'Yep, for what good it did us. Unfortunately, there was little hope of finding any clues when the evidence had been down with the fishes all that time, so we're now returning them to their rightful owners.'

'Are they any good?' asked Jack, knowing how immersion was usually a death sentence for aluminium left submerged for any length of time.

'Probably not, but it's procedure and it might just keep his nibs up the road off our backs.' The PC nodded in the direction of Fayre View.

'Ah yes, our celebrity chef.' Jack gave a cynical smile. 'I'm sure he'll be very grateful.'

'I won't hold my breath,' said the PC, raising his eyebrows, 'but, as you were instrumental in finding them, I thought you might want to be there.'

'Thanks. I'd like to have a chat with haughty Harvey again anyway.' On the way, Jack filled the constable in on his chat with Bailey and the estrangements within the Laydock household.

'So we won't expect him to be in the best of moods then,' groaned the PC as he swung the police vehicle up Fayre View's imposing drive.

He was correct in that assumption: Harvey Laydock was far from welcoming and decidedly unappreciative for the return of his outboard.

'Yes, well, a fat lot of good it's going to be now,' he snapped on the doorstep. 'I have to say that prompter action on the part of the authorities might have recovered it before it was ditched like that.'

'These motors were probably thrown into the broad within minutes of being stolen,' said Jack, through gritted teeth. He fixed Harvey's sleep-starved eyes with his own. 'Any idea why anyone would do that, Mr Laydock?'

'Who knows the workings of the delinquent mind these lawless days.' The celebrity suddenly realised the implications of the question. 'How would I? What are you implying, Fellows?'

'Just checking every possibility, Mr Laydock.'

'Yes ... well ...' Harvey closed one eye, '... you keep your misguided theories to yourself. As for this ...' he nodded at the outboard and then to the police vehicle, '... it's ruined now so take it away and dump it.'

'Disposal will be your problem, sir,' responded PC Meadows, trying hard not to tell Harvey Laydock what he'd really like him to do with his motor. Instead, some little devil prompted him to conclude, 'and when you write to the Chief Constable to thank him, I'm sure he'd appreciate a donation to the welfare fund.'

'Would he!' blasted Harvey, visibly bristling. 'He'll get a letter alright, telling him what I think of his force and its service.' He looked again at his outboard and the dogged expression on the face of the officer holding it. He nodded towards his garage. 'All right, stick it in there.' Then the door slammed shut once more.

'Makes you want to go home and shred your telly licence,' muttered the PC, as he and Jack carried the motor to the open garage. 'His lordship needs to learn to lock this as well or he'll be losing more than his outboard.'

There was indeed much to tempt a casual thief in Harvey Laydock's garage, not least a shiny sports car that Jack recognised as Amanda's late wheels. There was also the usual junk that most people seem to accumulate and which invariably finds its way to the car's domain. PC Meadows was scanning for a suitable place for this latest offering. 'We'll stick it here,' he finally decided, finding a space reasonably free of clutter except for one object covered by a piece of waste canvas. As the two officers manoeuvred the motor beside it, the canvas fell off to reveal what was underneath.

'Hello, now what do we have here?' PC Meadows was suddenly pleased he'd had to do Harvey Laydock's spadework, and four minutes later was again ringing the celebrity's doorbell.

'Yes, what is it now?' Harvey's impatience was veering on outburst. 'I'm a busy man, you know.'

'Not too busy to accompany me back to the station I hope, Mr Laydock.' The PC was suppressing an urge to smile. 'When we get there you can make a statement as to how a stolen outboard motor found its way into your garage.'

*   *   *

'Harvey Laydock - a thief - I can't believe it.' Audrey Fellows sat with her elbows on the kitchen table and her chin resting on her hands. Jack had arrived home half an hour before, but tonight the tea remained unpoured in the face of this latest report.

'Pretty astounding, I know,' admitted Jack, 'but not entirely unexpected. Of course, he wasn't doing it for gain, but just spite. He was confident the blame would be attributed to the youngsters from the Resolve Trust. The outboards were stolen and simply chucked in the broad until we began dredging. So, the last two had to be handled differently, with one hidden in his garage and the other planted in the Trust's dinghy. Or at least that's Stan's theory,' added Jack, remembering that every man was innocent until proven guilty. He finally poured the tea and slid Audrey's cup across the table.

'Thanks, love. You know, it must have been a horrendous shock to Laydock to find the game was up. What was his reaction?'

'Oh the usual display of aggrieved disassociation. Denied any knowledge and said someone must have put it there as he never bothered to lock the garage during the day. When that didn't impress Stan Meadows, he even tried accusing us of planting it!' Jack smiled to himself. 'Stan did let Harvey call his solicitor before leaving, but then took his time dropping me off at the staithe so Mrs Willows could catch a glimpse of our celebrity, looking somewhat sheepish, in the back of a police vehicle.'

'Which means it'll be all round the village by now,' sighed Audrey. 'So, what will happen to Harvey? Will he be detained?'

'Good gracious no.' Jack took a welcome sip of his tea. 'He'll have had to make a statement but, if he's got any sense, he'll let his solicitor do most of the talking. Then he'll probably be released with instructions to stay in the area, pending further enquiries.'

'But you think he's guilty, don't you?'

'I'm not sure, Aud,' confessed Jack. 'As we know, he certainly has more than one motive for seeking revenge by discrediting the Resolve Trust, but finding that motor in his garage took about five seconds flat, so why would Harvey let us wander in there unaccompanied if he knew we'd stumble on such incriminating evidence. And then there was the look on his face when Stan laid it on him. He really did seem genuinely taken aback.'

'But he's a TV star, Jack.' Audrey wasn't ready yet to give any slack to a man she positively disliked. 'He makes a living by putting on performances, and that's what he probably did for you.'

'I know, but I made my living by seeing through just that sort of deception and, to me, Harvey Laydock was a man who really didn't know he was concealing stolen property.'

'Well, if he didn't take it, then who did?'

'Goodness knows,' admitted Jack shaking his head. 'Harvey's got enough enemies for any one of half-a-dozen to put the finger on him – and that's just around here.'

'Oh dear. I suppose this will put the stoppers on him opening the frolic.'

'I should think that's the least of his worries right now,' said Jack with a smile, 'so don't worry, Aud, because he's probably committed to making the programme and, knowing him, will doubtless still have the gall to play the much-loved local resident as he declares the event open. Of course, if he proved his innocence before then, it would be all the better. Perhaps if I made a few enquiries of my own and ...'

'No Jack!' Audrey's raised finger and the look in her eyes had a firmness beyond discussion. 'No investigations. Just for once you're going to leave this to those who are paid to do it and let the law take its course. And besides,' she took his hand, her voice softening, 'we've got enough excitement in our lives for the next few weeks, the first of which is our sail in that wonderful old wherry. Let's forget Harvey Laydock for the moment while you tell me all about our little expedition.'

Jack sat back with his second cup of tea and talked enthusiastically about the forthcoming trip. He was excited at that prospect himself but, in spite of his wife's admonitions, his thoughts kept returning to the day's events. He had a strong premonition that Harvey Laydock was being framed. It might be just the beginning of a campaign against the chef. If so, even worse could follow.

He would never have admitted it to a soul but, much as Jack despised him, he was actually worried for Harvey Laydock.

*   *   *

Next morning, the man himself wasn't worried, but he was angry. He'd spent the previous afternoon at police headquarters making statements and listening to his solicitor deny all allegations. Finally they'd let him go with instructions to keep himself available for further questioning.

What had concerned Harvey most, as he emerged from the police station, was his public image. He'd had little doubt his plight had already reached the tabloids and knew enough about the ways of the media to guess that reporters would already be gathered outside the gates of Fayre View, awaiting his return. So he'd turned down the offer of a police car home, arranged for his own Jag to be delivered to a Norwich hotel, and there spent a peaceful, if sleepless, night.

This morning, with his spirits lifted by warm sun, Harvey dropped the roof of the Jag and sped homewards through country lanes, if not with a song on his lips, at least thankful to be still free, and confident he could weather the approaching storm. Drawing up in front of Fayre View's electronically-controlled gates, he was relieved to see the road devoid of pressmen.

He should have known better. Even as the decorative wrought-iron swung back, two figures emerged from their hiding place in the bushes opposite. One went straight to the front of the car, making flight impossible and raising a camera as expensive as it was intrusive, its motor-drive clicking off a whole series of Harvey's dishevelled features that would, doubtless, soon be staring out from some dirt-digging rag.

The second figure, meanwhile, had positioned beside him and was thrusting a small recorder into his face. 'Angelica Black, Mr Laydock.' She mentioned the name of a popular Sunday newspaper. 'Any comment on the rumours that your wife has left you and that you were arrested yesterday on criminal charges?'

Harvey groaned. He should have realised that "The Sundays" had later deadlines to pursue their sordid stories than the daily tabloids. He turned to tell this pushy bitch what she could do with her recorder and her paper.

But he never did. Angelica Black turned out to be a tall, shapely blonde whose tight leather trousers and low-cut blouse exuded sexuality. As his window purred its way down, Harvey smiled and pushed his sunglasses onto his forehead.

'Do you really want my story, Ms Black?'

She smiled back revealing perfect teeth. 'That's what I'm here for.'

'Then I'll give it to you ...' Harvey paused and nodded towards his home, '... but not here.'

'Where then?'

The celebrity's eyes narrowed slightly. 'Over supper tonight.'

*   *   *

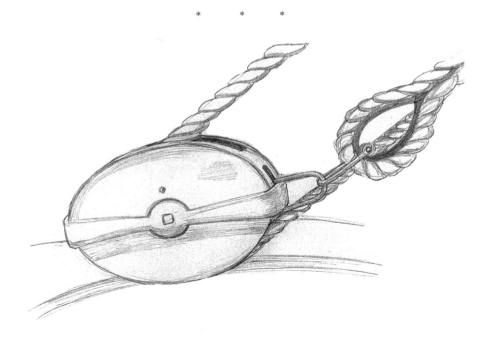

Chapter Eleven

Standing at Resolve's big tiller, flat cap pulled over his eyes against the bright morning sun, Alfie Rumball gave an almost imperceptible nod. It was the signal Greg had been waiting for. Through cupped hands, he shouted, 'Haul away,' to Freddie and Flinty up on the foredeck and soon the clank of the windless ratchet joined the purr of the tender's outboard which, until now, had been pushing them steadily downriver. With each turn of the windless, the mighty gaff rose ever higher and from it, rolls of black canvas unfolded as Resolve's sail was hoisted once more.

'Keep that peak under control,' Alfie ordered Gloria, who was feeding out the gaff line through a cleat atop the cuddy, at the same time trying to avoid the still-drooping spar from sweeping the cabin roof. But soon the gaff jaws were aloft with the main halyard starting to elevate the peak itself. A few more turns of the windless and the spar was pointing skyward at thirty degrees with its huge expanse of sail filling and drawing to the fresh southerly wind. Resolve was sailing again.

'Okay, come and secure this gaff-line!' shouted Greg to the foredeck crew and Freddie and Flinty, still breathing heavily from their exertions, unshipped the windless handles, came aft and took Gloria's line, looping it, as directed, through one of the mast hoops before taking a well-deserved rest.

'Phew! A pretty labour intensive operation that,' said Gloria, exercising stiff fingers.

'You'll soon get used to it,' assured Alfie with a knowing smile. He turned away as Resolve healed slightly to a fresh gust. 'Okay, ease the mainsheet.' Greg uncleated the controlling braided rope and allowed it to run through the huge wooden three-sheaved blocks on sail tack and iron horse, until Resolve came back to an almost-even keel and she progressed eastwards, even steadier and slightly faster.

'Right, let's get rid a that there racket,' said Alfie, nodding to the tender, as he put his back to the tiller in compensation for the wherry's bow paying off slightly. Seeing Greg's cut-throat signal, Damien instantly shut down the motor and clambered aboard the wherry where he eased the tender's ropes, allowing the boat to drop back and tow astern. Now the only sound was the creak of the blocks and the splash of breaking water as the Yare was thrust aside by Resolve's bow.

'How wonderful.' The words were Gloria's, but it was a sentiment echoed by the grinning faces of all the passengers huddled around the cuddy, well clear of the busy afterdeck.

There were several of them. To port, Jack and Audrey stood enthralled, but to Damien, who had just joined them, this was a dream come true. He turned to Jack, eyes gleaming. 'So, Mr Fellows, what do you think?'

'I think it's wonderful, Damien. She's a credit to you all.'

'You must feel very satisfied,' added Audrey, as thrilled as her husband at this unique experience.

'You bet. I'm just so lucky to have helped restore her.' Damien nodded to the expanse of the main hatches. 'Let's go and sit down.' He led them onto the old cargo hold. 'Like all trading wherries, the sail's loose-footed with no boom to come crashing over, so we're safe here,' he reassured them, lying down on the warm hatch boards and stretching out. 'This is just brilliant.'

'And your mum and sister seem to be enjoying it too,' observed Jack, sitting down himself and casting a glance to where Lucy Laydock lay chatting to Amanda further for'ard on the starboard side.

'Yes, I'm so glad they came. It'll do Mum good to get away from the village for a bit.'

'How's she handling things, Damien?' asked Audrey.

'Pretty well. She found being cooped up in Greg's flat a bit stifling at first, but now she's getting out helping Mandy, she's so much happier ...' he smiled as the boatbuilder joined his mum and gently touched her face, '... with that side of life.'

'Yes, she's certainly looking very contented and relaxed today,' agreed Audrey.

'You say your mum's doing work for your sister, now,' probed Jack.

'Yes, using my bike, which is so much better than a car.'

'Doing what?' persisted Jack.

'Oh ... collecting ...' Before finishing, Damien gave his apologies and jumped up in response to a wave from Rita who had just appeared on deck armed with her sketchbook and pencils.

'Saved by the bell,' said Jack. 'Why is everyone so evasive when it comes to telling me what sweet Amanda's game is?'

'Just relax and enjoy your day,' soothed Audrey, as she scanned the opening vista of the Yare valley. She looked for'ard to where Rita and Damien were laughing and chatting with all the tenderness of young love. 'They obviously are. It's good that he has someone to share this difficult time with.'

'Agreed, but I'd still like to know what his sister ...'

'Jack!' It was Gloria's shout that stopped the ranger in mid-sentence. She was still standing alongside Alfie, but beckoning with enthusiastic "come-over-here" gestures. He pulled himself to his feet and went aft.

'Go on, 'ave a go,' offered Alfie, indicating the big tiller. 'Time for a smoke break an' my mate seems to 'ave other things on his mind right now.' The old wherryman grinned and cast his eyes to where Greg and Lucy were engrossed in happy conversation. Amanda had joined Flinty on the foredeck and Freddie had disappeared completely. 'You'll find its yer back what do most of the work,' instructed the skipper, demonstrating with a couple of short corrections each way.

Jack took the old man's place and tried a couple of gentle tiller movements himself. There was certainly a lot of effort needed to move that great slab of rudder, but Resolve responded to it with such positive feel. 'She handles beautifully, Alfie. You'd never think she was over a century old.'

'Nah, built 'em good in them days.' He pulled the old pipe and a pouch of baccy from his tatty jacket, filled the bowl and lit up. Soon Resolve's passage was being marked by a trail of fragrant smoke as the miles passed by. 'Can't think of nowhere on earth I'd rather be right now,' he said, making a small adjustment to the mainsheet and taking another contented puff.

'Nor me.' Gloria folded her arms on the cuddy roof and rested her chin on top, as though surveying this realisation of her dreams. Jack could imagine the wonderful sense of personal achievement she must be experiencing as her attention went from the boat itself to the relaxed, happy, healthy-looking youngsters, so obviously benefiting from their new life afloat. The initial feeling of excitement on board had been replaced by an air of blissful contentment, which Jack shared as he fulfilled his own ambition of helming a wherry.

'You know, Alfie,' he said, turning to the slightly tired, but happy-looking, figure at his side, 'I reckon skippering wherries must have been a job in a thousand.'

'Yeah, it was an' all.' The skipper once more scanned aloft to the windvane, down to the sail's luff and back to the mainsheet, a sub-conscious routine as regular as the puffs on his pipe. 'But you're seein' it now jus' perfect. You try breakin' through a foot of ice in that there New Cut in winter or shiftin' forty tons a cargo by hand off Yarmouth Quay. It weren't so much fun then, I tell yer.'

Gloria was nodding in agreement. 'Goodness, it must have been a tough way to earn a living.'

Alfie took a harder bite of his pipe and nodded. 'An tha's if yer could make a living.' He gave a sigh. 'Trouble was, af'er the war, the wherries had finished and with 'em, any jobs for the likes a me. Best I could do was helpin' out in a boatyard, an' a part-time job on top a that, jus' to make ends meet.'

'Well, you're back sailing one, and for enjoyment now,' said Jack, putting his back harder into the tiller to follow another curve of the river. Just ahead, Cantley sugarbeet factory was coming into view. They were making good progress downriver. He turned to Gloria. 'What's the objective?'

'I'm hoping we can make Burgh Castle and moor up there for lunch.'

'No reason why we can't,' stated Alfie. 'Tide starts floodin' agin 'bout two, so we'll carry it fair both ways.'

The breeze remained steady also, and the weather fine. Freddie and Jenny were just appearing from below with trays of mugs and cookies. Like Alfie and Gloria, Jack couldn't think of anywhere else he'd rather be right now.

*　　*　　*

'These are delicious. Who made them?' asked Lucy, helping herself to another homemade biscuit.

Jack had handed over the tiller to Greg, and now lounged on top of the main hatch with the others, enjoying their morning break as river, boats and broadland scene slipped peacefully by. Damien had joined Greg and Alfie on the afterdeck.

'They're Freddie's,' replied Jenny, smiling towards her cheerful-looking crewmate sitting crossed-legged opposite. 'He baked them especially this morning.'

'Congratulations, Freddie, they're scrummy,' praised Audrey. 'Where did you learn to bake like that?'

'Oh, picked it up at one of my temporary jobs in a seaside café last year.' The young crewman seemed almost embarrassed at this unexpected praise. 'I found I really enjoyed cooking, but that job finished at the end of the holiday season and I found myself on the streets for the winter.'

'Perhaps you could enrol on a cookery course and take it up professionally,' suggested Audrey.

Freddie nodded. 'Love to, but chances for that sort of thing don't come to the likes of me.'

'Well they should,' said Lucy. 'I wish you could spend some time with my … er … husband. For all his faults, he's an ace with food and you'd learn so much.'

'Come off it, Mum,' protested Amanda. 'When has Dad ever done a thing to help anyone unless it's in his own interest?'

Further discussion was interrupted by Alfie, who had left Damien at the mainsheet and come for'ard. 'We need to harden that there forestay next time the sail's lowered,' he muttered to Gloria, pointing the stem of his pipe towards the mast's only stay, which was showing a perceptible slackness as Resolve ran before the wind on this northerly reach. 'If we start goin' to windward it'll rake the mast back a bit and she'll sail lousy.'

'I can't understand it,' puzzled Gloria. 'That was really tight when we last raised the mast.'

'Yep, so it was, but it's a new rope,' explained Alfie, "an new ropes always stretch. Tha's why we always stretched new uns the night afore usin''em in the mornin'.' He paused to wave to a hire cruiser, its crew busy photographing them as they passed. This would be the first time most river-users had seen Resolve sailing, and her stately progress this morning was producing more interest with every mile. 'Causin' quite a stir,' commented Alfie proudly. He turned again to Gloria. 'Reckon this old gal a yours will serve your cause well.'

But Gloria was miles away, scanning distant horizons before she realised Alfie was talking to her. 'Oh ... yes, Alfie ... I hope so ... that's the idea.'

'The frolic will give you some good publicity too,' enthused Amanda. She watched her brother rejoin Rita, who was still busy sketching on the foredeck. 'Is it true Rita is going to have a stall selling her artwork?'

'Yes, and I think she'll do well.' Gloria smiled as Rita flicked through some of her work for Damien's benefit. 'She really is a talented girl.'

'And quite keen on my son, by the look of it,' noted Lucy, helping herself to another biscuit. 'And I'm quite keen on these,' she added, with another smile to Freddie.

'Reedham Ferry just ahead!' shouted Greg from aft. Sure enough, a quarter mile away, the chain-link ferry with two cars on board, was making its slow way across the river. Greg put his back on the tiller and Resolve's bow swung a little towards the north bank the ferry had just left. 'She'll wait on the other side until we're clear,' he added as he brought the wherry back while Alfie re-trimmed the sail.

'How about the swing bridge though?' asked Gloria. The railway crossing was at the other end of Reedham's long waterfront, usually closed and certainly too low for their tall mast to pass beneath.

Greg checked his watch. 'Twelve fifteen. It opens at twenty past the hour, so we should be okay.' They were abeam the harbour master's office now, exchanging greetings with people on the town quay as Resolve glided past with stately grace. Even better, just ahead they could see the bridge's central span swinging steadily open until it lay along the river instead of across it. Five minutes, and they were sailing through the gap as several cruisers held off and the bridge controller came out of his cab to give them a friendly wave. Very soon were passing the entrance to the New Cut, maintaining their own course downriver, while Greg's hold of the tiller visibly relaxed. 'Right, time for someone else to have a go.' He glanced about. 'Where's Flinty?'

'Down below with his feet up,' answered Amanda with a smile.

'Well get him up top to do some helming.'

A few minutes later and a sleepy-eyed Flinty was making his somewhat reluctant way to the after deck.

'Don't know about this,' he grumbled. 'Never handled anything this big before.'

'You'll do fine, lad,' assured Alfie, pointing down the river, now lined entirely with reedbeds. 'I'll handle the sail if you just keep her goin' down the middle.'

Flinty took the tiller he had spent so many hours sanding and painting and soon his face was breaking into a satisfied grin as he realised he was actually steering this huge vessel and enjoying every minute of it.

'He's doing well, isn't he?' remarked Audrey to her husband.

'Having responsibility and the chance to discover his own capabilities is just what he needs,' agreed Jack, standing up and scanning the flat landscape ahead. On the far horizon, the low-lying silhouette of Great Yarmouth was coming into view, the tall chimney of the power station just visible. Another hour would see Resolve at Burgh Castle. The whole day was turning out perfectly.

Why then, pondered Jack, was something, strangely indefinable, causing him to worry? What wasn't right on this wonderful old vessel that offered such hope to so many? He sure it was something that had been said, but he couldn't think what. Still wondering, he went for'ard to help prepare the lines for mooring.

*   *   *

Well west of Resolve and miles from his own village, Councillor Wanstead stopped to soak up some of the morning's sunshine. Perhaps his mood wasn't quite as light-hearted as that of the wherry's crew, but he was, nevertheless, feeling the benefit of fresh air.

He had always enjoyed walking in the countryside but, these last few days, his leisurely ambles along favourite lanes had assumed more the nature of an escape. He had little doubt that vicious rumours would already be circulating in the village and, what they lacked in fact, would be more than made up for in wild conjecture. Not that it mattered anymore, because very soon he would doubtless be damned for all time by the villagers he'd tried to serve.

Henry paused to slip off his wax jacket that, together with a tweed cap and leather brogues, had become his standard walking attire. It was nearing midday now and very hot. He pulled out a large handkerchief and wiped some sweat from his brow.

It would have been nice to be sharing this walk with another like-minded companion, but that was a seemingly simple pleasure he hadn't enjoyed since losing his wife. He had known all along that his life as a respected pillar of the community was a sham, but had no reason to believe the truth would ever surface – until now. Perhaps the burden that weighed so heavily on his conscience was what had turned him into the officious, disagreeable, friendless person he had become. Only now did he realise how stupid he'd been.

He thought of the way Harvey Laydock had taken full advantage of his foolish obsession with the rich and famous, before dropping him like a hot potato when he was no longer of use. How he now hated that arrogant man. Then he thought of the other villagers happily planning the frolic and enjoying all the simple pleasures of shared endeavour. What an appalling error of judgement he'd made in his choice of friends. He felt the outsider, but it was too late now to change anything.

Or was it? Perhaps his time as a free man in this idyllic little corner of creation might be limited, but that didn't mean it had to be spent in enforced seclusion. If he could just help out with this frolic and enjoy a little of the camaraderie that had developed during the past week, then his last weeks of freedom might yet be pleasurable. Yes, he would attend the final planning meeting to be held at The Ferryman next week and humbly offer his help. Perhaps, by portraying a kinder, more amiable side to his nature, he might actually be accepted as part of the team.

Henry resumed his walk, but now with a slight spring in his step. Ahead, on the left, was a wood. In there it would be cool and peaceful. Henry slipped his jacket back on and strode into its dark and enticing interior.

*　　*　　*

Chapter Twelve

'Right, let her down.'

On Alfie's order from the stern, Freddie and Damien freed the windlass pall and, using a curved length of sprung steel as a simple brake on the drum, allowed the gaff and sail to start their smooth descent.

Just minutes before, they had glided by the flint walls of the old Roman fort overlooking the Waveney, and were now stemming the tide against the last hour of ebb as they slowly approached the mooring.

'Ease 'er in there, lad,' muttered Alfie, and Flinty, still at the tiller and with bottom lip firmly between his teeth, brought the wherry's bow in towards the quay. Water was sluicing past the hull, but the mooring was edging closer, inch by inch, as they crabbed towards it. 'Tha's good ... now helm right over ... bring 'er up.' Slowly and laboriously, the sixty-foot black hull came parallel to the staithe and stopped right alongside. At bow and stern, crewmembers jumped ashore with lines, urgently getting the head rope through a heavy iron ring and doubling it back to one of Resolve's timberheads before the tide once again exerted its relentless pull. There was a creaking and straining as these lines took the weight and then blissful peace and silence as Resolve settled to her mooring.

'Phew, never thought I'd do it,' admitted Flinty, wiping a drip of perspiration from the end of his nose.

'Well yer did right grand,' praised Alfie, once again pushing back his cap and tidying the coils of mainsheet that filled the afterdeck. 'Right, let's get that sail tidied an' things shipshape.'

All lent a hand furling the huge expanse of sailcloth that lay in heaps on the hatchboards. Soon it was secured to the gaff with ties and all spare lines coiled and stowed.

'It's such a beautiful day,' said Gloria, shielding her eyes against the midday sun, 'so let's have a quick run ashore and then we'll eat lunch as we sail home.'

Greg nodded towards a small riverside pub close by. 'How about drinks all round? You've earned it.'

'A good idea,' agreed Gloria. 'Resolve might be run as a dry ship, but I think the crew deserve a bit of a treat. In fact,' she announced, putting on a large straw hat, 'I'll even buy the first round, because I'm sure Alfie's ready for a pint.'

The old skipper smacked his lips, and Jack was licking his own when

Audrey smiled and said, 'If you don't mind, I'd rather go and look at the fort. I've never been here before and it's something I've always wanted to do.'

'I suppose I ought to come too,' said Jack through slightly clenched teeth as he put aside thoughts of an ice-cold lager.

'Would you mind if I joined you?' asked Jenny. 'One of my modules at uni was about the Romans and, once Flinty's back on track, I want to study the period in greater depth for a master's degree. This is a wonderful site and far too good an opportunity for me to miss.'

Damien also chose to forgo drinks in preference to wandering hand-in-hand with Rita along the riverbank towards Saint Olaves, while Lucy and Amanda walked with the others towards the fort. When they reached a dividing of the way, however, mother and daughter continued strolling beside the hedgerows, Lucy carrying the wicker shopping-basket they'd brought with them. After agreeing to meet up again on Resolve in an hour's time, the fort contingent continued their climb.

Still impressive, the Roman structure sat high on the rising ground, dominating the skyline and the estuary it had been built to guard all those centuries before. The side nearest the river had long since fallen into the marshes, but on the other three, twelve foot high flint walls with massive bastions at each corner enclosed what was now a large area of lush grass. In AD300 these battlements must have been a formidable sight to any marauding ships choosing to enter the vast estuary from the North Sea. Since then, nature had devised her own barrier across its mouth in the form of a sandbar on which the town of Great Yarmouth had been built. Now there was only a narrow entrance to the sea and the once-great estuary had become an expanse of inland water surrounded by tidal mudflats and marshland.

Standing in the grassy inner sanctuary, however, Jack's thoughts were far from amusement arcades, piers and fairground rides, as he tried to imagine life here seventeen hundred years before. It would have been a very different world then, a thought amplified by the intrusion of a helicopter, doubtless bound for a North Sea oilfield, clattering its way overhead. Jack looked up. 'I wonder what the Romans who manned this place would have made of that?'

'They were Greeks, actually,' explained Jenny. 'A detachment of elite Stablesian cavalry who had served previously in Holland and were well-used to marsh warfare.' She smiled apologetically. 'Sorry for the history lesson, but, knowing we were coming here, I looked up my notes on the subject.'

'I'm glad you did. It's all so interesting,' said Audrey, impressed, 'and you can't beat having your own expert guide.'

'I wouldn't say "expert",' protested Jenny, modestly, 'but, Emperor Claudius and his occupation of Britain has always fascinated me. I'm intrigued at the thought of all those men and women, far from their own warm country, serving in this cold, bleak edge of the empire.'

'Yeah, it must have been a bit of a naff posting,' agreed Jack. 'So, who were they guarding against, anyway?'

'Saxon raiders,' explained Jenny. 'The Romans called this "The Saxon Shore" and built a string of forts from Branodunum in North Norfolk to Portus Adumi in Hampshire. This was known as Gariannonum then.'

'You're a wealth of information,' said Audrey, sinking down onto the cool grass and stretching her legs. She thought of her own life spent supporting her husband, raising the family and running a home. 'It must be wonderful having the prospect of such an absorbing career ahead of you.'

Jenny lay down and cupped her chin on a hand. 'I suppose it will be when I get down to it, but I need to sort my brother out first.'

'Ah, yes, Flinty.' Jack was momentarily distracted by the distant figures of Lucy and Amanda, engrossed in conversation and picking items from the hedgerows, which they popped into the basket. He brought his attention back to the problem of John Flint. 'What a shame he couldn't have carved a career for himself like you hope to do.'

'But he did ... or was in the process of.' Jenny blinked at what were obviously painful memories. She turned and faced Audrey. 'As you've probably noticed, my brother's a pretty mixed up and sensitive lad, but he wasn't always like that. He took a trainee management position with a large supermarket chain when he left school and was doing really well before they assigned him to a spell in the accounts department. That's when he noticed that the cash taken and recorded didn't always tally, so he reported the discrepancies to the store manager, who promised to look into it. Unknown to Flinty, an investigation team came in, did a spot check of personnel lockers and found some marked notes in my brother's wallet.'

'But surely Flinty hadn't stolen them!' exclaimed Audrey. 'He'd hardly draw attention to the problem if he was taking the money himself.'

'Exactly,' said Jenny, her eyes welling up. 'My brother realised it was the manager himself fiddling the books and, knowing Flinty was onto him, he shifted the incriminating evidence my brother's way, getting him not only fired, but a police record and sixty hours community service.'

'Poor lad. A miscarriage of justice like that would leave anyone bitter,' said Jack, shaking his head. 'No wonder he's got a chip on his shoulder and a grudge against anyone in authority.'

Jenny nodded. 'It was the humiliation that hit him hardest. After the conviction and serving his punishment, he simply fled our area and disappeared off the radar.'

'Didn't your mum and dad worry?' asked Audrey.

'Our parents live overseas because of Dad's work,' explained Jenny. 'I didn't want to concern them so, having just graduated, I traced my brother to Norwich where he'd gone to try and start a new life. But, with his police record, he hadn't been able to get work anywhere and ended up living rough on the streets. He was in a terrible state when I eventually found him but, as luck would have it, I'd read an article about Resolve Trust and all the work Gloria Vale was trying to do for homeless youngsters like Flinty. So, I made contact with her and here we are.'

'Well, your brother certainly seems to be benefiting from the experience, judging by his performance today,' said Jack.

'Yes, he's gained so much self-confidence in just the last week,' agreed Jenny, 'thanks mainly to Amanda. She's really put herself out to help him.'

'Are they … involved?' asked Audrey.

Jenny hesitated. 'I'm not sure, and Flinty hasn't been too forthcoming about the whole thing. He simply says Amanda's just a good friend who's helped him more than anyone will ever know.'

'He's a lucky lad to have two such lovely girls caring for him.' Jack stood up and looked to see if Amanda and her mother were still foraging in the hedgerow, but they were nowhere in sight and must have already returned. 'Time we were getting back, or we'll miss our ship.'

As they ambled back to the staithe, they talked about the Resolve Trust in general and all the work and money Gloria had put into the project. 'She's done such wonders,' said Jenny, 'so it's really horrid that Harvey Laydock has tried to ruin it all. I can't believe he tried to cast blame on poor Flinty again the other night, by planting that motor in the Trust's tender?'

Jack shook his head sadly. 'Your poor brother must have felt that, yet again, he was being stitched up for something he didn't do, by someone with power.'

'Yes, I think he would have liked to have killed Harvey Laydock right then.' Jenny made an effort to force a wry smile. 'But now we hear that Harvey himself has been accused of the thefts, so perhaps this time justice will prevail.'

Jack hoped she was right, but didn't say it would probably be in a far different way than Jenny Flint envisaged.

*　　*　　*

Back on Resolve, they found the others, including Amanda and her mum, grouped around a newspaper spread out on top of the main hatch. 'Come and look at this, Jack,' shouted Greg who had bought the paper en route from the pub. 'I'm glad I didn't see it before I got my drink or I'd probably have choked.'

The paper was a popular Sunday specialising in tawdry gossip. "HARVEY LAYDOCK TELLS ALL", proclaimed its front page headline.

In the centre pages, Harvey did indeed do just that, with anguished poses of him outside Fayre View, and a full-length feature giving his somewhat jaundiced view of things. It was written by one Angelica Black, to whom Harvey had apparently confided his recent troubles, including the wife he had lovingly supported through her years of depression and alcoholism, running off with another man just two weeks before the filming of his next eagerly-awaited series.

'How dare he make out he's been the caring, long-suffering husband!' exclaimed Lucy, furiously. 'The lying toad! I'll throttle him when I get my hands on him.'

Amanda was peering over her mum's shoulder. She gave it a reassuring squeeze and glanced towards her brother, 'Well, we know it's a load of lies, and he certainly hasn't got our backing, has he Damien? "My children have been a tower of strength to me." He must be joking!'

Jack's attention was focussed on the paragraph relating to Harvey's "humiliating wrongful arrest" and the compensation he would be demanding when the police accepted that he'd been framed for the spate of local thefts. Harvey said he found it hard to imagine who could possibly bear him such a grudge and continued, "I have a wonderful relationship with the locals. In fact, I've generously volunteered to organise a village fete, and provide a free barbecue down at the staithe, as a thank you for their warm welcome." Angelica Black then went on to ask if his recent court battle and the heavy damages won in favour of Gloria Vale, could have anything to do with the fact that stolen property was found planted in his garage, but Harvey, very graciously stated, "I can't believe Gloria would be associated with such a thing. I've compensated her generously and she's even offered to help at my fete on Saturday." Angelica Black's article finished with the titbit that this event would be televised for the first instalment of Harvey's new series.

'Which, I suppose, guarantees the bastard huge viewing figures,' spat out Gloria with disgust, as she finished reading.

'"my fete",' quoted Greg, with equal loathing as he flicked-closed the paper. 'The bastard's gone and taken over our frolic to his own ends.'

Lucy started sniffing and got out a tissue. 'Typical. I notice he didn't mention any of the numerous women he's been playing around with for years.' She wiped her eyes and Greg was quick to draw her close with a comforting arm.

'Actually, this isn't all bad,' declared Amanda, trying to brighten the mood. 'It'll certainly bring in the crowds next Saturday.'

'Yes, but they'll only be coming to see what a dysfunctional celebrity family really looks like.' Damien shook his head in disbelief. 'Dad's really excelled himself this time.'

'Something like this was bound to come out,' said Jack, trying to calm down the highly-charged atmosphere. 'It could have been a lot worse.' He turned to all around him. 'I think the important thing is that no-one makes any statement in response. The media would love us to react, but we've just got to float above it all.'

'Which is more than this boat'll be doin' if we don't get away soon.' The voice was Alfie's from the sterndeck, and one glance at the mooring evidenced the wisdom of his words. The Waveney was well-down now, the bank high above them and the tide slackening.

Greg sprang into action. 'Right, let's get going.' He pointed to the river, flowing seawards. 'We'll use the last of the ebb to Breydon and then ride home on the flood.'

All seemed relieved to have something positive to do as an antidote to all the agro that article had induced. With what was fast becoming a well-oiled routine, the crew went to their stations and soon Resolve was off her mooring, sail raised and the southerly wind winging them northwards with the tide towards the old estuary. Audrey watched the ancient fort disappearing astern.

'That was a pleasant visit,' she mused. 'A pity that newspaper had to spoil it.'

'Just forget that and remember the nice bits,' suggested Jack.

'Yes, you're right.' Audrey looked back again to the fort. 'I learned so much, thanks to Jenny.'

Jack glanced to where the girl in question was already settling cross-legged on the cabin roof, strumming chords on her guitar. 'Yes, a smart girl with a promising future ahead of her.'

'Let's hope she'll soon be able to get on with her studies, now her brother seems to be getting his own life together.' Audrey glanced aft to where Flinty, under Alfie's keen scrutiny, was trimming the mainsheet as the wherry followed the curve of the Waveney's last half-mile. 'He looks really contented and enthusiastic, working this boat today.'

'A new man,' agreed Jack, remembering the surly, spotty teenager he'd met on his first visit to Resolve.

Elsewhere on the wherry, Gloria was chatting with Greg and Lucy while, up for'ard, Rita and Damien whipped the ends of a mooring rope on the side deck. The others had been down below, but were beginning to emerge as Resolve left the Waveney and stuck her clinkered bow into the open waters of Breydon for the first time in decades. With just a trickle of ebb left to flow out, and a following wind, it had been decided to sail its length before turning for home.

'It's almost like an inland sea,' commented Audrey, scanning the ever-widening vista of open water.

'Yes, but a very shallow one,' replied Jack, well aware of the extensive mudflats that lay just inches below the surface and ever-ready to snare any boat imprudent enough to stray from the main channel.

Hopefully this would not be a fate awaiting any of the dozens of boats traversing Breydon at this lowest point of the tidal range. There was a fresh feel to the day now, still sunny, but with the steady breeze bringing with it a definite scent of the sea. That sea, however, remained invisible behind the skyline of Great Yarmouth and Caistor, and was marked only by the forest of slow-turning wind turbines that sprouted like some ecological crop from the distant Scroby Sands. More pertinent to Resolve were the spans of Breydon Lifting Bridge, directly ahead now, marking the landward entrance to Yarmouth Harbour and the point at which they would be turning. With the southerly wind broad-reaching the wherry towards it at almost six knots, that time would not be long coming.

'Right, time for me to get some lunch on,' declared Freddie Catlin, who seemed to be enjoying his unofficial role of ship's cook. He disappeared below while Greg made his way aft to join skipper and mate.

Most of their way across Breydon had been sailed in slack water, but now little eddies were forming to landward of the channel marker posts. 'Tide's turned,' Greg remarked as he passed Jack and Audrey, 'and we'll need it as we close haul back. Ready about!'

Already Alfie was putting his back to the tiller and Resolve was turning slowly through the wind until she was heading homeward with the apparent breeze fresher over her decks and a slight heel in response to the harder-sheeted sail. There was more chop on the water too, causing small cascades of salty spray to break over the bow and squeals of good-natured protest from those on the foredeck, who beat a hasty retreat to a drier vantage point on the hold.

'Now the tide's turned, it's against the wind,' explained Jack to Audrey. Wind against tide anywhere usually created small overfalls, but on the wide shallow expanse of Breydon it was always more pronounced, providing a taste of the sea and some harmless thrills. But Jack had noticed something else, fast-approaching and with the capability of turning that water from choppy to alarmingly rough.

No act of nature, this, but a large cruiser speeding towards them. The two and a half miles of Breydon were free of any speed restrictions, but common courtesy still dictated a reduction in speed when passing other craft. Judging by the way the smaller boats ahead were plunging through three foot high wash, this obviously wasn't a consideration even occurring to the skipper of this big powerboat.

'I can't believe it ...' Damien was coming aft to join them, shielding his eyes against the sun as he watched the approaching boat, '... that's Great Taste.'

'Your father's boat? I think you're right,' agreed Jack as the powerful cruiser planed towards them at close on twenty knots. He shook his head. 'You'd think a chef would show a bit more consideration for people cooking lunchtime meals before causing that much turbulence.' Thoughts of hot pans on galley stoves suddenly reminded Jack that their own lunch was cooking below. 'Warn Freddie to stand by for some rolling,' he yelled to those closer to the cabin hatchway.

But, with only moments to grasp the immediacy of the situation, any

126

warning was too late. Within seconds, the offending craft was speeding by, creaming bow and quarter-waves peeling back from her sleek hull, and the easily identifiable figure of Harvey Laydock waving from the flying bridge.

'The bloody idiot!' exclaimed Greg, as Resolve rolled over the curling waves, her old timbers creaking and everything loose slamming and banging in protest at this unwarranted violation.

'Did I really see what I thought I saw?' asked Audrey, relaxing her grip on the cabin roof and shaking her head.

'That he had some dolly-bird with him?' Jack nodded. 'He did indeed, and proud to show us, if his smug expression was anything to go by.' He glanced towards Lucy and Amanda, who were edging along the deck to join them.

'He didn't waste much time did he?' remarked Lucy with a wry smile. She shrugged. 'Well, at least he's consistent.'

'And about to give us a second viewing,' said Jack, seeing Great Taste, close by Breydon Bridge, heeling over as she swung through a tight one hundred and eighty degrees that brought her speeding back to overhaul them once more. Soon she was foaming past, twin diesels roaring and hooter blaring. Once again, her owner waved enthusiastically, joined this time by the long-haired blonde at his side. Minutes later they were far ahead, the gleaming cruiser churning ever upriver at the head of an arrow of wash that rolled and broke over the outlying mudflats.

'What a pratt,' said Greg angrily, and no voice chose to disagree. Further for'ard, however, one voice was raised, and in alarm.

'Quick ... Freddie's been hurt!' The voice was Jenny's. She was standing half-out of the main cabin gangway and there was blood on her tee-shirt.

*   *   *

Chapter Thirteen

'When she rolled badly just now, I went to stop things shooting onto the floor, grabbed wildly and, I guess, one of them must have been the carving knife,' explained Freddie.

They were sitting at the mess table by the galley area, Resolve's volunteer cook somewhat white-faced and his injured hand wrapped in a towel that was rapidly becoming as blood-soaked as his shirt.

Jack had dashed for'ard in response to Jenny's alarm call, but he hadn't been quick enough to beat Amanda, who was first down the gangway and at the casualty's side. She had obviously taken on the role of first-aider and now she sprang into decisive action. 'Get my case,' she ordered her brother, who'd soon joined them. 'In the meantime, keep your hand raised, Freddie, and let's get this bleeding stopped.'

The towel seemed to have ceased to redden and now Amanda slowly unwound it. At Freddie's side, Jenny had her own hand soothingly on the lad's shoulder, her face showing a concern more akin to affection than mere friendship. Jack smiled to himself – Gloria was right when she said relationships could well blossom amongst Resolve's close-knit crew.

'I don't think it's too bad,' reassured Amanda, wiping blood away with a wad of damp cotton wool before rinsing the wound in the bowl of warm water, 'but no thanks to our moronic father.' She examined the three-inch gash across Freddie's hand more intently. 'Not too deep, so it won't need stitches, but just hold it up again and I'll put on some antiseptic.' She opened the metal case by her side, took out a glass bottle containing a yellowish liquid, removed the stopper and poured some onto a fresh wad of cotton wool.

'What's that?' asked Jack.

'Calendula officinalis ...' Amanda dabbed some into Freddie's wound, '... or Marigold, as it's more commonly known.'

'Is that an antiseptic?'

'Yes, and one nature provides free for the taking. I promise you, Mr Fellows, that this infusion will prevent infection just as surely as any of your expensive brand-names.' Amanda delved back into her case and brought out a small bottle of amber oil, poured some into a poultice and pressed it over Freddie's wound. 'Symphytum officinale – Comfrey – it stimulates and helps repair the skin cells.' She wiped away some of the surplus oil and covered the poultice with a bandage. 'That should take care of it, Freddie.' Amanda stood up, shut the lid of her case and gave the casualty a slap on the back. 'See how that goes. I'll put a fresh dressing on tonight and check it then, but I'm sure you won't need to see a doctor.'

'Thanks, Amanda, that's great.' Freddie went to stand up. 'I'd better get on with lunch again now.'

'No, you take it easy for a bit.' Amanda gently, but firmly, pushed her patient back onto the bench. 'We'll get lunch sorted.'

'I can do that,' volunteered Jenny, obviously relieved that this young man's injuries were less than she'd feared.

'We all can,' added Audrey, who, together with Greg, had joined them below. 'Freddie needs light duties for the rest of the day.'

'That inconsiderate bastard,' spat Greg, nodding in the direction of Harvey Laydock's long-departed cruiser. 'He ought to be hanged at the yardarm.'

Jack nodded agreement, though his thoughts were preoccupied with what he'd spied in Amanda's case before she'd closed and locked it. He was also trying to sort jumbled memories of things said that very day – casual words now suddenly, but inexplicably, significant and crying out for recall. What were they and why had such recollections just been triggered? As always happens, the more he searched, the more the connection evaded him and, in the end, he gave up and went on deck to enjoy the breeze while it lasted and feel Resolve surging homeward under its power. Later, he'd have a quiet private word with Amanda just as soon as the opportunity presented itself.

* * *

'You're practising herbal medicine aren't you, Amanda?'

The evening meal was long past, Resolve still gliding upriver with the tide beneath her, but the wind predictably dying as the sun started its inexorable descent. Amanda had joined Jack on the foredeck and now she paused to answer, her lips tightening slightly at this unexpected confrontation, before merely nodding.

'And have you had any training in herbalism?'

'No, but I've studied it for years.' Amanda sat down on the carling hatch. 'It all started at school where chemistry was always my favourite subject. We had a bout of sore throats going about and I'd read of this old remedy, so I pinched some sage from our school herb garden, mixed it with vinegar and got some of my friends to gargle with it three times a day. It worked.'

'And that inspired you to further research?'

'That's right. One of my classmates suffered a lot from hay fever, so I tried making up teas for her using elderflower and plantain and, gradually, the symptoms improved. Later I tried using nettle as well, which relieved things even more. I began to realise there was a market for herbal remedies and they really did seem to work, so I secretly decided, instead of training to become a doctor, I'd like to become a herbalist. Already I've been able to do some good and make a bit of spare cash on the side.'

'You take money for this?' asked Jack, impressed that this young woman's medicinal skills were apparently matched by business acumen.

'Not from my friends,' Amanda hastened to explain, 'but one day I helped someone in the village with a problem and word soon got around about my little treatments. More and more people asked for help, so I started charging, but it wasn't just for the money. I loved carrying out experiments, secretly, on my Dad's boat, and wandering about in the countryside finding the plants and herbs from which to make up remedies.'

'So, what sort of ailments have you been treating?'

Amanda shrugged. 'Everything from bronchial and digestive problems to infertility and impotence.'

'Good heavens!' Jack's imagination tried to grasp this sweet young girl doing her bit to enhance local sex-life. Then, thoughts of other conditions brought him back to more immediate questions. 'How about skin conditions, Amanda – do you treat those?'

She nodded again. 'I know what you're thinking, Mr Fellows, and, yes, I have been trying to help John Flint with his acne.'

'Rather successfully, from what I can see.'

'Skin conditions are notoriously difficult to treat,' explained Amanda, 'but, in Flinty's case, it was linked to stress. I treated his skin with oils of marigold, chickweed and dandelion, but I'd read that nervous tension weakens the immune system and reduces energy levels, so I prepared him tinctures of camomile, passionflower and valerian and, not only is he feeling better, but his acne's cleared up too.'

'Is that what you were doing on Great Taste that night we had our meeting?' asked Jack, keen to find answers to other open questions.

'Yes, but of course Father came to his own wrong conclusions which ended in an almighty row, leading to the family break-up.'

'But why didn't you tell your father the truth?'

'I think that would have enraged him even more than thinking Great Taste was my illicit love-nest.' Amanda rolled her eyes. 'Remember, he's got big plans for me to go to medical school, so imagine what his reaction would be if he found out that I was going around dishing quack cures and planned to make it my career, especially as I was manufacturing them on his precious boat. Added to that, some of my clients have rather sensitive personal issues, so I thought it better to keep the whole thing secret.'

'I saw you and your mum collecting from the hedgerows this morning. Were they herbs for your remedies?'

'Yes, dandelions, nettles and some feverfew. Mum needs something to occupy her time right now, so I'm teaching her to be my collector.'

'Good idea,' agreed Jack, 'but is all this legal, Amanda?'

'I'm not sure,' she admitted hesitantly. 'Henry VIII made a charter that gave the right for anyone to practice herbalism, so, strictly speaking, it's not illegal. But, without recognised training, you can't join one of the associations and without that membership, you can't get insurance against any malpractice.'

'In other words, if someone reacts badly to one of your prescriptions, you could be in deep mire.'

Amanda blinked and nodded. 'Possibly, but I really am careful. There's a strong lobby to have herbalism regulated which must be good but, until it is, I don't think I've broken the law.'

'... until something goes wrong.' Jack put on his sternest voice. 'No, unless you want to find yourself in deep trouble, leave the prescribing until you've had proper training and got your qualifications.' Further discussion was ended by the ringing of his mobile.

'I'll leave you in peace,' said Amanda, seemingly glad of the excuse to scamper away.

Jack checked the caller. 'Hello Bailey. Good to hear from you. What's happening?'

'Not much,' admitted the young detective, 'but I thought I'd bring you up to date. Any chance of getting together sometime soon?'

'I'm at The Ferryman for a meeting tomorrow night. How about we have a drink together before six?'

'Sound's good, sir. See you there.'

Jack rang off and sat back on the dead hatch to enjoy the rest of Resolve's progress upriver. It was late evening now, the sun a glorious red as it began its final dip below the western horizon. From below came the lilting chords of Jenny's guitar and the rather more uncertain notes of her brother's harmonica. They formed a pleasing background to the chat and laughter it carried with it.

'They all seem happy enough again,' murmured Audrey, sitting down beside her husband to share this magic moment of twilight at the end of a blissful day. At earth's edge, a lingering red reflected off the few stratus clouds way out to the west, a dramatic contrast to the deepening blue that filled most of the heavens above the masthead and stilled wind vane. With the sun setting, a chill was descending on the river now, and it was good to feel Jack's arm fold around her and the warmth and reassurance it gave. 'You had a good chat just now?'

'I did indeed.' Jack relayed all that he had learned from Amanda, who was now with the others below.

'My goodness, I hope she knows what she's dabbling in,' was Audrey's reaction. 'Well, at least now we know just what that young woman's been getting up to.'

'It's answered some of the questions,' said Jack, without admitting the feeling that Amanda hadn't been totally forthcoming about her clandestine activities. But now was not the time to break the magic of the moment as, below them, Resolve's clinkered bow chuckled ever slower in the evening calm. Very soon, and they'd be starting the tender's engine and the tranquillity would be gone. Jack glanced astern to where Gloria, at the helm, was using her slight frame to make ever bigger corrections to compensate for the loss of steerage. Beside her, Alfie puffed contentedly on his pipe, his eyes aloft at the vane. Jack guessed he was deciding if it was time to down the sail. He gave them a wave and they smiled and waved back – a middle-aged woman fulfilling her dreams and an old man enjoying his last.

This was indeed a night to savour and Jack wished he hadn't that old familiar feeling that something soon would dash those dreams for ever.

*   *   *

Chapter Fourteen

'Thanks, sir. Good health.' DS Bailey raised his pint glass of lager to Jack's and, with eyes closed, took a few mouthfuls followed by a long out-take of breath. This had been long-awaited through a day of frustrating non-achievement.

The pair had found a quiet corner in The Ferryman, a discreet distance from the locals and holidaymakers sharing tall tales around the bar. 'Things dead-ending a bit?' enquired Jack, sympathetically, knowing all too well how, early on, investigations frequently hit a blank wall.

'You could say that,' admitted Bailey, pulling a face. 'I've tried making the odd discreet enquiry locally, but the story is always that Alice Wanstead did a runner to Canada with her fancy man eight years ago. The only mystery in people's minds around here is why she left it so long.'

'So, who lured her away?'

'No-one knows. Just some bloke from up north, is what our good councillor told everyone.'

'And no-one has heard from her since?'

Bailey shook his head. 'Not so much as one Christmas card.'

'Have you tried over there?'

'Yep.' Bailey took a longer sup of his lager, 'The RCMP is trying a trace, but Canada's a big place and some areas are pretty remote.'

'How about DNA?' asked Jack. 'Have they extracted any from the skeleton?'

'Forensic Science Laboratory's working on that, but there seems to be something they're not prepared to divulge just yet.'

'Hmmm. Of course, it wouldn't help identify the remains anyway, unless they can compare it with DNA from one of Alice's relatives. Have you made contact with any of them?'

'Not yet,' confessed Bailey, well aware his report so far had been pretty negative. 'Our only hope is their children in Australia and New Zealand, but the councillor hasn't a clue if they still even live there. If they do, the same problems apply as Canada.'

'Big countries and lots of isolated corners,' agreed Jack, before giving the DS a smile of reassurance. 'I see your problem, Bailey, but stick with it. Something will turn up when you least expect it.' He nodded in the direction of the broad. 'Like the skeleton itself.'

'And that wouldn't have surfaced if you hadn't got that dredging under way,' acknowledged the young detective. It seemed a good note on which to change subjects. 'How's that going, by the way?'

'On schedule.' Jack was glad at least one of them had something positive to report. 'Should be finished in the next couple of days, which is just as well, as we have our frolic this coming Saturday.'

'Your water-fete thing,' remembered Bailey. 'Is that all panning out okay?'

'I'll let you know that after tonight's meeting,' promised Jack. 'You are coming on Saturday, I hope?'

'Absolutely, wouldn't miss it. I called Stan Meadows at BroadsBeat this morning and he mentioned he'll be there with the RIB as well.'

'Good. The more the merrier. We might be glad of them if things kick off.'

'Why, what trouble are you anticipating?'

'None I hope, but we'll be having some pretty explosive factions there enjoying more than the odd drink, and you know where that can lead ... talking of which ...' The pub door had just opened to admit none other than Harvey Laydock and friend. The celebrity was obviously pleased to be the object of more than one glance of recognition from the holidaymakers, though Jack guessed it was the shapely blonde on his arm really turning heads. He nudged Bailey and pointed his glass towards the TV star. 'Recognise him?'

'I do indeed.' Bailey sipped his drink slowly while studying the celebrity over the rim of his glass. 'Doesn't look quite so glamorous in the flesh, does he? Perhaps it's the worry of being caught red-handed with one of those stolen outboards.'

'You know all about that then?'

'Of course. Not unconnected to my murder investigation, seeing as the skeleton was dredged up in the same place. But it's hard to believe someone in his position should risk it all with petty thieving.'

'Depends on the motive. He's had domestic problems of late and word is he's all set to go bottoms-up financially. Not that you'd guess by looking at him.' Harvey had removed his roving hand from the young woman's waist just long enough to produce a fifty-pound note for another round of drinks. Then, ushering her to a corner table, he spotted Jack and gave a forced smile of recognition, which the ranger reciprocated just as insincerely, while taking a closer study of the celebrity's companion. For this was no giggling blonde fan, but an intelligent, self-assured young woman obviously appraising the clientele of The Ferryman as keenly as they were her.

Bailey had also been studying the pair. 'She doesn't seem to be enjoying his advances that much.'

'No, and I think I know why.' Jack had seen that investigative look before.

She surely wasn't police and that left one other main option. 'I bet she's a journalist.'

'Do you reckon, sir?' Bailey raised his eyebrows. 'Well, whatever, our Harvey seems to be handling his broken marriage pretty stoically.'

'And her,' said Jack, grinning. He proceeded to tell Bailey about the Sunday newspaper story written by Ms Angelica Black.

'And you reckon that's her?'

'Has to be.' Jack went on to explain how Harvey was effectively taking all the credit for arranging the frolic for his own gain.

'Good publicity, though,' said Bailey, trying hard to put a positive slant on things. 'You'll have thousands there just to see him in the flesh.'

'Which wasn't the idea of the thing at all,' grumbled Jack. 'I suspect he's only attending the meeting tonight so he can tell us what parts we have to play in front of the camera on the day.'

'Well, I hope you have a good one,' quipped the DS mischievously as he finished his drink and stood up. 'My round, sir. Can't miss this opportunity to say I bought a drink for a TV star.'

'Very funny,' laughed Jack as the young detective headed for the bar.

It wasn't the only laughter in The Ferryman that night. Over on the other table, Harvey and friend seemed to be warming up to an even merrier night ahead.

Jack glanced at his watch. The others would be arriving shortly. He doubted they would see the joke.

*   *   *

'Well, I'm glad that's over with.' Audrey stood with her husband on the village staithe, the Resolve team having just departed after a somewhat heated meeting in The Ferryman.

'Yes,' agreed Jack, 'the frolic itself will be a doddle after that.'

He'd known that tempers were bound to flare with such divisive characters and highly emotive underlying issues coming together in one small room. Some had even wanted to exclude Harvey altogether, but the proposed TV coverage had to be discussed, and the celebrity had done this with relish once the more mundane aspects of the day had been covered.

'That can't have been easy for Lucy, having her estranged husband sitting opposite while she had Greg by her side.'

'Well, at least Harvey left his latest squeeze in the bar.' Jack smiled and shrugged. 'No doubt she used the time to jot a few notes for her next scandalous exposition.'

'You really think she is Angelica Black, the journalist who wrote that article in the Sunday?'

'I'm sure of it, and I bet she's going to hang around for any other tasty bits of Harvey-life she can get her hands on.'

'How can the stupid man be so gullible? She'll take him to the cleaners.' Audrey gave a deep sigh. 'And to think we came up with this idea as a means of bringing people together. At one point in there tonight I thought we were going to have a punch-up.'

'Yes, old Greg did get a bit heated, didn't he?'

'And with good reason. All the work everyone's put into this just so Harvey can step in and manipulate the whole event to film his cookery programme.' Audrey didn't often get worked up, but this evening her patience had been pretty stretched. 'And he isn't the only one trying to jump on the bandwagon now. Fancy Councillor Wanstead coming to offer his services by doing the accounts, after all the trouble he's given Resolve Trust.'

'He's a lonely man with a lot of worries of his own right now,' conceded Jack, begrudgingly. 'He probably feels the need of a bit of fun, which is what this whole thing is about. Anyway, he's welcome to the accounts. It's Harvey's TV coverage that worries me.'

'In what way?'

'Just that people won't act naturally, knowing it's being televised.'

'Well, Harvey's convinced it'll be good for everyone, including Gloria and her team. And, give him his due, he did agree to young Freddie working with him at the barbecue.'

'Very reluctantly,' Jack pointed out, 'and only because Lucy made it pretty clear that if he didn't, she'd push to give an interview, telling her side of the story.'

'Yes, I think Lucy is quite enjoying her new-found independence,' said Audrey, turning up her coat collar against the chill wind now blowing across the marshes.

'And not only Lucy,' said Jack. 'I might be wrong, but I have the feeling there were others there tonight determined our celebrity won't have it all plain-sailing on the day.'

Audrey raised her eyebrows. 'Who, and in what way, for goodness' sake?'

'Oh, I just sensed those youngsters from Resolve had something up their sleeves. I noticed the look they were giving each other when Harvey was spouting on about his "natural screen presence".' Jack tried to keep a straight face. 'I reckon those monkeys are cooking up some scheme to ensure dear Harvey falls flat on his famous face on his big day.'

'You're painting devils on the wall again, Jack Fellows,' scolded his wife, wagging a finger in mock disapproval. 'Harvey Laydock might be a pain in the neck, but at least he's going to ensure we have a good turnout on Saturday.'

Jack rested a foot on a mooring post and looked out across the broad. The dredger was close in by the staithe now, a reminder of how water had so often hidden sinister secrets from the conscious eye.

That water was now suddenly being swept by increasingly sharp gusts of wind as a black and rolling line squall seemed all set to make its rain-spewing passage.

'I just hope we have good weather on the day,' said Jack as he turned and led Audrey to the car.

*   *   *

Chapter Fifteen

Once again, Jack rested a foot on a mooring post and looked out across the broad. The dredging team had moved to their next job, the broad shone in blissful sunshine and all around, final preparations for the frolic were going on in an atmosphere of industrious enthusiasm. It was Saturday and their big day.

With the channel deepened to 1.8 metres, Resolve now lay alongside the staithe, just ahead of Jack's launch, paintwork shining and colourful bunting flying from her masthead.

'Looks right good, don't she?' Alfie stood beside Jack, admiring the vessel in whose rebirth he'd played such a significant part. He turned to Gloria on his other side. 'You ought to be real proud?'

Resolve's owner smiled and nodded. 'I am, Alfie, but she wouldn't be here today without all your expert advice.'

'Or all the work them kids of yours 'as put inta her,' commended the old skipper, lighting his pipe. He turned and looked back to the encampment of stalls and displays growing behind them. 'An' they're still at it.'

They were indeed. At one stall, Rita Wakefield was setting up her display of artwork, while on the next, Amanda and her mother were laying out samples of herbal skin and hair products. She'd taken Jack's advice to avoid any medicinal treatments, but he saw no problem with creams and ointments, which would doubtless sell well. Further along the staithe, Damien was helping Greg prepare rowing boats and canoes for public hire, while on Resolve itself, Jenny and Flinty were making final preparations for the many visitors expected onboard to view the old vessel at close hand.

'Yes, I'm proud of all of them,' admitted Gloria. 'They're living proof of what the most destitute youngsters are capable of, just given the chance.'

'The problem will be moving them on when they're ready to return to mainstream life,' pointed out Jack. 'Resolve will be a pretty hard act to follow.'

'Yes, I know, but they've all developed new skills, and my hope is that they'll be keen to go out into the world and put them to good use.'

'Let's hope so, and talking of skills,' Jack remembered, 'it's time I went to help Audrey set up her cake-stall. I'll catch up with you later.'

He hurried off and found his wife already unloading containers of appetising, freshly-baked goodies. 'There should be plenty here to tempt the customers, Jack.'

'Certainly will. Where do you want these flapjacks, love?'

'Right here, thanks, and if you've got time before officially being on duty, perhaps you could go and fetch poor old Spike from the car.'

Jack wandered off, happy to have an errand and the chance to greet other stallholders selling such things as homemade preserves, second-hand books and bric-a-brac. There was even the chance to have handwriting analysed or fortune told. The results of a few here today would make interesting reading, Jack thought, smiling to himself as he made his way to the edge of the display area where men were stacking straw bales to serve as butts for the airgun range. Nearby, the inevitable splat-the-rat and hoopla stands stood ready for customers, as was the tombola with an array of teddy-bear prizes. The sight of these reminded Jack he was soon to be a grandfather. He'd certainly return and buy some tickets once the opening ceremony had taken place.

Other preparations were rather less pleasing. Just inside the entrance, a cameraman and sound technician were readying their equipment while, nearby, Laydock himself was in intense discussion with the clipboard-holding producer. One slightly harassed-looking young woman was attempting to put last touches of make-up to the personality's ageing features.

A world of make-believe, thought Jack, while acknowledging that in one respect at least, the celebrity had been absolutely right, because already a crowd of followers were gathering at the entrance, eager to see their hero in the flesh.

There would indeed be a good turnout for the frolic.

*　　　*　　　*

'... and so I happily declare this water frolic open ... and I'll be serving local-ly-sourced food from the barbecue later in the afternoon, completely free of charge, and this will be followed by a fantastic waterside firework display.' Harvey Laydock posed momentarily in front of the camera before cutting a ribbon to release a net of brightly-coloured balloons, triggering an outburst of spontaneous applause from the surrounding crowd. As the balloons rose gracefully into a cloudless blue sky, the local brass band struck up a jolly tune and the fun commenced.

'Free barbecue, heh,' commented PC Meadows, rubbing his stomach. 'By the end of the day I'll be ready for that.'

'Yeah, well just make sure you have some of my Aud's cakes as well or I'll never hear the end of it,' warned Jack. With Spike happily trotting beside them, they headed back to the moorings and their respective boats. The PC had arrived with another constable in the BroadsBeat RIB, more as a PR gesture than any need, but Jack was glad of the company of this cheerful copper and pleased to see another familiar face waiting by the launch.

'Morning, Bailey. Glad you could make it.'

'Couldn't miss this chance to sample your wife's home-baking,' smiled the DS. He nodded towards the stalls. 'I was just about to treat myself.'

'I'll show you where she is,' offered Jack, pleased of the opportunity for a quick word alone. 'Any developments?' he asked as they made their way.

'None,' said Bailey with a disgruntled shake of the head. 'No word of the kids from the Antipodes, and here even the bone-boffins are holding back on their findings for some reason.'

'Well, if it's frustrating for you, it must be fraught for him,' said Jack, indicating the somewhat forlorn figure of Henry Wanstead wandering amongst the stalls. Jack told Bailey of the councillor's offer to look after the event accounts. 'He just yearns to feel wanted really.'

'Well he will be – by us, just as soon as I have some concrete evidence,' promised the detective with grim humour.

Arriving at Audrey's stall, they found Harvey and the rest of the production team already there. 'We just need a quick shot of me trying your cakes,' the celebrity was explaining. As the camera recorded, he picked up one of Audrey's scones and took a bite. 'Hmmm, lovely ... you must give me the recipe.' Then he put the half-eaten scone down and turned back to the production team. 'Right, let's get a shot of me scoring a bullseye on the range before I have to start cooking.' Without a word of thanks to Audrey, he was gone.

'Typical,' said Jack.

'I'm sure he's very busy,' defended Audrey, chuffed to bits that her scones could well feature in the programme.

'We all are,' said Jack, pushing Bailey ahead of him. 'Give our hard-working DS here something scrummy, Aud, while I go and check how young Freddie Catlin's doing learning skills from the lord and master.' He gave Spike a scratch on the head. 'Come on, old boy, let's see if we can get you a treat.'

At Harvey's large barbecue station, Freddie was unloading boxes from a pickup truck while chatting with Amanda.

'The idea is that Dad lets you do some of the cooking, Freddie,' Amanda was declaring, 'so don't let him just use you like a skivvy.'

'Well, these have to be unpacked anyway,' explained Freddie, lifting another box of frozen hamburgers from the truck. There were plenty more yet to be unloaded: boxes of sausages and mushrooms, catering packs of ready-prepared onions and bread rolls.

'You look busy,' said Jack as a way of breaking into the conversation.

'Oh, just preparing,' explained Freddie, shrugging his shoulders.

Jack turned to Amanda. 'How's the herbal business going?'

'Very well – a dozen or so bottles sold already.' She looked up from fussing Spike, and over to her stall where Lucy was busy serving yet another customer. 'Mum's really loving having a useful role to play at last.'

'And your dad's adoring fans don't seem put off by recent events either,' added Jack, glancing towards the airgun range where the celeb, in front of camera crew and fascinated onlookers, was making a third attempt at even hitting the target.

'Unfortunately not. This has worked out perfectly for him in every way … so far.'

'What did she mean by "so far"?' Jack asked Freddie, as Amanda hurried back to her stall.

'Oh, just a little scheme she's thought up to bring her dad down to size.'

'What "little scheme"?'

Freddie paused to give Spike a sausage, smiled noncommittally and said, 'You'll see.'

'Yes, well, as long as it doesn't spoil anyone else's pleasure,' warned Jack. 'This is a day for reconciliation, remember.'

Back at the boats, he paused to take in all the revelry. Greg and Damien were busy launching the public in rowing boats and canoes, most of which were already out on the broad, mindfully watched over by BroadsBeat in their RIB. Close by, Resolve was alive with visitors, on deck, atop the main hatch, in and out of the cabin, pausing only to ask questions of the crew. Even Flinty seemed to be entering fully into the spirit of the occasion, looking animated and more confident, while old Alfie puffed away at his pipe, enthralling a never-ending audience with tales of life in the old black-sailed traders. Gloria sat at a table by the boarding gangway, telling of the work of the Trust and encouraging people to make a donation.

It was all going far better than they could ever have wished for.

Jack just hoped it stayed that way.

*   *   *

'Phew! I'm exhausted.' Audrey sat down on one of the table bench seats and stretched weary legs. 'Baking cakes is certainly less tiring than selling them.'

'It is when you've had non-stop customers all day,' agreed Jack, sitting down with his wife. 'Sold many?'

'Every last crumb.' Audrey gave her husband a disarming smile. 'Didn't even have one myself, so I'm looking forward to a hotdog.'

'Me too.' The enticing aroma of Harvey's sizzling food had been tantalising Jack's taste buds for a while now, but he could stave off hunger a little while yet. 'We'll let the queue die down a bit first and then get ours.'

It was early evening now and the stalls had closed after a busy day's trading. The holders were at last free to mingle with the public, the majority of whom had remained to enjoy Harvey's free barbecue and firework display. Amongst them was Rita, happy with her sale of paintings and sketches, and Amanda, who had joined Jack and Audrey at their table.

'Yes, a complete sell-out for me too,' she explained happily in answer to the ranger's question. 'Mum's gone off to help Greg clear up, but I'm ready to eat when you are.'

'Which had better be now,' declared Jack, seeing the last of the queue move off with full plates, while Freddie Catlin started clearing up. Harvey was chatting to the recording crew who'd lain down their equipment and were scoffing hotdogs before filming the final sequence of the celebrity evaluating the day and lighting the first firework. 'Hello, two more hungry mouths.'

It was Gloria and Alfie, equally exhausted from the non-stop queue of visitors to the wherry. 'You sit yourself down, Alfie,' said Gloria, ushering the old skipper onto the bench. 'I'll get yours for you.'

Leaving Spike in Alfie's care, they all went to the barbecue counter where there was still a fair amount of food remaining, '… except mushrooms, I'm afraid,' Freddie apologised. 'We ran out of those just before you came.'

'Oh, that's a shame. Alfie loves mushrooms,' grumbled Gloria.

'I'll take Dad's plate for him,' offered Amanda. 'Did you make sure there's nothing missing like I asked, Freddie?'

He had, and Amanda took her father's ready-plated up meal along with her own.

'I'm hoping we can get Dad and Gloria actually eating together,' she confided to Jack as they made their way back to the table and settled down ready to eat. Spike sat up, his nose sniffing tantalising smells.

'Don't give him anything,' ordered Jack. 'Rule is, he's never fed from the table.' Spike sank back, duly disappointed.

Skipper Alfie wasn't so easily placated. 'Yer forgot the mushrooms,' he complained to Gloria, whose explanation didn't totally appease. 'Yer know they're my favourites and, anyway …' he pointed to Harvey's plate, '… how come he got some.'

'That's because Freddie put some on one side for him earlier,' explained Amanda.

'Bloomin' privilege,' mumbled Alfie.

'Well, he did provide it all for free, so you can hardly begrudge him chef's perks,' pointed out Audrey.

In fact, there seemed some doubt whether Harvey would taste his own food at all. Standing some distance off in discussion with the production team, he seemed disinclined to join them. 'It's because Gloria's with us,' explained Amanda quietly to Jack. 'He might listen to you, though. You and Audrey come with me and see if you can persuade him to join us.'

They went over to the group, but Harvey was still reluctant to make any concessions.

'What, eat with that witch, after all she's done to me,' he hissed quietly, while giving a superficial smile for the sake of the film-crew.

'I know what's gone on between you two,' stated Jack, firmly, 'but can't you try and put all that behind you, for the cameras at least.' He indicated the table with Gloria and Alfie left sitting alone. 'Come on, bury the hatchet.'

The celebrity chef was definitely wavering. In the end his indecision was cut short by Gloria herself leaving the table and joining them.

Speaking deliberately loudly, for all around to hear, she said, 'Harvey, you and I have had our differences, but today shows what we can do together. We are grown ups and it's time we started behaving as such.' She held out her hand. 'Peace?'

He hesitated only seconds before offering his own hand and nodding. 'Peace.'

'Great.' Jack slapped both on the back. 'Now let's go eat.'

Back at the table everyone sat down in relieved companionship. Even Harvey was smiling, though his face slipped into mock annoyance when he looked down at his plate. 'Hello, someone's nicked my mushrooms.'

'Well you did have some,' protested Amanda with concern, 'Freddie put some on one side for you. Someone must have…' Her voice trailed off as everyone at the table realised there was only one person who could have "nicked" Harvey's mushrooms. Somewhat amused, they all turned their gaze to Alfie, but any humour in the situation stopped right there. The octogenarian was looking anything but well.

'Alfie, are you all right?' asked Audrey.

'No … not really … my guts …' mumbled the old skipper. He pulled himself shakily to his feet. 'I think I'll go an' lay down.'

'I'll come with you,' offered Jack.

'No … no thanks … rather be alone.' Alfie staggered off as fast as he could back to Resolve.

'Poor Alfie,' sympathised Audrey.

'Well he has eaten rather a lot,' said Gloria, looking at the skipper's empty plate.

'Including my mushrooms,' laughed Harvey. 'That'll teach him.'

It did indeed seem poetic justice, though Amanda clearly wasn't amused. In fact, Jack couldn't help noticing the teenager seemed on the verge of tears. Gloria also was still worrying about her skipper. Finally she stood up. 'I'm just going to check how he is, poor dear.' She left her meal untouched and hurried off to the wherry.

'I hope he's okay,' said Audrey, voicing all their concerns.

'He will be,' reassured Jack, 'he just needs to get rid of his meal.'

But any comfort Jack's words may have given were instantly negated by a yell from Gloria on Resolve's foredeck. 'Help! Something's happened to Alfie!'

Jack dropped his fork and ran, joined en route by PC Meadows and DS Bailey who had also heard the cry. But none of them were quick enough to beat Flinty, who was first on Resolve's foredeck where an almost hysterical Gloria was pointing to a figure lying face down in the broad. 'It's Alfie. He must have fallen overboard!'

Flinty didn't hesitate, but dived straight in fully clothed. By the time he had turned Alfie face-up, Jack had thrown a bowline which Flinty slipped over the old skipper's thin shoulders, supporting him while those on deck warped them both back alongside. Soon, strong arms were lifting the wherryman up onto the foredeck.

Straightway, Jack was kneeling down beside the skipper's cadaverous form, inert and pathetic in a gathering pool of water. With one hand under Alfie's jaw, he tilted back his head, pinched the nose between thumb and forefinger, inhaled deeply and then breathed straight into his mouth. He repeated this process five times before PC Meadows placed fingers on Alfie's neck, looked directly at the ranger and shook his head.

In desperation, Jack placed his hands just below the old skipper's breast-bone and gave five firm compressions. While he paused, the PC repeated the mouth-to-mouth, but there was no sign of life. Bailey felt for a pulse, but turned and shook his head sadly.

Jack went to start another cycle of compressions, only to be stopped by Bailey's comforting hand on his shoulder. 'It's no good, sir, he's gone.'

Jack stood up. Beside him, Gloria clasped a hand to her mouth. On shore, Audrey wiped a tear, but it was Amanda who was the most stricken. Her own tears had now grown to gasping sobs, but it was the words between that most startled all around her.

'I killed him ... I killed him ...' was all she could utter between outpourings of uncontrolled grief.

Standing watching, a little back from the staithe, Councillor Wanstead shook his head, sighed deeply and turned for home.

*   *   *

Chapter Sixteen

DS Bailey turned to a new page in his notebook and took out his pen. 'Right, Miss Laydock, would you care to elaborate on what you were telling us earlier.'

Outside, in the gathering dusk, all was now quiet. It had been left to PC Meadows to disperse the crowds who had quickly gathered around the scene. With the firework display cancelled and an air of tragedy hanging over what, only hours before, had been a place of merriment, the public had gradually melted away leaving only the Laydocks and the crew of Resolve to linger around the unfolding drama. While paramedics, and then the coroner's men, dealt with Alfie, Amanda had gone below. She was soon facing DS Bailey, the detective keen to take a preliminary statement.

He sat facing Amanda across the messroom table, Jack beside him and Lucy opposite with an arm around her distraught daughter. It was the mother who answered, straining to keep a check of her own emotions. 'I think we should get our solicitor.'

But Amanda shook her head. 'No, Mum, I need to tell the truth.' She wiped away more tears. 'But ... I ... I didn't mean to. It was all a mistake.'

'Start from the beginning, Miss Laydock,' said Bailey.

'All right.' The teenager gave a big sniff. 'It was all a bit of a joke, really ... on Dad. He was the one meant to have the mushrooms.'

'You intended to poison your own father?' Bailey leaned closer across the table. 'Why?'

'Not to poison,' protested Amanda, between tears. 'Just to make him a bit high, that's all.' She turned and faced Jack. 'He was being such a pain, taking over our frolic, so we thought we'd teach him a lesson and make him look a fool in front of the cameras.' Amanda gave another sob. 'We never for a minute guessed that poor Alfie would pinch them and ...'

'You keep saying "we". Who else was in this?'

'All of us on Resolve,' admitted Amanda. 'We got our heads together and thought it would be a giggle.'

'Did Gloria know about it?' asked Lucy, with increasing dismay.

Amanda nodded. 'Yes, she knew what we were planning, but wasn't part of it.' The teenager shrugged shoulders now rounded by anguish. 'Gloria's had her own issues with Dad, so I suppose she didn't feel particularly inclined to put the brakes on us. She thought, like the rest of us, that it would just embarrass him and trash the TV programme. If she'd known it would kill ...'

'I'll be interviewing Miss Vale later,' interrupted Bailey. 'Tell me about these mushrooms with which you intended to poison ... to inconvenience your father.'

'Amanita muscaria.'

'Amanita what?'

'Muscaria, or fly agaric as they're more commonly known. I picked them myself from the woods last autumn and kept them dried. They contain the toxins ibotenic acid and muscimol, but they would never kill.'

Bailey held up his hand. 'We'll sort the chemistry later. What I want to know right now is why you'd picked these mushrooms last autumn, when you're telling me this little scheme was only cooked up in the last few days?'

'I collect all sorts of mushrooms and herbs for my remedies,' explained Amanda, rather hesitantly. 'Most are only there in autumn, so I collect them then to dry store and ...'

'... sell as hallucinogenics?' Bailey sat back and fixed Amanda through narrowed eyes. 'Are you aware, Miss Laydock, that it's illegal to even possess such substances, and that dealing in them carries a sentence of up to life imprisonment?' Amanda's face turned white and she glanced despairingly towards her mother. Stunned silence, however, was the last thing Bailey wanted right now, and Jack wasn't surprised when he moderated his tone and added, 'but we won't dwell on that for the moment. Just tell me how these fly agaric mushrooms got onto your father's plate.'

'I only had two left anyway, so I got Freddie to cook them and slip them on.' Amanda's face was almost pleading now. 'Believe me, he never would have if he thought ...'

'Yeah, well we'll see what he has to say about that,' said Bailey bluntly. He turned as the bulky figure of PC Meadows appeared in the gangway entrance. He gave the DS a nod. Bailey turned back to the young girl before him. 'Amanda Laydock, I'm satisfied there has been a crime committed here and that you're going to have to accompany me to the station for more questioning. You don't have to say anything, but it may harm your defence ...'

'But you can't arrest a girl for just playing a trick,' protested Lucy, standing up.

'Mrs Laydock,' intoned Bailey gravely, 'there's a man dead thanks to your daughter's "trick", and possible charges of involuntary manslaughter to answer for.' He turned back to Amanda, '... but it may harm your defence if you do not mention, when questioned ...'

Amanda listened to the rest of the caution before slowly getting to her feet.

She turned to Lucy, stunned with distress and apprehension. 'It's all my own stupid fault, Mum, so I need to go and get it sorted.'

Up on deck, darkness lay heavily over the scene of tragedy, the ashen faces of fellow crewmembers all the more ghostlike in the flashing blue light of the police car. They watched numbly as it drove off, taking with it, not only a friend, but all their hopes and dreams that this day might bring an end to acrimony and rancour.

Overhead, the flags strung from Resolve's masthead fluttered in the first stirrings of a new weather system. Somehow they seemed to symbolise the futility of trying to change the ways of fate.

*   *   *

'What a disaster.' Jack was speeding homewards, his occasional knuckle-whitening grip of the steering wheel, the only indication of the grief and distress he was feeling. In the back, Spike slept, oblivious to it all, but Audrey was feeling as dejected as her husband.

'Yes, it was the worst possible end to such a lovely day.' She turned and placed a hand on Jack's arm.

'Poor old Alfie,' went on Jack, glumly. 'He wouldn't have even been there if I hadn't talked him into skippering Resolve.'

'You didn't "talk him" into anything,' protested Audrey. 'Thanks to you, Alfie spent the last weeks of his life doing the thing he loved most, and I'm sure he wouldn't have changed that for anything.' She glanced out of the window. It was only a mile to home now. 'He was an old man, Jack, who probably hadn't many years ahead of him anyway. We all marvelled that he'd survived this long without his wife.'

'That's not the way the police and courts will look at it.' Jack slipped a gear and turned into the by-road to their village. 'Those mushrooms were planted deliberately in food. It's only the fact that they were aimed for someone else that will prevent Amanda facing a possible murder charge.'

Audrey shook her head. 'The silly girl. I can see those young people wanting to embarrass Harvey, but I don't suppose it will help Amanda if the police establish she was going around selling magic mushrooms as hallucinogenics?'

'It certainly won't,' agreed Jack, 'but from what I know of that girl, it must have been through misguided motives. I thought at first she might have been pushing something for Flinty, but now we know she was just giving him medication to help his nerves.'

'... which, it seems now, might have included fly agaric mushrooms in small doses. But, talking of Flinty, didn't he show courage tonight, the way he dived in to try and rescue Alfie?'

'Yep, quite a little hero, and I'm sure Gloria will be proud of him. Sadly, that's about the only positive thing to come out of today as far as the Resolve Trust is concerned.' They were driving down their own lane now, Jack slowing as the cottage came in sight. 'I'll drop off and see them tomorrow … after writing my report.'

'But tonight we're going to have a stiff drink and try and get some sleep,' prescribed Audrey as they came to a stop outside their cottage. She turned to the border collie, curled fast asleep behind her. 'Come on Spike, wake up, we're home now.'

But Spike still lay comatose on the back seat.

'He's usually jumping up and down before we even arrive,' frowned Jack. 'Not like Spike to oversleep.' He got out, opened the rear door and bent down beside his companion of many years. 'Spike, wake up … Spike …' He stroked the old dog's head but Spike remained motionless.

'Is … is he all right?' asked Audrey, opening the other door and seeing the concerned look on her husband's face.

'He's breathing all right,' reassured Jack, lifting the dog's head in his hands and pushing up one eyelid to reveal dilated pupils, 'but otherwise dead to the world. Get in, Aud. We're taking Spike to a vet.'

*　　*　　*

'So, my own kids concocted this little plan to make a fool of me on my special day?' Harvey sat back into the plush upholstery of Great Taste's saloon and took a deep gulp of whiskey.

Seated with him were Lucy, Damien and Greg. The boatbuilder's presence on Harvey's cruiser would have been anathema to both parties a few hours ago, but the drama just enacted had at least temporarily outweighed personal grudges, though not petty squabbles.

'That's typical of you,' retorted Damien angrily. 'Talking of our water frolic as "my special day" is just the sort of attitude that inspired us to make a fool of you in the first place.'

'Stop this!' shouted Lucy. 'Our Amanda is in a police cell right now, and all you two can do is argue over words. It's all so petty.'

'I hardly call attempted patricide "petty",' protested Harvey. 'It's only a chance of fate that it's not me lying on the slab at the morgue instead of that other old buffer.'

'We're talking of the dead, Laydock, so I'll thank you to show some respect,' warned Greg jumping to his feet, the blood vessels in his forehead pulsating their own warning. He took a deep breath and his seat back beside Lucy. 'And stop this stupid talk of murder. The kids planned to get you high in front of the cameras, that's all.'

'Yes, well you try telling that to your precious Alfie Rumball,' countered the celebrity. 'I doubt if he's seeing the joke.' He looked again at Lucy. 'My own daughter turning on me after all I've done for her. Did you know of this stupid jape?'

Lucy shook her head.

'But I did, Dad, so you can direct your venom on me.' Damien leaned forward and fixed his father with unblinking eyes.

'It'll be directed all right,' warned Harvey pointing a shaking finger at his son. 'And presumably you also knew about this happy-mushroom scam that Amanda has been running under our very noses?'

'Yes, but it's not what you think. Amanda just loves researching herbal remedies to make people feel better …'

'… and making some easy money on the side distributing fungi classed as a prohibited substance,' snapped Harvey.

'No,' persisted Damien, 'but some of the young village lads asked if she could get some magic mushrooms for a laugh and, on her next collecting spree, she did, knowing that their effects would be harmless and non-addictive, especially in the tiny quantities she gave them. By the time she realised she was dealing in a Class A substance, they'd got the squeeze on her and it was too late to stop.'

'Yeah, well she's been stopped now, hasn't she?' Harvey lowered his head in his hands. 'God knows how we can get her out of this.'

'By getting on to our solicitor to start with,' suggested Lucy, relieved that her husband had at least started considering their daughter instead of himself.

Harvey nodded. 'Not easy on a weekend, but I'll try and contact him first thing tomorrow.' Then he looked questioningly at his wife. 'I don't know about you, Lucy, but I'm dreading the thought of a night alone. Are you coming home?'

Lucy wanted to ask what had happened to her husband's lady-friend, but instead said, 'No, Harvey. I won't be coming back to Fayre View ever again. I'll be with you in whatever we have to do to get our daughter out of this mess, but my life now is with Greg.'

Harvey sat silent for a second as though fighting some inner turmoil. Then, with an effort, he shook his head and smiled. 'Fair enough … I deserve that. I know I'm a pratt and that all this is down to my own pig-headedness.' Wiping something in his eye, he stood up and went to the built-in bar. 'I guess we could all do with a drink.' He turned to Greg. 'What what can I get you?'

For a few seconds the boatbuilder seemed taken aback. Then he simply said, 'Well … if you're sure, I'll have a beer, please, Harvey.'

'And I'll have a coffee,' said Lucy, standing to give her husband a reassuring hug. 'I think we're all determined never to go back to our bad old ways.'

*   *   *

'Poisoning?'

Jack faced the veterinary surgeon across Spike's inert little body. Audrey stood silently beside him. They'd called the after-hours number en route and been directed straight to the animal hospital.

The vet removed his stethoscope and nodded. 'Looks like it. Has he eaten anything suspicious?'

'Possibly fly agaric mushrooms.'

'Okay ... hmm ... well, he's certainly showing all the symptoms, but just to make sure, we'll get this analysed.' Spike was still lying on the blanket he'd been carried in, a patch of recent vomit adhering to its woollen surface. Using a small wooden spatula, the vet scraped some into a plastic container and sealed it. 'In the meantime, we'll keep him in tonight and see what we can do.'

'Will he ... be all right?' asked Audrey, fighting back the tears.

The vet straightened up and looked over half-rimmed spectacles. 'Difficult to say. Amanita Muscaria is often fatal in dogs, but some respond to treatment. Basically he's got acute gastro-enteritis, but otherwise he's pretty fit, so we'll keep our fingers crossed, give him nothing but water for twenty-four hours and try and purge the toxins. In the meantime we'll check his blood and urine for toxic amanita metabolites and give him supportive and symptomatic therapies, but ...' he paused to pull the blanket back over Spike's still form, '... we can't promise anything.'

Audrey gulped.

'Do all you can for him,' said Jack, 'whatever it costs.'

'Of course. Leave him with us. If there's any problem during the night, we'll call you. Otherwise, you call us in the morning.'

They both gave the old dog a gentle stroke and left.

*   *   *

Also not eating was Amanda Laydock. In her police cell, she pushed aside the untouched meal on the tin tray, drew knees up to her chin and contemplated a future bleak beyond imagination.

The reality of her stupidity had been brought home on arrival at the station where she had been formally detained, pending charges of "involuntary manslaughter". Lodged in a cell now with nothing to do but think, she dwelt on the shame all this must be causing her family. She had only sought to embarrass her father, but with solitary time in which to contemplate her actions, she thought of all the things he'd provided over the years and which she'd simply taken for granted. Then she reflected on the comfortable home they'd all enjoyed, and glanced about the bare brick of her cell. So many times on television she'd heard of people being arrested, but never in her wildest dreams did she think she would ever be one of them. Now she missed home and family more than she ever thought possible.

How long would she be here? Tomorrow was Sunday, but the young Detective Sergeant had said she should be ready to make a more formal statement sometime during the day. On Monday she would appear before the magistrates who might bail or remand her.

A message from her mum said they were trying to contact the family solicitor and she was to give no further statements without him present. Amanda knew that legal representation would surely cost her dad another small fortune he couldn't afford, and was it worth it anyway? She and the police knew she was guilty, so what was the point of fighting it? She would tell the magistrates the truth, like she'd told everyone else, and accept the consequences. She guessed that hearing would be after the post-mortem on Alfie.

Amanda wiped away another tear. Oh poor Alfie – she'd really loved that kindly old man and they'd all learned so much from the expertise he'd brought to Resolve. She still couldn't start to comprehend how she was responsible for his death. She thought of his slender frame lying there, face-down in the water, and shuddered. If only they hadn't run out of mushrooms and he hadn't taken her father's. If only he hadn't been left alone at the table and given that opportunity. If only his constitution had been better placed to handle those toxins and if only someone had gone to the wherry with him when he felt so ill. So many "if only"s, but the biggest if only was that she hadn't played this stupid prank in the first place. How Amanda wished she could turn back the clock.

Now, she could forget her future hopes and aspirations – all the travelling she was going to do in her gap year, researching herbal remedies around the world. What had that detective said? "Seven years to life for dealing in prohibited substances." Well, in the morning the whole sorry tale would be headline news and the family name would really be shot to pieces, only this time she couldn't blame her father. Amanda rolled on her side and buried her head in her arms.

But she didn't sleep. For one thing, the cell light continued to burn all night and for another, she was racked by thoughts of how it could have come to this and how Alfie had died. But, why had he died? She knew fly agaric mushrooms were hallucinogenic and produced effects akin to LSD – that was why she slipped those two in for her father. Several might produce unpleasant symptoms like convulsions and disorientation, but it would take many to result in death. Alfie was certainly an old man and perhaps not in the most robust health, but she still couldn't believe those two little mushrooms could wipe him out so quickly. Had she used the wrong ones?

It was a mistake almost impossible to comprehend. She had studied fungi so assiduously, always been so careful and well aware that some could be deadly. Her hands clenched her tissue as she thought of Alfie's post-mortem, when her ignorance and irresponsibility would be laid bare.

Amanda buried her head deeper into her arms and tried to imagine Resolve and her crew. Where was the wherry now? What were all her friends doing and thinking? What effect was all this having on Damien and her mum?

Instead of comfort, just the thought of those she loved produced another outburst of uncontrolled sobbing.

*   *   *

'Here's your tea, Jack.'

Amanda was not the only one experiencing a sleepless night. In the Fellows' household, both Jack and Audrey had found that blessed state ever elusive as their thoughts dwelt on the events of the day and Spike fighting his own battle in the animal hospital. Finally, Audrey had got up and put the kettle on.

'Thanks, love. I haven't slept a wink.'

'Nor me.' Audrey climbed back into bed and checked the time - two-thirty. She tapped the nature book she had brought up with the tea. 'While I was waiting for the kettle, I looked up Amanita Muscaria or fly agaric as everyone calls it.' She turned to a marked page. 'It really is a beautiful-looking mushroom, just the sort you associate with elves and fairies.'

'And away with the fairies is where you'd be if you sampled it,' warned Jack, cynically. 'Some tribes still regard it as almost sacred for its psychoactive effects.'

'According to this, its toxicity isn't reduced by cooking, freezing or drying, so you can see how Amanda managed to keep it from last autumn.' Audrey closed the book and frowned. 'If she only put two on her father's plate as she said, how on earth did our little Spike manage to get some?'

'That's what's been puzzling me,' admitted Jack. 'He was hanging around the table, but I can't see Alfie letting him have them, seeing as mushrooms were his favourite and the one thing lacking by the time he got his barbecue. That's why he pinched Harvey's.'

'And we know Spike wouldn't take them himself,' added Audrey. 'He's been trained better than that and, anyway, we were there and would have seen him do it.'

'Yep …' Jack took a sip of his tea, '… but, on the other hand …' His sentence trailed off into deep thought.

'What are you thinking, Jack?' asked Audrey, who knew only too well how easy it was to lose her husband completely once he started a mental process. 'Something's occurred to you, hasn't it?'

'What? Oh, just a thought,' shrugged Jack. 'Nothing of consequence.'

'I can't keep my thoughts off poor Spike, lying there far from home,' said Audrey, taking a gulp of tea, which temporarily eased the lump in her throat.

'Me too,' agreed Jack, at the same time reminding himself that someone had to keep up the family spirits. 'But we have to take comfort from the fact that they've not called us, which they said they'd do if things worsened.'

As if almost on cue, the bedside telephone rang its dreaded toll.

*   *   *

Chapter Seventeen

'The two-timing little bitch!'

Harvey Laydock stood in the village store, glaring at the Sunday rag in which Angelica Black's report had once more made the headlines. Quickly flicking to the inner pages, he found the rest of her article was even worse.

After a night in Great Taste, knowing he couldn't do anything to help Amanda until the morning, he'd chosen to obliterate the horrors of the day by downing a full bottle of rum.

That was after Damien had gone off to be with a girl called Rita, leaving him onboard with his estranged wife and her lover. A strange trio, but he'd been glad enough of their company and, considering the circumstances, they had got along surprisingly well.

Lucy, free from the grip of alcohol, but worried beyond words at what might be happening to their daughter, had been a rock of common sense. Harvey had felt incredibly emotional, not just because his beloved daughter was languishing in a police cell, but that it had taken something like this to finally bridge the gap that had grown between him and his wife. If they'd just found some unifying endeavour earlier, perhaps it would never have come to this. Sadder yet was the realisation that this understanding had come just that bit too late.

Even more amazing was the fact that, despite Greg's influence on both his wife and Damien, Harvey found he actually liked the man and had to admit, if only to himself, that this boatbuilder was just the sort of person he'd always strived to be and never quite managed.

For the first time in his life, Harvey faced up to painful reality. On screen, he'd always been portrayed as the tough, no-nonsense hard man. That was the persona orchestrated by the media and one which even he had started to believe. Perhaps it was the effort of constantly trying to be someone he really wasn't that had made him such a bastard to live with.

Kennard, on the other hand, was a man totally devoid of pretence who derived his pleasure from the world about him with no urge to seek fortunes afar. Building and sailing wooden boats, giving love to those who loved him – that would be enough for Greg Kennard. Harvey could well understand why both Damien and Lucy had fallen under his spell and, talking to him last night, discussing practical ways to help Amanda and being assured of his support,

Harvey felt himself slipping under that same incantation. Finally, sometime in the early hours, he had fallen into a drink-induced sleep and woken groggily this morning to find his company gone.

That awakening had taken a few seconds in which to orientate himself and only one more to remember the miasma engulfing his family and the need to do something about it. Rolling off the saloon couch, he'd stumbled to the galley to discover an empty coffee-jar and the clock showing ten-thirty.

It was only a short walk to the village store, but an epic of endurance that had jarred red-hot pokers of torment through his throbbing skull and brought sympathetic glances from villagers clearing up the staithe. On the public moorings, Resolve's bunting hung lank and bedraggled. Some of her crew were mopping the decks, but the whole boat seemed wrapped in an air of mourning. He recognised Damien amongst them and felt the urge to go and talk with this son he had so patently failed to understand and help. In the end, he stayed resolutely on course for the store, more to avoid Damien seeing him hung-over, than his need for caffeine. The shop bell sounded like a thousand Big Bens, but the newspaper stand gripped his immediate attention.

FATAL FOOD POISONING AT TV CHEF'S FROLIC FIASCO proclaimed the headline. OWN DAUGHTER ARRESTED.

Scanning the lurid account of yesterday's tragedy, Harvey finally knew what it was to be taken advantage of. Having thought he was on the threshold of a budding romance, he now knew that Angelica Black had simply used him. How could he have been so naive as to parade her in front of the village? No wonder they'd been giving him sympathetic looks. Instead of the glowing publicity he'd planned, the tragedy that had unfolded had now been shared with the rest of the nation.

Harvey groaned. All the recording work they'd done yesterday was doubtless already being sold to the news channels instead of for his new series. He'd worried that he might be in the evening of his career. Now he knew that evening was swiftly turning into terminal sunset and, what was more surprising, realised he didn't even care. What was the point of a career compared to his family? All his effort now had to be channelled into helping Amanda.

Harvey paid for the paper, threw it straight into the waste bin and headed home to Fayre View. He needed to call his solicitor.

*　　　*　　　*

The Fellows, on the other hand, were feeling the euphoria of relief.

That telephone call had not been the harbinger of some awful deterioration in poor Spike, but from their son-in-law to say that Jo's baby was finally on the way. Audrey had promised to head straight down.

'... but you'll have to stay here for Spike,' she agonised to Jack, after putting the phone down. 'In fact, I won't go myself until I know the little chap's all right.'

'I'll call them at eight,' promised Jack and, when he had done so, been unutterably relieved to hear that the collie had come through the night okay. 'The vet says he's responding to treatment, but they want to keep him in a while yet to make sure.'

'Oh, thank goodness.' Audrey uttered a silent prayer and then applied her practical mind to how they'd cope. 'I'll go by train and leave the car for you, Jack,' she decided. 'I know we'd planned to go together, but things …'

'Don't you worry, love,' reassured her husband, genuinely anxious for his beloved dog, but not overly disappointed at not being involved in imminent childbirth. 'As soon as I know Spike's really on the mend, I'll come and join you. In the meantime, I have a few other things to check here.'

'What sort of things?' In all their discussions through that long worried night, Audrey had sensed that her husband had other suspicions. Of what? Everyone knew what had happened and, bitterly regrettable as it was, the facts were inescapable. But she also knew her Jack. 'You're on to something aren't you?'

'Not really. Just some aspects that don't quite gel.'

'In what way?'

'Can't say at the moment, Aud. I just need to think about them.'

'Well, while you're thinking, I've got a bag to pack,' said Audrey, springing into action in the knowledge that her husband would never discuss facts until he was sure of their validity.

Jack opened his laptop. 'I'll google train times for you.' As he did so, the realisation came that it had been many years since he'd been at home without Audrey. Seeing her pull out the suitcase, and knowing Spike wouldn't be there either, brought home to him just how empty the house would feel without them both.

But his wife was correct on one point. He was on to something and the next few days might disclose just what.

* * *

The female police officer led Amanda Laydock into the interview room, but it wasn't DS Bailey awaiting her.

'Dad!'

'Hello Amanda.' Harvey stood up, but a glance from the escort had him back in his chair. 'Sorry you're having to go through this.'

Amanda managed to force a smile. 'My own fault, Dad, for playing the fool.' She sat down and looked earnestly at her father's drawn face. There was a table between them with a line across its centre. 'I'm just so grateful you've come to see me. I didn't expect you to.'

'Your mum and Damien wanted to come as well,' explained Harvey, 'but the police were making concessions to allow even one visitor, so I'm afraid you're stuck with me.'

There was a lot Amanda wanted to say, but the welling tears kept it to just a short, 'I'm sorry, Dad.'

'Don't be for me.' Harvey shook his head, sadly. 'I've been a crap father, Amanda, I know that. You were right to try and knock me off my pedestal. It's just unfortunate that the old boy ...' But Harvey stopped when he saw a fresh stirring of emotion clouding his daughter's usually blithe demeanour. Amanda had been born pretty, but her big hazel eyes were ringed with dark shadows, while her long glossy hair hung now in dull, lifeless tangles. She ran her hand through it distractedly.

'I ... I can't believe I killed a man, Dad.'

'Stop thinking of that, Amanda,' ordered Harvey, struggling to control his own emotions, 'and stop saying it as well. In fact don't say anything more to anyone until you've talked to our solicitor.'

'You shouldn't run up legal costs for me, Dad. It's all a horrible mistake, but it's all my fault and I've got to accept the consequences.'

'Yes, well, you're going to be represented whether you like it or not,' said Harvey with mock severity before leaning as close as the demarcation line allowed. 'You've never been too good at doing as I tell you, but this time you'll have to.'

Her smile this time came naturally. 'Right, Dad. I suppose I had to start sometime.' She wrinkled her nose. 'What are Mum and Damien doing this afternoon?'

'Damien's on the wherry with his girlfriend ... what's her name ...?'

'Rita Wakefield. She's a lovely girl and very artistic.'

'Yes, I saw some of her work at the frolic yesterday. There are a few clever people on that wherry ... like Greg Kennard. Your mum's with him now.'

'That can't be easy for you, Dad,' sympathised Amanda.

'Oh, I don't know.' Harvey gave a sad little shrug. 'It's just good to see your mum enjoying life again, and Kennard's a good type. We all had a drink together last night. Made me think that perhaps I might ...' The policewoman had glanced suggestively at her watch and Harvey nodded back. 'Time to go. I brought you these.' He held up the bag of clean clothes sent by Lucy and smiled. 'Can't have you coming home looking a mess.'

'Thanks, Dad.' Amanda felt just a little of her despair returning. 'I wonder when that will be?'

'Soon,' said Harvey.

He left the police station hoping more than he'd ever hoped before, that he was right.

*   *   *

'Jack – DS Bailey.'

Jack was sitting at home, an oven-ready meal untouched on the plate before him. Thirty years of Audrey's delicious home-cooking had spoiled him completely for anything out of a packet.

It was ten hours now since he'd dropped her at the railway station, and in that time he'd walked alone by the river, thought much of the events of yesterday and received a welcome call from Audrey on his mobile to say she'd arrived safely. She was at the hospital where Jo was still in labour, but promised to let him know just as soon as things happened. Back home, he'd opened a can of lager, started drafting his official report, microwaved his freezer meal, rejected it just as quickly and tapped his fingers as he awaited news on the mothering front. Even DS Bailey had been surprised at how promptly the phone had been answered.

'That was quick sir. Were you expecting a call?'

Jack explained.

'I won't keep you long then. Just thought I'd let you know what's happening.'

'And …?'

'… and, not much further than yesterday regarding Laydock's daughter. We had a call from the family lawyer to say he's coming tomorrow and not to question her until he's there. So, instead, I went and took statements from all the wherry crew.'

'Anything new?'

'Not really. Only supports what the girl originally told us.'

Jack glanced down again at his rapidly congealing meal. 'Just the same, Bailey, I'd like to know what they all said. How about meeting me for some grub and a pint at my local? My treat.'

'Sound's good, sir. Give me an hour.'

'See you there.'

Jack went and scraped his meal into the bin and was just pouring the lager down the sink when the phone rang once more.

*   *   *

'I think I'll go for the steak and kidney. How about you?'

'Same for me,' agreed Bailey, handing back the menu.

Jack held up his glass of local brew. 'Well, you can congratulate me.'

Bailey eyed him suspiciously. 'You're not telling me …'

Jack's grin widened further. 'Yep, I'm a grandfather for the first time. Aud called just after you rang off. It's a boy.'

'That's wonderful, sir … Jack.' Bailey raised his glass. 'All well?'

158

'Just fine, both of them. Trouble is, Aud wants to know when I can go down and see them.'

'Nothing to stop you is there?'

Jack explained about Spike's mystery poisoning.

'Sorry to hear that, sir. Is he going to be okay?'

Jack held up crossed fingers. 'Hopefully. I rang again this afternoon and the old fellow seems to be responding to treatment. They suggest I leave him another couple of days though, which would give me time to nip down to London.'

'There you are then. Nothing to stop you.'

Jack stroked the rim of his glass with his finger and frowned. 'I suppose not. When I rang, the vet told me they'd had the results of Spike's test which confirmed poisoning by Amanita Muscaria.'

'Fly agaric mushrooms,' sighed Bailey, 'just like Miss Laydock admitted. We'll have our own pathology results tomorrow, but, as far as I'm concerned, it's an open and shut case.'

'You're that sure are you?'

'Of course.' Bailey raised his eyebrows. 'Why shouldn't I be, with police witnesses and a virtual confession? What more can we want?' He frowned and leaned slightly closer. 'You don't have any doubts, do you, sir?'

'I'm never sure about anything until I have all the data,' explained Jack. 'Tell me how you got on this afternoon with the Resolve crew.'

'They all confirm the original story,' explained Bailey, pausing only to drink. 'The youngsters are all pretty distraught, but admit they hatched this scheme to get Harvey high on the day. Apparently they were cheesed off at the way he seemed to be taking over the frolic and thought they'd make him look a fool in front of the camera. Amanda had two fly agaric mushrooms left over from the ones she'd dry-stored the previous autumn. Young Freddie Catlin was going to be helping out on the barbecue stall, so he had the job of cooking them before slipping them onto Harvey's plate, which, of course, he did. What they didn't allow for was that the real mushrooms would run out and Alfie Rumball would pinch the magic ones when no-one was looking. Needless to say, they're devastated at the way things turned out. There's no doubt they all had genuine affection for that old skipper and can't believe they've played a part in his death.' Bailey shook his head. 'I guess they're going to have to live with that guilt for the rest of their lives, not to mention any charges we might be bringing.'

'How about Gloria Vale?' asked Jack. 'Where did she stand in all this?'

'Admits she knew about it, but didn't play an active role.' Their meals had arrived now and the detective paused until the waitress was well clear. After a couple of appreciative mouthfuls he continued, 'Gloria confirmed that the initial idea came from Amanda, with the other youngsters all happy to share in what they thought was just a good giggle. She admits not trying to stop them, because she'd had a lot of grief from Laydock herself in the past and felt disinclined to avert any heading back his way.'

Jack nodded. 'Understandable. Did she know much about Amanda's little herbal enterprise?'

Bailey paused again to enjoy his steak and kidney. 'Only that she was glad to have someone with medical knowledge on board. Like any group, they had their aches and pains and Amanda was good at treating them. She'd even helped that Flint lad overcome his negative, rather belligerent attitude to life.'

'Yeah I know.' Jack thought for a second before asking, 'That metal case where Amanda kept all her herbs – did you check it while you were on board?'

'Of course, sir, but there was nothing significant in it apart from a few innocent herbs like valerian, comfrey, rosemary and the like.'

'No mushrooms?'

'No, sir.'

'None at all?'

'None.'

'Hmm … interesting.' Jack continued his meal, but feeling a little guilty at enjoying this celebratory meal while Spike lay in the veterinary hospital and Amanda, in a police cell. He told Bailey something of how he felt.

'Spike'll be home again soon,' reassured the DS, 'and, as for that young lady, it's all her own doing.'

'Possibly.'

Bailey looked perplexed. 'There's something about this business you're not sure about, isn't there, sir? Want to tell me, because I'm blowed if I can see it.'

'I've already told you.' Jack pointed his fork towards the young DS. 'Spike's poisoning.'

'But, that's already confirmed as fly agaric, so only goes to confirm what Amanda said.'

'Which was that she only supplied two mushrooms which we know Alfie pinched, so where did Spike's come from?'

'Titbit from Alfie or he licked the old man's plate afterwards,' suggested Bailey.

'No, I've already dismissed those ideas, but there is another possibility.'

'Which is?'

'That there were more mushrooms to start with.' Jack paused. 'But, let's wait and see your lab results before I stick my neck out any further.' He finished off the rest of his steak and kidney and, as a way of changing the subject, asked, 'How about your other investigation?'

'The skeleton in the broad?' Bailey shrugged his shoulders. 'I wish that were as straight forward as this poisoning case. The Forensic Science people have promised a report in the next few days, but even if I get DNA, it still won't be of use.'

'Not located either of the Wanstead children yet?'

Bailey shook his head, swallowed a last mouthful and pushed away the plate. 'Amazing that we've got two murders at the same location at the same time. He looked at Jack quizzically. 'You don't think there's any connection, do you, sir?'

'Not directly, but remember you've also got Harvey Laydock accused of nicking outboards and dumping them in the same location as the remains, which kind of closes the circle on this whole strange business.'

'Could all be a coincidence, sir,' offered Bailey. 'I saw Councillor Wanstead at the frolic, but he seemed keener to find friendship than draw more grief down on his head.'

'He's a lonely man with worries,' agreed Jack.

'And he'll have a lot more just as soon as I get an ID on those remains.'

'If you get an ID.'

Bailey waited while the waitress cleared their plates and took orders for coffee. 'I will, sir, but with this latest business to deal with, I'm quite content to let Mr Wanstead stew in his own juice for a while yet. Give him enough rope, and he'll hang himself.'

'Not literally, I hope.' Jack absentmindedly moved the condiment set about the table, only to be stirred out of his introspection by the waitress bringing the coffees. When she'd gone, he said, 'Call me tomorrow when you've got the path results. It'll be interesting to hear what the medical people say.'

'Pretty predictable, if you ask me, sir.'

'I'm not so sure.' Jack took a sip of coffee. 'I'll bet you a pint it won't be quite as you think.'

*   *   *

Chapter Eighteen

Resolve had shifted her mooring to mid-broad when Jack arrived next morning. The bunting had been lowered, but freshly mopped decks and topsides shone as she swung at anchor in the morning sunshine. Only Gloria Vale, however, came to take his lines as he came alongside.

Jack sprang on board. 'Crew not jumped ship, I hope.'

'No, but I've sent them all off to give the farmer a hand.' An air of great melancholy seemed to be hanging over the wherry, mirrored by the sadness in Gloria's eyes as she added, 'Keeping them busy seemed the best policy under the circumstances.'

'Yes it's a pretty dire time all round.' Now didn't seem the time to mention Spike's poisoning. Besides, a call to the veterinary hospital first thing had confirmed that the collie was well on the mend and could be collected in days. Jack had relayed that glad news to Audrey as icing on the top of her grandmotherly cake, but that was another subject best avoided now in the face of another's grief. Instead he forced a smile and asked, 'Can we have a chat about all that?'

'Of course.' Gloria ushered Jack for'ard. 'I'm having to force myself onto this foredeck now,' she confessed, squatting down on one of the timberheads, 'with all its horrible memories.' She nodded to the cuddy. 'Same with my cabin. I spent many happy hours down there chatting with Alfie, and listening to the wonderful stories of his sailing days.' She closed her eyes as though trying to erase all that had happened. 'I just can't believe he's gone.'

'No, he was the last of that old school, but at least he relived happy memories before crossing the bar.' Jack sat down on the timberhead opposite. It was time to talk about things neither of them wanted to. 'You knew all about this magic mushroom caper, then Gloria?'

She nodded. 'Yes, but only in a peripheral way. Amanda herself told me what they were going to do and I just laughed and said "Good luck".' Her eyes met Jack's. 'I know I should have stopped them right there, but Laydock had given me so much grief in the past, that ...'

'Yes, I know,' interrupted Jack. 'Did Amanda tell you where she actually got those fly agaric mushrooms?'

'Picked in a wood around here in autumn and then kept dry-stored.

162

Apparently, she had just two left and decided to use them …' Gloria ran a hand through her red hair, '… with disastrous results.'

'She kept them in a metal case down below, didn't she?'

Gloria nodded. 'The youngsters have wooden trunk-type lockers in the main cabin. When Amanda came to join us she asked if she could keep her case in one of those and carry on making herbal medicines on board. I agreed.' She glanced towards the cabin hatch. 'That Detective Sergeant checked it yesterday, but if you want to look …'

'No, that won't be necessary,' assured Jack, standing up, 'but I have got one favour to ask.'

'Which is?'

Jack pulled out his small digital camera. 'I'm writing a small obituary of Alfie in our parish mag. It would be nice to include some photos of Resolve to go with it. Particularly places on board where he spent happy hours, like the afterdeck and your cabin.'

'A lovely thought, Jack.' Gloria nodded towards the cuddy. 'A bit of a mess, but help yourself.'

'Thanks.'

The photos took only minutes and when Jack rejoined Resolve's owner on deck, it was to find her staring wistfully at the staithe, now empty of all the stalls and gaiety that had filled it the day before. 'We all had such hopes for the frolic, didn't we? If only I hadn't left Alfie alone to steal those mushrooms when I wasn't looking.' She turned and faced Jack with stricken eyes. 'When Harvey seemed reluctant to have his meal, I thought the youngsters' plan was going to fail. That's why I was so keen to have him join us and get eating. If only I'd …'

'Hindsight is always 20/20,' cut in Jack, anxious to avoid any more emotion and looking towards the staithe himself. 'We never did have our fireworks, did we?' Climbing down into the launch, he turned and smiled. 'When this is all over and sorted, we'll see old Alfie off by having them then.'

'That's the least we can do for him,' agreed Gloria, before slipping Jack's lines and handing them over, 'but it won't bring him back.'

*   *   *

Jack had barely reached the main river again before his mobile rang. It was DS Bailey.

'Can we meet at your local again tonight, Jack?'

'Yeah, but it will have to be later. I'm going to visit Spike and then pack for London tomorrow. Is it urgent?'

'It might be for you, sir. I owe you a pint.'

'As you said, sir, not quite what I expected,' admitted Sergeant Bailey, putting down his glass and fixing Jack with suspicious eyes, 'though how you guessed that, is beyond me.'

'I never guess, Bailey.' Jack sat back in the quiet corner of the lounge bar, took a small folded paper from his pocket and laid it on the table between them. Then he raised his glass to the DS. 'Cheers. Now tell me the findings.'

'That Alfie Rumball died of a heart attack following near-drowning, but we knew that anyway,' explained Bailey dismissively. 'It's what they found in his stomach that was the real shocker.'

'Not magic mushrooms?'

'Oh, they found mushrooms all right,' acknowledged Bailey, 'but they weren't fly agaric like we expected. They were …'

'… these,' interrupted Jack, pushing across the note.

Bailey paused, seemingly confused, before opening the slip and reading aloud. 'Amanita virosa.' He threw the note back on the table in sheer frustration. 'How the devil did you know that, sir?'

'I didn't know, I surmised,' said Jack, leaning forward. 'Amanita virosa, or destroying angel, is one of the most poisonous fungi in the world.'

'… with no known cure,' added Bailey. 'I've consulted a forensic mycologist myself, sir. He told me they and Amanita phalloides are responsible for ninety per cent of mushroom related deaths.'

'Yep, the death cap is the worst,' acknowledged Jack, 'but I knew it wasn't that they'd find.'

Bailey scratched his head. 'I'm baffled you knew it wasn't fly agaric, so goodness knows how you worked out which of the two deadliest ones it was going to be.'

Jack smiled and tapped the side of his nose. 'Deduction. I'd already surmised that Alfie hadn't eaten a magic mushroom, but tragically been fed one of the deadly ones. I consulted our nature book at home and found that death caps are usually olive-green in colour whereas destroying angels are white and easily mistaken for the button mushrooms we all enjoy with our meals.'

'And so, the perfect one with which to fool your victim,' concluded Bailey. 'But, of course, this has completely altered the whole nature of our investigation. What we thought was a childish prank on Harvey Laydock is now beginning to look like someone definitely trying to murder him.'

'Have you interviewed Amanda on the subject?' asked Jack, keen to swing this conversation away from his own suspicions.

'This afternoon.' Bailey sat back, happy to inject his own concrete facts. 'Of course, she denies trying to murder her father and could only think it must have been a horrible mistake on her part. But, she admits picking a destroying angel, although she can't imagine how she could have given that mistakenly to young Freddie Catlin to cook and feed to her dad.'

'Neither can I,' said Jack. 'That girl knows her stuff when it comes to herbs and fungi, but did she say why she picked that deadly one anyway?'

'She did, and how about this for a near-confession? She reckons she was so fed-up with her father mucking up all their lives that she did just contemplate how much simpler their own might be with him out of the way. At that very same time she spotted a destroying angel. Apparently it's so rarely found this early in the year that she picked it, but swears she could never have used it in earnest. But she would say that, wouldn't she?'

'But, by the same token, if she really had, she certainly wouldn't have admitted she picked it,' Jack hypothesised. 'Surely, her honesty reinforces her plea of ignorance.'

'Not really,' argued Bailey. 'She stored that destroying angel in her box, safely sealed and labelled "poison", with the other ones. Everyone had seen it at some time or another and would be bound to spill the beans eventually.'

'… or use it themselves,' said Jack. 'You didn't see it in the box when you checked it did you?'

'No,' confirmed Bailey. 'As I said before, not a mushroom left.'

'Exactly. There's more to this than we first thought, Bailey.'

'There are certainly more serious charges to be answered, which is why Amanda Laydock has now been charged with the attempted murder of her father as well as the manslaughter of Alfie Rumball. We got a late hearing with the magistrate who's sent her for trial at Crown Court.'

'Serious stuff indeed,' replied Jack, sadly. 'Has she been remanded?'

Bailey shook his head. 'Released on police bail until the session next month.'

'Some time yet then,' said Jack, thoughtfully. 'Look, Bailey, I'm off to my daughter's tomorrow for a couple of nights, so give me a ring there if anything significant turns up.'

'Will do,' agreed the DS, before indicating towards the dining area. 'Time to eat, sir. My treat this time.'

'You're on,' enthused Jack, knocking back the rest of his beer and standing up. 'The sooner I get Aud back the better. This'll be the first decent meal I've had all day.'

'Well I'm definitely going to give the mushrooms a miss,' confided Bailey, following the ranger to a table. As they took their seats he said, 'It was interesting to hear what that mycologist had to say on the subject. Apparently, mushroom poisoning's been used several times over the centuries to polish off the unwanted.' He paused in selecting his meal. 'Do you know sir, an Amanita virosa was even used to assassinate Emperor Claudius in ancient Rome.'

*   *   *

Chapter Nineteen

'I've missed you, Aud.'

Stepping into their daughter's small east London lounge, Jack and his wife were feeling the warmth of renewed togetherness, though Audrey's response could well have given a different impression.

'Rubbish. If I know you, Jack Fellows, you've been far too busy sussing out the Laydock case to even notice I was gone.' Then she took her husband's hand, smiled warmly and admitted, 'But it is good to have you here, Jack.'

'Right, you two, that's enough of that,' teased daughter Jo. 'Now, before you do anything else, come over here, Dad, and have a peep at your grandson while he's asleep.' William looked very settled in his Moses basket and Jack was quite overcome with emotion as he stroked the baby's tiny hand, willing the little chap's eyes to open so he could be picked up and cuddled. 'We should enjoy a few minute's peace now, so sit yourself down next to Mum and fill us in on how poor Spike's doing.'

Jack reluctantly tore himself away and joined Audrey. 'He's on the mend at last, thank goodness, so we should be able to collect him on the way home. He'll soon be running beside his river again.'

'But, in the meantime, you have a new grandson to get to know,' said Jo, standing up as, on cue, noises could be heard coming from the basket. 'Mum, would you like to pick William up and introduce him to his granddad while I go and pop the kettle on?'

'She'll make a good mum,' said Jack proudly, as their daughter left the room. He gave a down-turned smile. 'Better than the dad I ever was.'

'You were a great dad. You just had a demanding job, that's all,' said Audrey, gently laying the baby on her husband's lap. 'That's it, put your arms under him and lift him up. He won't break.'

'I know.' Jack sighed, as he gave William a tentative little jiggle. 'Chasing villains certainly took its toll on time with the family.'

'And even when you were with us, your mind always seemed to be at work,' remembered Audrey, recalling their family years spent in the shadow of Scotland Yard. 'Thank goodness all that's behind us.'

'Yep,' agreed Jack, genuinely glad to be policing the Broads instead of London's underworld. Even so, he was unsure how to broach the next phase of this conversation. 'But, talking of The Yard, Aud, I need to pop in there tomorrow.'

'What!' Even the baby jumped slightly, but Audrey didn't notice. Instead, she'd turned to face her husband with a look that had cut through more than one meeting of the Parochial Church Council.

Jack was on dangerous ground here, and he knew it. 'It's just I need to check some facts with some of my old mates, love.'

'You're here to spend precious time with your daughter and new grandchild.' Audrey scowled at her husband. 'I know you're not an "earth father", Jack, but don't think you're going to escape the baby thing this time by disappearing back to your old haunts.' She nodded down to their grandson. 'It's only two days, for goodness' sake. Can't you just give us that time?'

'Not when a young girl's liberty's at stake. There's something about this Amanda Laydock case that doesn't gel and I need to get it sorted.' Jack met his wife's eyes. 'She's her mother's daughter too, you know.'

Audrey thought for a few seconds before lowering her head and nodding. 'I know. We need to help that family.' She looked up smiling. 'And Jo and I would probably be better off with you out of the way, anyway. You and nappies never went well together.'

Jo returned carrying three mugs of tea. Jack gingerly handed the baby over to Audrey and settled back with the best cuppa he'd tasted in days. Tomorrow evening he'd be the perfect grandfather … just as soon as he'd checked what was bothering him most. He turned to Jo. 'Can I just use your laptop and print off some photos?'

*   *   *

'Thank goodness he's dropped off at last! Well done, Dad. You must have a special touch, because Mum and I have been trying to soothe him for ages.'

William was draped over his granddad's shoulder, having suffered a particularly bad bout of colic. Jack had had his day at The Yard, found what he'd wanted, and now was the time to do the "grandfather thing", which he was surprisingly eager to do. He felt rather smug to think he'd succeeded where both mother and grandmother had failed, and walked up and down the room with William at last contentedly sleeping – or at least until his mobile rang right next to the baby's ear. 'Sorry about this,' he apologised, hurriedly handing back the now-screaming offspring and exiting into the privacy of the kitchen.

'Yes, Bailey; what've you got?'

'Not rung at a bad time, have I?' asked the DS, detecting the slight brusqueness in the ranger's voice and hearing the sound of inconsolable crying in the background.

'Only family relations put back another two decades,' Jack removed the muslin cloth still covering his shoulder and threw it onto a chair, 'but I'm sure you've got good reason.'

'The final autopsy report on our skeletal remains, if you're interested,' explained Bailey, without further apology.

'I certainly am,' said Jack, pulling up a kitchen stool, family disruption temporarily forgotten. 'What did they find?'

'Not what we expected at all.' Bailey gave Jack the full findings from the Forensic Science Laboratory.

'You're right, it's an eye-opener,' agreed Jack, taking a few seconds to assimilate the information he had just been given. 'I guess this alters things somewhat, as does what I discovered today.' He explained his visit to Scotland Yard and the results obtained.

'Blimey, that is a stunner.' Bailey seemed a little disenchanted. 'Nothing seems to be turning out quite how we expected it, does it sir?'

'The trick is not to "expect" anything until you have all the facts, but keep an open mind,' said Jack, sagely. He paused for a few seconds. 'Bailey, we need to bring things to a head and get this cleared up once and for all.'

'I agree, sir, but how?'

'Here's my suggestion,' said Jack.

*   *   *

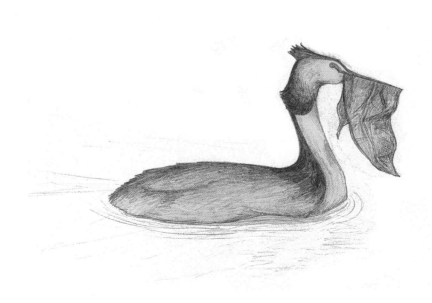

Chapter Twenty

'Well, this is one way to visit Norwich.'

Gloria was looking upwards to the harsh steel arch of Carrow Bridge as it slid by above their heads.

'Just the Friendship Bridge to go under now,' said Jack. 'We'll moor shortly after that.'

Resolve was in Norwich for the first time in over half a century, but this was a very different city to the one she must have sailed to in her trading days. Now, luxury apartments rose in place of old warehouses while, just coming into view ahead, the new riverside development promised an evening of varied nightlife for the youngsters on board. With her mast lowered since the Postwick Viaduct and powered by her tender, the wherry was soon sliding under the curved span of the next crossing, a cycle and foot bridge built to commemorate Norwich's link with the Serbian city of Novi Sad. Everyone was on deck now, enjoying Resolve's entry into the "fine city". Even Amanda, out on bail, was making the most of her freedom, though still somewhat subdued by the burden of her forthcoming trial.

That was an anxiety shared by the rest of her family – Damien manning the tender, Lucy staying close to Greg, and Harvey, a little self-conscious on this, his first trip aboard the vessel he'd schemed so hard to scupper. Another surprising guest on board for this evening cruise was Henry Wanstead, a man Harvey seemed to be going to great pains to avoid.

'Not quite the life and soul of the party, is he?' commented DS Bailey, standing beside Jack by the aft cuddy, but nodding towards the haggard figure of the councillor, standing alone in the wherry's bows.

'Probably contemplating imminent arrest and life behind bars.' Jack turned to the wherry's owner, standing quietly beside Greg at the helm. 'How does it feel, Gloria, bringing Resolve into the city for the first time since her rebirth?'

'Great.' Gloria's smile turned just as quickly into an expression of sadness. 'But I just wish Alfie was still here to share it.'

'Yes, he would have loved this ... though perhaps not the changes,' added Jack, looking to starboard as they passed the bars, cinemas and clubs of the new development. 'I somehow don't think this would have been quite his scene.'

'No, but he would have approved of showing Resolve off to young people.'

The idea of taking Resolve right into Norwich's heart had been Jack's, but one finding immediate approval from adults and youngsters alike, who seemed more than ready for a change of scene. Once alongside, the crew would be moving amongst the clubbers and revellers of Riverside, explaining the ideals of Resolve Trust and, hopefully, raising some funds for future work. Jack's suggestion of including Harvey, Wanstead and DS Bailey in their party had raised some questioning eyebrows, but personal harmony continued to be one of the Trust's aims and no-one could very well object too strenuously. Nevertheless, some pretty confrontational parties were now finding themselves in close confinement and Jack knew they had to proceed with caution, especially considering what he had planned.

'Julian Bridge coming up,' announced Greg, glancing to where the new crossing, named after Norwich's fourteenth century mystic recluse, was spanning the river ahead of them. The guests kept tactfully out of the way as Resolve's young crew prepared lines. Damien brought the tender's engine to stop as Greg steered them in towards the old dock wall. Ten minutes had the wherry smoothly alongside, and soon evening revellers were gathering at the quayside to admire this enchanting anachronism nestling in the shade of twenty-first century evolution. From a nearby nightclub came the steady beat of modern music and Greg could see that the youngsters were keen to get amongst it. 'Let's get the mast up again first,' he ordered, and soon the mighty length of pitch-pine was arcing back to the vertical and the masthead weathervane swinging level with the surrounding buildings.

It was Rita who brought out the bunting that had last flown at the frolic, seemingly a lifetime ago. 'How about rigging this again?' she asked Gloria. 'If we're here to show the flag, we may as well have some to show.'

'Good idea.' Gloria watched as the strings of signal flags were hoisted once more, to flap lazily in the last movements of the evening air. 'That looks better. Now we really look like a vessel on a goodwill visit.'

Keeping that goodwill onboard would be the greater challenge, thought Jack, as he made his way to Gloria's side. 'Before we go ashore, I'd like to have a word with everyone …' he glanced at the crew already exchanging banter with the onlookers standing on the quayside, '… below.'

Resolves's owner gave a quizzical look, but by this time DS Bailey had joined them and Gloria realised something more serious than a mere chat was in the offing. 'Right you lot,' she shouted light-heartedly, 'let's have you all below.'

Everyone, guests included, made their way down the gangway into the wherry's old hold, the youngsters showing limited enthusiasm at this delay to their evening's run ashore, the adults somewhat bemused at what this unexpected convention was all about.

Jack was the last one down the gangway. He knew what it was all about and that this night would end in sadness rather than joy.

*   *   *

'Last Saturday, we lost Alfie Rumball, a good friend of this vessel and all of you,' began Jack, casting an eye towards Amanda, nervously biting her top lip. She blinked several times before taking the hand of her mother sitting beside her.

Jack was seated on the gangway steps. It saved him having to stoop beneath the low deckhead and placed him just a little above the rest of the group seated around Resolve's large mess table. It was certainly made up of a mix of people, but all were anxious to see where this meeting was heading, and Jack wasted no further time showing them.

'Initial investigations pointed to Alfie's death being a tragic accident, the result of a practical joke planned for Harvey Laydock, who you youngsters decided needed teaching a lesson.' Jack glanced towards the man in question sitting at the other end of the table, but the celebrity remained expressionless and silent. 'You concocted a scheme between you to get him on a high in front of the cameras using magic mushrooms picked by Amanda. But the scheme backfired. Alfie Rumball ate those mushrooms instead and died as a result.' Jack paused to scan the expressions of guilt and regret on the faces before him. 'Or at least, that was the theory until DS Bailey here received the full autopsy findings, and it was then we realised the intention was far more serious. Those findings revealed that Alfie had been poisoned, not with hallucinogenic fly agaric mushrooms, but with one far more deadly, a destroying angel. So, that meant we were dealing with not just the involuntary manslaughter of Alfie Rumball, but also the attempted murder of Harvey Laydock, for which,' said Jack, nodding towards Amanda, 'his daughter here has been charged.'

Amanda raised her head, visibly drawing on her old spirit. 'But I didn't. I had no intention of killing my father.' She looked Jack straight in the eye. 'I would never do a thing like that.'

'Why not?' Jack was meeting the teenager's eyes with steely ones of his own. 'You had the motive and opportunity. You'd just had a big bust-up with your father and he'd taken away your car, driven your mum into someone else's arms and, on top of that, was possibly about to lose the family home paying off the damage award to Gloria. That debt could well disappear with him on death, and therein lay your biggest motive.'

'You think I'd do such a thing just for money?' Amanda's raised voice was a mixture of indignation and confusion. 'I've admitted I'm responsible for Alfie's

172

death, but it was all just a horrible mistake. I was sure I'd given Freddie here the Amanita Muscarias to put in Dad's food, but I must have given him the Amanita Virosa instead.' She shook her head. 'I'd been so careful to keep the destroying angel safely stored and labelled. I can't believe how I made such a mistake.'

'And perhaps you didn't,' responded Jack, with just a hint of compassion. 'Virtually everyone else here knew about the deadly mushroom you kept in that herbal box of yours on board Resolve, and could easily have slipped it in with the others for Freddie to cook. Your own mum, perhaps?' Jack turned his attention to Lucy, still holding her daughter's hand and with Greg on her other side. 'You had the same motives as Amanda and you wanted shot of Harvey to start a new life with Greg here.'

'What, and let my own daughter carry the can for it?' protested Lucy, furiously. 'What sort of mother do you think I am?'

'She's a wonderful mother.' It was her son, Damien, speaking up from his place beside Rita. 'If you're going to lay the blame for this on our family, Mr Fellows, I had as much motive as anyone.'

'Indeed you did, Damien,' agreed Jack. 'You so badly wanted to be a boat-builder like Greg, but your dad was intent on pushing you into a career you dreaded. And then, on top of continually cheating on your mum, you found he was trying to put Greg, a man you truly admired, out of business. You must have felt very bitter, Damien, and you knew your sister Amanda had the means to sort it once and for all.'

Before Damien could even answer this charge, the voice of Greg Kennard joined the fray. 'There were plenty others of us harbouring grudges against Harvey.' The boatbuilder was half out of his seat now, those tell-tale veins once more pulsing red in his neck. He pointed a threatening finger at the ranger. 'Don't pick on women and kids, Jack. If anyone had motive to bump off Laydock, it was me.'

'How right you are, Greg.' Jack's voice remained calm. 'Harvey had long been a thorn in your side. He was trying to undermine Resolve Trust every way he could, as well as scheming to have you evicted from your premises and put out of business. And then you fell deeply in love with his wife and wanted to marry her. If only for that oldest motive in the world, having Harvey dead and gone would, for you, be the best thing that ever happened.'

Greg shook his head. 'I thought you knew me better than that, Jack and, anyway, it wasn't just Harvey who was plotting against me.' He paused to point an accusing finger at the chairman of the council. 'That bastard Wanstead was the one doing all the dirty work.'

'Only to have his hero turn against him when the chips were down,' continued Jack. He transferred his gaze to the dejected figure sitting alone and almost hidden at the aft end of the cabin. 'Yes, Wanstead, you do indeed have a lot to answer for. You idolised Harvey Laydock and were prepared to do anything to gain his friendship. He asked you to find underhanded ways to discredit the Resolve Trust and you willingly obliged by faking the theft of outboard motors and throwing the blame the Trust's way. You simply dumped them in the broad or, like the one you lifted off that sailing cruiser at the staithe, stashed them in incriminating places where you knew they'd be found. You did the same with that one we found in Harvey's garage because, by now, he was treating you with the contempt you deserved and, in your eyes, was deserving of a bit of retribution in return. You were already in the police frame on other matters, needed to divert some of that suspicion and decided to shift it right back to the man who'd triggered it in the first place.'

'How dare you.' Wanstead was on his feet now, some of his old blustering ways finding new life in the face of direct accusation.

But Jack was having none of it. 'Sit down, Wanstead, and don't waste our time protesting your innocence. You know you could very well be facing more serious issues than perverting the course of justice . . .' Jack paused to let that sink in, '. . . including the attempted murder of Harvey.'

'Me? You're trying to pin that on me too?' Wanstead was on his feet once more, but there was contrition in his voice as he admitted, 'All right, I admit I took and dumped those motors, but . . .' he stopped and pointed at the celebrity he'd once so admired, '. . . it was his idea. Yes, you're right, it was me who planted that one in his garage, but . . .'

'. . . when it seemed that wasn't going to work, you decided to give him a taste of something else,' suggested Jack. 'A destroying angel mushroom, perhaps?'

'I've never even been on this wherry before,' protested the councillor, 'and knew nothing about that poison mushroom they had here.'

'No, but you're a keen rambler,' replied Jack. 'Everyone in the village says how much of your spare time is spent walking the country lanes or through the woods, so you could just as easily have found a deadly Amanita Virosa of your own.'

'Rubbish. I've given years of good service to my village and you have the nerve to accuse me of something like this. It's them . . .' Wanstead waved a shaking hand over the young people sitting staring at his florid face, '. . . these young misfits you need to be investigating.' His pointing finger came to rest on the impassive face of John Flint. 'Like him . . . young tearaway . . . he'd poison you as soon as look at you.'

'You pompous old git.' It was Flinty on his feet now. 'People like you are always quick to pass the blame onto people like me.' He indicated Harvey, still sitting silently on the edge of all this discontent. 'Why would I want to kill Amanda's dad?'

'For a number of reasons, actually,' answered Jack, turning towards the young man. 'Having been given a rough ride by society so far, and now, having found a sanctuary on Resolve, here comes another person with power bent on destroying you and all the good work Gloria is trying to do. By this time you've formed an attachment to Amanda, who's trying to help you with her herbal remedies, but she too becomes a victim of her father. And then, that night at the staithe, another stolen motor appears in the boat you were supposed to be guarding and Harvey Laydock is hovering around. You must have been sure it was him trying to set you up. You were consumed with bitterness, knew about the mushroom jape and, doubtless, had access to Amanda's box. What easier way for you to extract a bit of retribution on someone who's been harsh on you and the girl you love.'

'Why do I have to take the blame for everything?' There was old bitterness in Flinty's voice, but it was his sister who put a calming hand on his shoulder before turning to Jack.

'Why can't you leave him alone?' She glanced around her fellow crew-members. 'We were all in on that silly trick, so we could all be equally guilty of swapping the mushrooms.'

'Except you could be guiltier than most, Jenny.' Jack swung his gaze from brother to sister.

'Me?'

'Yes, you, who has made a special study of ancient Rome and, in particular, the reign of Emperor Claudius, who met his own end poisoned by Amanita virosa.' He gave Jenny a questioning shrug. 'What more poetic way to dispatch the man persecuting your brother and others you have become very close to …' Jack glanced at Freddie, '… than one from the very period you admit to having a fascination for.'

'When it comes down to it, it was me who cooked those mushrooms and put them on Harvey Laydock's plate.' It was Freddie Catlin speaking up now, the young budding chef who, Jack had noticed, was becoming increasingly close to Jenny. 'If you're going to blame anyone, Jack, why not me?'

'Stop this!' Gloria had jumped to her feet. 'Stop all this soul-searching.' She turned to Jack. 'And stop attacking these young people. They've put up with enough in life without us tormenting them as well.' Gloria's red hair seemed a good indicator of her disposition right now as she pointed to herself and said, 'If anyone had reason to want Harvey Laydock dead, it was me.'

'That would be true, Gloria, but for the fact that you also have the best of motives for keeping him alive.'

'You mean the balance of the damages, he owed me,' conceded Gloria. 'I agree, we need the money, so I would have been a fool to kill off that quarter-million along with Harvey.' She shook her head. 'And why are we going through all this anyway? Poor Alfie's death was just an accident. You've got Amanda paying the price for that. Isn't that enough?'

'It isn't when Amanda didn't poison anyone.'

'Not intentionally she didn't.'

'She didn't poison anyone, intentionally, accidentally or otherwise,' repeated Jack, sparing just a second to flash the girl herself a reassuring smile. 'She only thought she did.'

'I knew Amanda would never try to kill me,' spoke out Harvey, for the first time, from the aft end of the cabin. 'I've been a lousy family man …' he glanced around the assembled group, '… and probably a real shit to just about everyone else, and I'm truly sorry for that, but who the hell would try to wipe me out? I haven't been that bad, have I?'

'A good question, and one I'm about to answer.'

Twilight was giving way to darkness now, the lights of Riverside casting shadows across the old quay. From the nightclub alongside, a kaleidoscope of revolving lights threw startling colours into Resolve's open hatchways. Jack took a deep breath. He'd created enough acrimony this evening. Now was the time to reveal just why.

*   *   *

'The main problem in sorting this mystery,' explained Jack, 'was the very thing we have just discovered again now – that almost everyone here had reason to hate Harvey Laydock and had access to the means to kill him. In the end, it was poor Alfie who paid the price and Amanda actually confessed to triggering the chain of events that led to his death.' He paused to scan the silent faces intent on his own. Gone now was that impatience to be enjoying the evening ashore. Everyone here wanted the solution – everyone that is except one.

'But certain things didn't quite add up. Amanda was sure she'd given Freddie the fly agarics to slip into her father's food, but Alfie died from eating a destroying angel. Had she given the wrong mushroom by mistake? But then my own dog was poisoned by fly agaric, so how did Spike get them and where from? Poor Amanda here was so sure she'd been the cause of the tragedy that she straightway made a confession and that, in a way, was what threw us for so long.' Jack turned and glanced briefly at DS Bailey, still standing silently behind him, 'It's a golden rule of detection that you never try and make the events, as you see them, fit the facts as they are, but that was just what we were doing. Someone had tried to murder Harvey and instead poor Alfie had died. But what if we took those events at face value? Alfie Rumball was dead. What if he really was the intended victim from the start?'

'Alfie?' Greg was shaking his head, but speaking for everyone there. 'That's crazy, Jack. We all loved old Alfie. No-one would have wanted him dead.'

'Someone did,' replied Jack, bluntly, 'and, I'm afraid, the facts prove it. There's no disputing the pathology findings that Alfie was suffering the effects of Amanita virosa poisoning. Now there is one big problem with that fitting the scenario of tampered food at the barbecue. Destroying angels are fatal all right and with no known antidote. Eat those and you are dead as surely as if someone put a knife right through your heart, but – and this is the big "but" – their effects only start to become apparent twelve hours after they've been eaten.'

'Twelve hours,' repeated Jenny. 'In other words ...'

Jack nodded. '... Alfie Rumball must have eaten that mushroom long before the evening barbecue.'

'But he only ever ate on Resolve,' protested Freddie. 'Twelve hours earlier must have been breakfast that morning and I cooked that, and we didn't even have mushrooms.'

'Did Alfie actually eat with you in this messroom?' asked Jack.

Freddie thought for just a few seconds before shaking his head. 'No, come to think of it, he ate like he often did, with Gloria in her cabin. Gloria actually ...' Freddie's voice trailed off as he realised the implications of what he was saying.

'... cooked his breakfast for him,' completed Jack. He turned to the wherry's owner. 'Yes, Gloria, it was you, as you often did, who gave Alfie his breakfast that morning, but what he didn't realise was that he was tucking into his own doom. It was you who fed Alfie that fatal destroying angel.'

There was an audible gasp of shock from the others.

'This is insane.' Gloria looked around her, an uncomprehending smile finding sympathetic disbelief in all her crew. 'Why on earth would I want to murder Alfie?'

'I'll come to that later; for the moment let me explain how. A lot of this is surmise, but I'm sure you'll tell me if I've got it wrong.' Jack folded his arms. 'You admit you knew all about this little trick the others were going to play on Harvey here. That may have been the catalyst for coming up with your own nasty little plan, because you knew Amanda had a destroying angel in her herbal box, probably flicked through her books on the subject, and found out how deadly that particular fungus was. You may even have glanced through Jenny's history books and read how Emperor Claudius got murdered the self-same way. Whatever, you decided to take that destroying angel and feed it to Alfie for breakfast on the day of the frolic. You knew mushrooms were one of his favourite foods, so he took no encouragement to eat it.'

'This is ridiculous.' Gloria looked around for support. 'I can't think anyone here is prepared to listen …'

'Let him finish,' interrupted Harvey.

Jack continued. 'You would've found out that it took twelve hours before the effects of eating a destroying angel became apparent, so I'm sure Alfie's breakfast was timed to make that happen at the end of the barbecue. Knowing that Harvey would, by then, be feeling the effects of having eaten the fly agaric mushrooms, Alfie's sickness would simply be put down to the same cause. But things didn't go quite to plan, did they? What you never anticipated was that they'd run out of mushrooms and those planted on Harvey's plate would be the only ones left. You had to think fast, Gloria, and what you decided to do was discard Harvey's mushrooms when you were left alone at the table with Alfie. You simply threw them onto the grass. We didn't see you do it, so I'm sure Alfie didn't either. The only one who did was my poor old dog Spike. He sniffed those magic mushrooms out of the grass, wolfed them down, and nearly died as a result.'

'This is an entertaining tale, Jack,' said Gloria through tight lips, 'but how can you expect anyone to believe all this dribble? Why would I throw Harvey's mushrooms away? Surely Alfie needed to eat them if they were supposed to be blamed for making him ill.'

'Yes, but everyone assumed he did. As they were missing from Harvey's plate, we all thought the old boy had pinched them when no-one was looking. The fact that a post mortem would determine them as destroying angels instead of fly agarics would be put down to Amanda's mistake, and then she'd be left to carry the can and you'd be in the clear.' Jack shrugged. 'Alfie was all set to spend an agonising couple of days of lingering death. As it was, back at Resolve he stopped to vomit over the side and fell in – or at least that's what you told us. Whatever, he'd have drowned if it wasn't for Flinty here diving in to rescue him. But near-drowning for an old man of nearly ninety isn't going to be survivable and it must have been a big relief for you when his heart gave out and he was gone. That, at least, prevented him having to tell the doctors what he'd eaten in the last twelve hours.'

'This all sounds very plausible, Jack,' said Greg, 'but it doesn't even begin to explain why Gloria would want to kill a harmless old man who'd done more than anyone to get her project going.'

'Exactly,' agreed Gloria, thankful for her boatbuilder's support. 'I loved Alfie like everyone else. Why would I want to harm him?'

'That,' replied Jack, 'was something that eluded me at first, but which I'll now explain.'

*   *   *

'There were a few clues early on,' began Jack, 'but they didn't mean anything to me and probably only triggered alarm bells with you, Gloria, until you'd confirmed them later. That's when affection for a kind old man turned to hatred.'

Gloria simply shook her head. 'What are you talking about, Jack?'

'I'm talking about revenge, Gloria.'

'Is this all a charade or what? What could little Alfie Rumball possibly have done to make me want to murder him?'

Jack's voice remained an emotionless monotone. 'He killed your father.'

Gloria's eyes fixed on her accuser's. 'My father died just two years after I was born, Jack, but it's not a subject I care to discuss even now.'

'I can understand that ...' Jack took some papers from his bag and laid them on the table before him, '... considering the nature of your father's death.' He glanced at a photograph lying amongst them. 'I'm sorry, Gloria, but I was a bit underhand the other day when I asked if I could photograph Resolve, including the interior of your cabin. What I was really after was this, a copy of the framed print you told me was of your parents' wedding.'

Gloria's expression hardened. 'I'm disappointed in you, Jack. I really thought I could trust you, of all people.'

'You can always trust me, Gloria ...' Jack paused for only a second, '... to pursue the truth. You see, there was something familiar about your father's face, the first time you showed me that photo. Things said later reminded me why, and other events made it significant, so I photographed it, took it to London, and my old mates at the Yard soon provided the rest.'

Gloria sat back and folded her arms. 'I never wanted any of this to come out, but as you seem determined it should, then perhaps you'd better share it with us all.'

Jack nodded. 'It's not a nice story, so I'll keep it short. Your father's name was Fenner – Charlie Fenner – and he was involved with the Manchester underworld. In the early sixties, Charlie was one of a gang that raided a warehouse. Things didn't go quite to plan though, the police got wind of the job and were soon at the scene. Unfortunately, your dad had a firearm, used it and ended up in court for murdering a copper. They didn't take kindly to that sort of thing back then, and your dad was eventually hanged for his crime. I was a brand-new PC myself at the time and I remember it well. It just took a while to connect the face to the story.'

The stunned silence filling Resolve's main cabin was finally broken by Greg. 'Good grief, Gloria ... we didn't know ... you never told us.'

'There was no need to.' Gloria raised her chin in defiance. She hadn't come through so many traumas in life without knowing how to handle adversity. 'I was only two at the time, but the stigma went on forever. Life for Mum was intolerable and, in spite of changing our name, it was a continual struggle.' She held her hands out in desperation. 'But I can't see what any of this has to do with Alfie Rumball.'

'I think you do, Gloria, and you did the very first time I mentioned his name. I noticed the shocked look on your face, but you explained it away by saying you were just concerned at the thought of asking a man his age. And, I'm sure even you had doubts about him being the same person. But you realised it was, on the day we sailed Resolve to Burgh Castle. Certain things were said that day and you knew fate had finally presented you with one of the men who'd brought such misery to your early life.'

'I still don't get it, Jack.' Greg was speaking for them all. 'How could Alfie be involved? What things were said?'

'The first was an innocent enough remark,' explained Jack. 'Alfie was talking about the old days, sailing wherries, and telling us how things were so tight money-wise after the war, that he had to take a part-time job.'

It was Lucy Laydock who spoke up this time. 'You're not going to tell us that dear Alfie was a villain ... a member of that gang?'

Jack shook his head and smiled. 'Far from it. Alfie Rumball was as law-abiding as you and I. In fact, he had a very well-developed sense of right and wrong and was prepared to act on it.' Jack paused. 'Do you remember when we were sailing downriver, how the forestay slackened off and Alfie said it would need tightening?'

'I remember it well.' Lucy searched her memory for Alfie's actual words. 'He said it was due to the rope being new and needing stretching.'

'And ...'

Lucy scratched her head for further recall. 'Oh yes, he mentioned how, in the old days, they always stretched ropes overnight before using them in the morning. So, what was wrong with that?'

'Only that it was poor old Alfie having a senior moment and doing what many of us do as we get older. He was getting just a bit confused with events from his past.'

'And I'm getting confused with events of the present,' admitted Greg.

'So was I at the time. I'd certainly never heard of sailors pre-stretching ropes, but couldn't think why it disturbed me. Then it was you, Greg, much later on, who gave me the clue that joined those loose ends together.'

'Me?'

'Yes, after Harvey came roaring past us in Great Taste, and you said he ought to be hanged from the yardarm.'

'Well?'

'Just that, the answer to Alfie's strange remark and the realisation as to which group of men always pre-stretched their ropes prior to using them in the morning.'

Jack knew none of the young people would know what he was talking about, but Gloria did and it was she who now provided the answer.

'You're talking about hangmen, Jack.'

The ranger nodded. 'Exactly, Gloria, and the one who hanged your father was ...'

'... Alfie Rumball.' Gloria Vale turned to meet the stares of all on board. 'In later years I had the money and means to find the names of all those who'd had a hand in my father's death. He was weak and easily led and that was why he'd been given the gun the night of that warehouse robbery. They needed a fall-guy if things went wrong and Dad was their perfect foil. He didn't deserve the end the state gave him and I vowed, if the chance ever came, to seek revenge on any who'd had a hand in it.' She glanced at Jack. 'I knew the hangman was called Alfred Rumball, and couldn't believe it when that was the name of the wherryman you knew. But, I'd learned how those executioners worked and that remark about stretching ropes told me this really was my man. Fate had given him up to me and I was going to see it through.' She turned back to the group. 'The question was, how? And then the silly idea to make Harvey eat hallucinogenic mushrooms on his big day, provided the perfect cover. I took the destroying angel from Amanda's box and fed it to Alfie for breakfast that last morning.' Gloria gave a humourless chuckle. 'Ironic isn't it, that the condemned man was always given a hearty breakfast before he met the hangman, and that's exactly what I gave the one who took my father's life in the name of justice.'

From the corner of his eye, Jack could see DS Bailey keying a text into his mobile. Then the detective stepped forward. 'Gloria Vale, I'm arresting you for the murder of Alfie Rumball. You don't have to say anything ...'

As the caution was read out, a flashing blue joined the disco lights as a police car drew slowly onto the quay. Jack's voice was softer now, almost kindly.

'Time to go, Gloria.'

She got up, but just as Bailey went to escort her up the gangway, she paused. 'What a waste. I had so much to offer young people who'd had a rough deal from life ... just like me.' She turned to Jack. 'How I wish you'd never come near this wherry.'

Jack could only nod in agreement. 'Gloria, as long as we live, you'll never wish it more than me.'

A female PC had come to stand at the head of the gangway and, within minutes, Gloria was being ushered into the back of the police car, but she paused for one last look at her beloved Resolve. Then she simply shook her head, climbed in and was gone. Bailey joined Jack once more on the aft deck of the wherry.

'Good result in the end, sir.'

'You could say that.'

Bailey could see there was no satisfaction in this result for the ranger. 'I should spare her any sympathy, Jack. She was prepared to see a young girl banged up for something she didn't do.'

Jack nodded and smiled. The youngsters were emerging from the cabin now, shocked into silence, but finding comfort in shared sadness. 'They'll get over it – and I will too.'

Bailey nodded. 'Bit of a turn up, the old wherryman being a hangman as well.'

'All the hangmen the state used for judicial executions were part-timers,' explained Jack. 'Old Alfie must have been finding it hard to make ends meet, but his knowledge of ropes and knots made him a good candidate for that grim task.'

'Definitely not a job to boast to your mates about,' said Bailey with a shake of his head, 'though I sometimes wish we still used them. There's a few I'd like to see with appointments in the eight o'clock book. Like him, for instance.' He nodded towards the furtive figure of Henry Wanstead, just stepping ashore and about to wander off into the nightlife. The DS smiled and nudged Jack. 'He must think we've forgotten him. Come on, Jack, just a little more business to conclude before this night's through.'

They soon caught up with the councillor who jumped nervously as Bailey's hand went on his shoulder. 'Going somewhere, Mr Wanstead?'

'Oh … I thought you'd just about wrapped everything up.' Henry Wanstead's eyes had the look of a man hoping beyond hope that he was right.

'Not everything, councillor. There are some issues connected with your good self that still need sorting.'

'I … I've told you everything I know.'

'Have you now?' Bailey nodded back towards Resolve. 'Well you certainly opened up somewhat in there, so I'd like you to come to police headquarters first thing tomorrow where, I warn you, you will probably be charged with theft and attempting to pervert the course of justice.'

Wanstead nodded, but he was waiting for the next part, the charge he had been dreading these last weeks. '… and …?'

The DS stood in silence for a few seconds, seconds in which he knew the man before him was going through all the torments of hell. Then he simply cocked his head and said, 'That's all. You can go.'

It was Wanstead's turn to stand in silence, mouth agape. Then he managed to blurt, 'Thank you … thank you,' and he was gone.

'Phew!' Bailey glanced to where one of the bars heaved with young carefree life. 'Not quite the atmosphere of your local, Jack, but I bet they still serve a good pint.'

'Which is what I could really do with right now.' Jack put his hand on Bailey's shoulder. 'Come to think of it, you do owe me one … remember?'

They headed for the bar.

*   *   *

Epilogue

'Oh, that was pretty. I wonder what's next?' As the last star of the first rocket dipped to extinction in the broad, Audrey gave her husband's hand another squeeze. 'We needed this, Jack – to see people enjoying themselves again.'

The ranger nodded. 'Yes, this is how the frolic should have ended. If only …'

'Life's full of regrets, Jack. We all think we can control life, but we have to accept that sometimes it controls us. It's not what we'd choose, but there it is.' Audrey turned and gave an appealing smile. 'Nothing will bring Alfie back, but the important thing is that the others have come through this experience the better for it.'

'And here's one of them now,' indicated Jack, as Harvey Laydock came strolling up to join them.

The celebrity gave a sincere smile before handing across polystyrene cups of steaming soup. 'Here you two, have something to warm you up.'

'Mmmm.' Jack breathed in the appetising smell of leak and potato. 'Perfect for a night like this.' He glanced towards the hog roast sizzling over the barbecue. 'It's good of you, Harvey, putting on such a feast for everyone again.'

'And it was a wonderful gesture to rearrange the firework display – and we all know you did it for the right reasons this time,' said Audrey as a further succession of rockets were launched from their floating pad.

'Just glad to give a little something back to the village.' Harvey looked up as the rockets erupted into cascades of multi-coloured flashes, their light revealing a certain sadness in the personality's tired features. 'A pity Alfie and Gloria aren't here to share this.'

'Yes, we were just saying the same.' Jack turned and gave a quizzical look, 'But I'm surprised that you of all people Harvey, aren't allowing yourself a little gloat at how things turned out.'

'With Gloria, you mean?' Harvey seemed puzzled himself. 'Funny how our attitudes change isn't it? Probably the old fable of slaying the dragon and then missing it.' He shrugged. 'Gloria Vale was a victim of her circumstances like the rest of us, but it's how you handle the result that matters.'

'Well, I heard what you did regarding that last court payment,' divulged Jack, turning to face the man who weeks before had been the biggest thorn in his side. 'You could have used her conviction as an excuse to avoid that, but instead you paid it anyway to the Trust. That was a noble gesture.'

Harvey seemed almost embarrassed. 'Well, they're going to need all the funds they can get to keep up all the good work Gloria started.' He nodded towards Resolve, Japanese lanterns hanging in the rigging and her crew on the hatch top enjoying the show. 'I'm on her Board of Trustees now, would you believe? One of my first jobs was appointing Greg as the new chap in charge.' He gave a sad smile. 'A bit of extra money will come in handy for him and Lucy, and I wish them happiness.'

Jack sensed it was time for a change of subject. 'And I hear one good spin-off from the frolic is that a Norwich firm's prepared to sponsor the youngsters building a couple of those rowing skiffs Greg so badly wanted?'

Harvey made a visible effort to brighten. 'Yep, we've got a new bunch of needy youngsters joining us next week, so we'll need something to keep them busy. They'll be using Greg's workshop, which will help him ... and my son too.'

'So Damien's not doing his A-levels or going to university?' asked Audrey, although she already had an inkling of the news.

'No, instead I've got him onto the boatbuilders' course he always wanted.' The celebrity shrugged philosophical shoulders. 'He's happy now and I've finally come to realise that doing what you want and not what you think you should, is one of the essentials for a contented life. That's why Amanda's off on her herbalist's course instead of going to medical school.'

'A wise choice,' agreed Audrey with a smile. 'I wonder if she'll stay friendly with young Flinty?'

'Probably,' sighed Harvey, with resignation. 'They have great plans to open up their own clinic and, with his experience in retail and Amanda's own little entrepreneurial flair, they'll probably do well together.'

'Just as long as Amanda's sold her last magic mushroom,' proclaimed Jack, frowning.

'Don't worry, she's had her scare.' Harvey nodded in the direction of Bailey, queuing up for his soup. 'Our good detective sergeant tells me they're going to drop any charges in that respect ...' he paused and smiled, '... and any further action against me regarding the stolen motors.'

'Which is more than our Councillor Wanstead can hope for,' Jack replied, indicating the lonely figure down by the edge of the staithe.

'Ex-councillor,' corrected Harvey. 'With his forthcoming hearing, he decided the only decent thing was to resign as chairman of the council.' The celebrity shook his head. 'But I'm going to pay his legal costs, seeing as the silly fool was only doing it to try and please me.'

Jack gave a chuckle. 'The way things are turning out, it wouldn't surprise me if you put up for election yourself.'

'No way,' insisted Harvey with firm determination. 'In fact, I'll be a thousand miles from here by the time they get round to that.'

'Really? Somewhere nice?' asked Audrey, surprised at this one piece of unknown knowledge.

'Greece in Great Taste.' Harvey nodded towards the big cruiser, briefly illuminated by yet another explosive starburst. 'I'm living on board her now Fayre View has been sold. The plan is to offer cookery courses afloat in the Cyclades.' He smiled. 'I've had enough of living a false life for the media. Hopefully, out there, I'll finally discover the real me.'

'I'm sure you will,' agreed Jack, 'but Greece is a long haul. Are you taking any crew?'

'Freddie Catlin is coming as deck hand and getting some chef training thrown in.' Harvey turned and indicated the lad himself, busy handling the food counter on his own. 'In fact, I'd better be getting back to check how things are going.' He shook Jack's hand, kissed Audrey's cheek and was gone.

'Not such a bad type in the end,' said Audrey.

'He'll do,' said Jack.

The display had reached its finale, an ear-splitting spectacular crescendo, which seemed to reverberate for miles around, before dispersing slowly into the night sky, leaving behind only a sulphurous smell and an eerie silence. After a moment of stunned awe, the crowds erupted simultaneously into loud applause.

'A good job we left Spike at home.' Audrey took her hands from her ears. 'The poor little chap would have been scared stiff by all these bangs.'

'Not as big as the scare he gave us.'

Audrey nodded agreement. 'I don't know how many lives a dog has, but he must have used up his full quota this time.'

'On the other hand,' countered Jack, 'if dear Spike hadn't gone and eaten those fly agarics Gloria chucked off Harvey's plate, we might never have got to the bottom of things at all and she could well have got away scot-free.'

'Like some other people we know,' complained Audrey, glancing towards Henry Wanstead, engaged in cheerful banter with some fellow-villagers. 'He has every reason to be relieved.' She turned to her husband, frowning. 'You were so sure that the skeleton in the broad was his wife Alice, so how come Bailey isn't pursuing the investigation? Surely Wanstead must have done it?'

'Only if he was a Viking.'

'What?'

'That's who we think murdered that poor woman.' Jack turned and faced his wife. 'Those remains turned out to be a thousand years old, Audrey.'

'A thousand …'

'… years,' Jack repeated, 'which just about puts them right at the time Sven Forkbeard and his gang were sailing their longships up the Yare to attack Norwich. Our poor woman was murdered all right, but probably with a Norse battleaxe …'

'… and has lain in that broad ever since.' Audrey sighed. 'Well at least now we can give her a Christian burial.'

'And Henry Wanstead is off the hook,' concluded Jack, almost with regret. He shrugged. 'You can't win 'em all.'

'It's hard to imagine anyone "winning" when there's murder involved,' said Audrey sadly. The evening was drawing to its close now and people were starting to make their way home. She turned to her husband. 'Back on the northern rivers again next week, Jack, but you won't forget this spell in the south.'

'Not in this lifetime,' said the ranger, taking his wife's hand and joining the departing throng. 'Come on, Aud, let's get ourselves a drink.'

The water frolic was finally over.

*   *   *

But one figure remained, Henry Wanstead standing alone by the water's edge. Out on the broad, pyrotechnical smoke still lingered, an almost-ghostly veil lying blanket-like in the anti-cyclonic air. Henry was hoping a similar veil could now be drawn over the whole business of strange remains and missing wives.

It had just been a ghastly coincidence, that victim from the eleventh century being found right where he'd dumped the motors. Coincidence or not, it had triggered a lot of awkward questions from that keen young sergeant, though Wanstead had constantly told himself he had no reason to really worry.

The ex-councillor looked across to the far corner of the broad, a secluded inlet well clear of the main channel and one location they would never attempt to dredge. They would never need to, for few people realised that the water there hid an ancient pool that sank to seemingly bottomless depths. No-one would ever find her there.

Henry Wanstead allowed himself just one self-satisfied smile and turned for home.

THE END